The second b

]

Can you turn the clock back on your first love? Would you even want to try?

Alex McCann and Teodora "Ted" Vasquez left Cambio Springs together. Ted came back. Alex didn't.

Now, years later, the future alpha of the McCann wolves has returned with plans to bring new life to the dying desert community. Plans that could change everything for the isolated enclave of shapeshifters in the California desert. Some love the plan. Others hate it. The two former lovers are at each other's throats, and everyone is watching to see what happens.

But when murder once again strikes Cambio Springs, can they overcome their past to help the community they both call home? And can the love they shared once burn again when so many stand against it?

Praise for Elizabeth Hunter...

"Hunter is an author to watch!"
—RT Book Reviews

"Elemental Mysteries turned into one of the best paranormal series I've read this year. It's sharp, elegant, clever, evenly paced without dragging its feet, and at the same time emotionally intense."
—Karina, NOCTURNAL BOOK REVIEWS

"Hunter is an absolute pro at giving us steamy, heart-melting romance."
—Mandy, I READ INDIE

Desert Bound

A Cambio Springs Mystery

Elizabeth Hunter

Desert Bound
Copyright © 2014
by Elizabeth Hunter
ISBN: 978-1501079580

All rights reserved. No part of this book may be used or reproduced by any means, graphic, electronic, or mechanical, including photocopying, recording, taping, or by any information storage retrieval system without the written permission of the publisher except in the case of brief quotations embodied in critical articles and reviews.

This is a work of fiction. Names, characters, places, and incidents are the products of the author's imagination, or are used fictitiously. Any resemblance to actual persons, living or dead, business establishments, events, or locales is entirely coincidental.

Cover art: Damonza
Cover design: Damonza
Edited: Cassie McCown
Proofread: Linda at Victory Editing
Formatted: Elizabeth Hunter

The scanning, uploading, and distribution of this book via the Internet or any other means without the permission of the publisher is illegal and punishable by law. Please purchase only authorized electronic editions, and do not participate in or encourage electronic piracy of copyrighted materials. Your support of the author's rights is appreciated.

For information, please visit:
ElizabethHunterWrites.com

For Sarah

You deserve to have
at *least* one book dedicated to you
for all that you do.
You're a gem. Always.
-E.

ALSO BY ELIZABETH HUNTER

The Elemental Mysteries Series

A Hidden Fire
This Same Earth
The Force of Wind
A Fall of Water

The Elemental World Series

Building From Ashes
Waterlocked (novella)
Blood and Sand
The Bronze Blade (novella)
Shadows and Gold (novella Fall 2014)

The Cambio Springs Mysteries

Long Ride Home (short story)
Shifting Dreams
Five Mornings (short story)
Desert Bound

The Irin Chronicles

The Scribe
The Singer
The Secret (Winter 2015)

Contemporary Romance

The Genius and the Muse

Chapter One

Teodora Vasquez threw back her head and let the slow spin of beer and music and crowd wash over her. She was almost there. Almost to the buzz that would let her forget the past week. The past month. Maybe the past year…

"Ted!" Tracey shouted from the other end of the bar. "Can you help me with this?"

The waitress was carrying two trays of empties and trying to maneuver behind the bar as patrons at the Cave called out orders. The blues-rock band playing that night started another set, and the volume just got louder.

Ted stood and made her way over to Tracey. "You know I'm not working tonight."

The waitress managed to put the tray on the back counter and turn to glower at the pushy patrons sitting at Ollie's long oak bar. Ollie was at the other end, pulling pints and keeping an eye on the crowd. No one shouted orders at him. They didn't dare.

"I know," Tracey said, "but Jena had to leave, and I can't imagine this is harder than surgery, right?"

Ted glanced at the rowdy crowd. "Not too sure about that."

"Please?" The woman's gaze was desperate.

"Fine." She stepped behind the bar, and Tracey hurried to hand her a spare apron as Ted yelled at Ollie, "You owe me one!"

Ollie grunted but didn't look away from the taps.

Waiting tables and making drinks wasn't harder than operating the small medical clinic in Cambio Springs. The buzz she'd almost caught had disappeared with Tracey's plea, and Ted couldn't think of anything better than the whirl of activity at the Cave to quiet her mind.

"You're a lifesaver!" Tracey fixed her mop of wiry curls into a ponytail and washed her hands before she started mixing the list of drinks she'd written on her pad. "Sandra was supposed to work tonight. She was a no-show. I have no idea why Jena had to run out, but it must have been an emergency. —Ollie, I need two Blue Moons and a cider!— She didn't even ask. Just told Ollie she was leaving. —And a Fat Tire when you get a chance!— He didn't argue."

He wouldn't. Jena wasn't a regular employee. Like Ted, she helped out when Ollie needed her, and she wasn't a flake. She was a chef and owned the only other restaurant in town, the Blackbird Diner. She also had two boys at home and another on the way, thanks to her hot-as-sin new husband, Caleb Gilbert.

"Hope it's nothing serious." Ted tried not to worry too much. If it were medical, her phone would already be ringing. She was the only doctor in town.

"I'm sure it's fine."

"He call anyone to help behind the bar?"

"Yeah."

Ted grabbed a pad and headed out to the floor, nodding along to the music. It was a new band—some boys from Las Vegas—and they were good. The Cave was Ollie's bar, but all of his closest friends helped out occasionally. It was fun to hang out on quieter nights, and they always drank for free. Jena and Caleb usually got a babysitter for the boys and were there on the weekends when live music filled the bar and things were busier. Jena waited tables and made drinks with Ollie while Caleb would hang out and keep things from getting too crazy. Having the Cambio Springs Chief of Police in the corner of the room tended to keep out the wilder elements.

Well, the wilder *human* elements. There wasn't anything they could do about the shapeshifters. The visiting humans mixed among the locals, never suspecting the large man who served them drinks was a bear on full-moon nights. Or the lean guy at the pool table slid into a rattlesnake to sun himself on the hot desert rocks that surrounded the small town. The three brothers nodding along to the band howled at the moon on Friday nights.

And that wasn't just a figure of speech.

She was picking up empties when she felt warm breath on her neck. She was about to turn and bare claws when she heard his voice.

"Hey, Ted."

Son of a bitch.

Alex McCann leaned down and gave her neck an obvious sniff. Ted tried not to roll her eyes. Wolves. It was all about the nose.

"What are you doing here, Alex?"

He took another deep breath and smirked. "Pissing you off and, apparently, turning you on a little."

"Go away."

"I'm also helping out Ollie. He called and said Jena had to take off. He knew I wasn't busy tonight."

"Well, Tracey asked me to help, so you can go home."

He looked around the chaotic bar, and Ted tried to keep a straight face. They were still short-staffed. The Cave wasn't a large bar, but that night, they were stretching the fire code with all the people crammed in to hear the music and let loose at the end of the week.

Apparently Alex thought so too.

"I can stay."

"Don't you need to get home?"

He cocked his head. "No, I told you—"

"I mean Los Angeles." She lifted an eyebrow. "Work's done for the week. Shouldn't you be scurrying back?"

He looked close, a quiet expression of challenge on his face. "I am home, baby. You'll get used to it eventually."

She stepped on the toe of his boot and ground her foot down. "Don't call me that."

It didn't do anything but bring up painful memories.

He clenched his jaw, and Ted could see the faint golden glow behind his eyes. "Don't go furry now, McCann."

"Then keep your claws in, Vasquez."

She stepped back and smiled. "You only wish my claws were in you." She was fairly sure there was an old scar or two on his shoulders that proved it.

Alex stepped back, and people cleared a path for him. They always did.

"Patience is a virtue… *baby*."

Ted turned back to finish picking up the tables.

The work kept her too busy to think about Alex. Too busy to think about their history or how she still—even after years apart—turned toward his side of the bed to reach for him at night.

She'd devoted years to her feelings for him. Years to making a relationship work that probably never should have started anyway. She'd loved him. Almost felt desperate with it sometimes, and Ted hated that feeling. The raw need for him still clawed at her when he was near, as if the wildcat inside her were tearing to get out.

To hurt him? To drag him back? She didn't know. And she was a person first, not an animal.

Luckily she was too busy to examine it closely when she was balancing a dozen empty glasses on a tray.

Too busy to think about her struggling practice. Too busy to think about her family or the rumbling in the cat clan her mother and great aunt were trying to quell. And definitely too busy to think about the new spa resort Alex was building in the heart of Cambio Springs, the place the Vasquez clan had called home for generations.

Some in town hoped the resort would use the natural mineral springs that gave the town its name to draw wealthy visitors to the luxury resort that McCann Holdings was building. Others worried the secrecy the seven original families of the Springs had carefully maintained for over one hundred years would crumble and humans would discover that one of the springs, the one hidden in the canyon walls, had turned the original town founders into shapeshifters.

Cats, wolves, snakes, birds, and bears. There had been others married in, but the seven original families had passed on their strange quirk to their offspring, and now the isolated desert town was unique for more than just the mineral springs. It didn't matter if your mom or dad married a human. If one of them changed into a bobcat on the full moon, you would too.

"Hey, can I get a beer here?"

"Miss? Miss?"

"Another round when you get a chance?"

The shouts, laughs, and mild chaos around her had the odd effect of quieting Ted's mind as she focused on the immediate task. It was what had made her so good in trauma. She'd been in her element during her time in the ER. Part of her hated that she'd had to go into general practice, but that was what the town needed.

And what Cambio Springs needed, Ted gave. That's the way it had always been. And if giving that meant sacrificing part of her heart, she made the sacrifice.

"Why's it so slow tonight?" a whiny voice at her next table asked.

"It usually isn't. Oh my… He is so hot."

Ted smiled at the table of clueless human women who ordered four margaritas and couldn't take their eyes off the singer in the corner. He was cute, but Ted had to admit he didn't hold a candle to the eye candy standing behind the bar, laughing and mixing drinks with a smile and a wink to the girls. Ted knew she wasn't the only one who noticed.

Ollie and Alex had been friends for years, and while the men didn't look a thing alike, the easy camaraderie was obvious. At almost six and a half feet tall, Ollie Campbell was a giant. Big arms. Big shoulders. His sun-darkened olive skin was covered with tattoos from wrist to collar. He'd trimmed his beard back to a thick stubble for the summer, and it was still growing out.

Alex, on the other hand, was getting scruffier. Not as tall as Ollie, he still stood an impressive six feet. His frame was leaner but strong in a way that didn't come from a gym. Sandy hair and piercing blue eyes. The Southern California business gloss was slowly wearing off the longer he stayed in town, and Ted tried not to notice how good it looked on him. It reminded her of when they'd been living together when she was in medical school. He'd been working construction then, not closing real estate deals. Rough and callused, when he came home dusty at night, he reminded her of home.

That animal attraction hadn't lessened between them; Ted had just gotten better at ignoring it.

She also ignored all the women flirting with Alex.

The Cave was the unofficial boundary line of Cambio Springs, so humans came in to drink the beer and listen to the quality bands that the Cave managed to pull in, but they didn't linger in town. Most were just passing through. The few who showed more interest were quietly discouraged, mostly by Ollie or any of the other bears in her friend's clan who acted as the unofficial guardians of Cambio Springs.

She saw Ollie smile at her and knew he'd caught her watching Alex. She rolled her eyes and rushed to another table. Ollie might have been Ted's second or third or fifth cousin, but he was one of Alex's best friends too. And he had opinions. Quiet opinions, but he hadn't held them back.

"He's back now, Ted. Work your shit out. You guys belong together."

Simple problem. Simple solution. Typical bear.

Sure, Alex was back. Until the resort was finished, and then Ted had little confidence he'd stick around. He'd misled her too many times.

"When are you coming home?"

"As soon as I can."

"Don't say we need to move on."

"Give me a little more time, Téa."

"Soon."

"Soon" had turned into seven years. Seven years since Alex McCann had broken her heart. Then he had come back and gotten her hopes up before disappearing again. Ted had learned her lesson.

No more Alex. No third chances. Time to move on.

But Ollie wanted the people around him content and happy, and she knew he missed when Alex and Ted had been together. She was his family, and Alex was his best friend. In Ollie's opinion, the solution was obvious.

Get over it and move on with their life together. The problem was Ollie believed Alex was staying in the Springs—which Ted didn't, even a little—and the bear's heart hadn't been broken one time too many by the wolf behind the bar.

She sidled up to the bar with a pad full of orders just as the band started in on an edgy rock cover of "With a Little Help from My Friends." Ted risked a glance at Alex. It was one of their songs. She remembered dancing in their tiny kitchen in Venice Beach, Alex singing the lyrics in her ear after a particularly bad day.

They'd grown up together, been friends before they were lovers. And sometimes she missed that most of all.

"Take a break."

He stood behind her; she didn't even need to look to know. The band had taken off at midnight, and someone put a Lucinda Williams tune on the jukebox. Fast enough to dance to but slow enough to hold your partner close. Exactly the kind of music Alex had always liked.

He knew what he was doing.

"Can't." The crowd had died down. She and Tracey were cleaning up the floor. It was after midnight, and her mind was clear. If she went home now, she'd sleep well. If she danced with Alex, she wouldn't sleep well for a week. As much as she hated it, he still had that effect on her.

"Dance with me, Ted." He slipped a hand around her waist to pull her back from the table she'd been clearing. "Just a… friendly dance."

She scoffed. "Right."

"Friends dance." He leaned closer, his heat pressing against her side. She could smell more than a hint of bourbon on his breath and wished it didn't draw her in. By the ease of his voice, he was buzzed and close to being drunk. At that sweet, goofy place that made him even harder to resist.

She patted the hand at her waist. "Make sure you get Jim or Ollie to drive you home."

"One dance."

"Alex—"

"You told me we were friends, remember?"

She had. In a moment of weakness, after Ted had loaded her oldest friend into her Jeep so Caleb could drive her to the hospital in Indio. In those moments when the prospect of losing Jena had terrified them both, she'd turned to Alex. Held on. She needed a friend, and he'd been there.

"Yeah, so? We can be friends."

"Friends dance with each other, Ted."

"Fine. One dance." Just to prove she could. She dropped the rag and turned to him, letting Alex guide her between the tables and toward the small open floor by the jukebox.

He held her loosely, and Ted set her hands on his shoulders.

One dance. Between friends.

She ignored the happy purr of her lion and tried to lean away from his body, but Alex still managed to surround her. With his arms, his scent, and that indescribable hum that always seemed to follow him. Like a live wire, her body reacted. She could feel the spark of awareness as he scented her.

Damn wolf.

He leaned in, his rough voice licking along her nerves.

"You smell good."

"That's surprising, considering how hot the bar is."

His grin was lazy. "You always smell good."

"You lived with me long enough to know that isn't true. Are you getting senile in your old age?"

"Why are you so mean to me?"

So I don't fall for you again. "Habit?"

"Why do I like it so much?"

"Definitely habit."

He laughed, his chest rumbling against hers, and Ted felt her skin light up, ready for his touch. She could feel the hair on the back of her neck rising and her arousal spiking. She started to push away, but Alex took a deep breath and pulled her tighter. He leaned down, his eyes narrowed on her face and his lips coming dangerously close. He blinked, and she knew he was feeling the bourbon he'd been sipping all night behind the bar.

"Téa—"

"Don't—"

"When we get back together, would you be okay with adding on to your house, or should I look for a bigger place before we have kids?"

She dropped her arms. "Right. No more dancing."

"What?"

"'This is your idea of a friendly conversation?'"

Even drunk, he still had a comeback. "Friends get married, have lots… and lots of mind-blowing sex, and procreate. Are you saying I shouldn't look for a bigger house?"

"Friends don't have sex."

"*Mind-blowing* sex."

She didn't even respond, just turned and walked back to the table.

"Ted!" He tried to follow her, laughing a little, only to trip over the leg of a chair that Tracey had propped up while she cleaned. Ted ignored him and darted into Ollie's office, intent on escaping before Alex could catch up with her.

She almost ran smack into the bear. Ollie held up his hands in defense. "What's chasing you, kitty cat?"

Only Ollie was allowed to call her "kitty cat" and survive. Mostly because he could smush her, even when she was a hundred-pound mountain lion.

"An annoying mutt you asked to help at the bar tonight."

"Ah." Nodding, Ollie stepped aside. "You know he misses you, right?"

"Yeah, it must be hard to lose your fallback plan." She gathered her purse and grabbed for the light sweater she carried to ward off the night chill. She started pulling it on as Ollie stood in the hall.

"Is that what you think? Really?"

She didn't say anything. *Put on sweater. Grab keys. Ignore rational bear.*

"Come on, Ted. Things are different now. Have you considered talking to him about it? You know he's not moving back to LA."

"No." She gripped her purse in both hands and clenched her eyes shut. "I don't know that."

"He says he's back for good. You don't believe him?"

"No." Even though a part of her heart wanted it to be true, she didn't trust that part. Her heart had let her down too many times.

"Ted—"

"I can take a lot of shit, Ollie." Her voice was hoarse; she cleared her throat. "But I've been down that road before. More than once. I'm not setting myself up just to get knocked down again."

Damn Alex. She'd come out tonight looking for a little peace among the crowd, not an emotional slap in the face. Ted shook her head and walked to the office door, only to see Ollie pressing a hand to Alex's chest, holding his friend back. His friend who had obviously been listening to their whole conversation.

Ted ignored the bare pain on her former lover's face.

Not again.

She looked up at Ollie and whispered, "Thanks a lot. Don't call me for a favor anytime soon."

Neither one said anything when she walked out the door.

If the crowds didn't work, then maybe wine would.

Ted took a long sip of red wine and leaned back in the recliner she'd stolen from her mom's house. It had been her dad's. On days she missed him, sitting in it felt like the big warm hugs that had filled her childhood. She'd had her eyes closed for approximately thirty seconds when the knock came at the door.

"Oh, for the love of…" She swung her legs down and marched toward the door.

If it was Alex, she was going to kill him. She'd done grunt work at the medical examiner's office in LA. She read Patricia Cornwell. She could figure out how to kill someone and make it look like an accident. Probably.

If not, the jail time might be worth it.

"Alex, for the last time—" She realized it wasn't Alex before the door swung all the way open. "Allie?"

The petite blonde's face was swollen and red. She sniffed but said nothing. Her eyes shone with tears in the lamplight.

"Allie, what on earth?"

Ted started pulling her into the house, every protective instinct on alert. A car door slammed in the dark. Then Jena was walking up the path.

"Hey."

"What's going on? Is someone hurt?"

"Not exactly. Do you have wine? Please tell me you have wine." She put a hand on her five months' pregnant belly. "I'm out, and Caleb only drinks beer."

Jena looked exhausted too, though not as wrecked as Allie. Both walked into the house in silence.

Ted said, "Will someone just tell me—"

"Joe left me."

Allie's voice was so soft Ted barely caught it.

Her mind wanted to scream, *Oh, thank you, Lord. Finally!*

Luckily, she held back.

"What happened? I mean, I knew you guys were having problems, but —"

"He just took off. Left me and the kids. Walked out while we were sitting down for dinner."

"Um…"

"It was meatloaf."

"You make excellent meatloaf."

"He said he didn't want to be married anymore. Like it was no big deal."

Ted was going to kill him. But not before she neutered the scrawny coyote.

Jena said, "That's why I left the Cave. Kevin called my cell."

Allie started to cry. "What kind of man leaves his fourteen-year-old son to clean up his messes?"

"A shit one."

"Ted!" Jena said, making hugging motions with her arms and pointing toward Allie.

"What?" she hissed. "You know I'm not good at the comforting thing. Joe is an asshole, and Kevin is an awesome kid who shouldn't have to deal with his father's shit. He's a douche bag." She huffed out a breath. "Man, that feels good. I've wanted to say it for years."

Jena said, "Glad to know it's all about you, Ted."

"That's not what I meant."

"My babies…" Allie didn't even hear her, but Jena glared. "Oh God. He was a jerk to me, but they loved their daddy. What am I gonna do?"

It was true. Joe had gotten Allie pregnant her senior year and planted three boys and a girl in her before Allie finally said "enough" after the birth of Loralie four years before. Joe seemed to love being a dad, and Allie had four kids under the age of fourteen. Before the base had closed and he lost his job, they'd struggled, but they'd all still laughed a lot.

But laughter over the past three years had been scarce, and Ted had suspected more than once that Joe was stepping out on her friend. They'd been friends once. All of them. Close friends. But Ted hadn't thought of Joe as anything but Allie's asshole husband in a long, long time.

"Friends get married, have lots of mind-blowing sex, and procreate."

Alex's words—meant to tease—now taunted her.

Talk about a lesson learned the hard way.

No, Alex. Never again. Even if he really did stay in town and they could manage to be friends, it could never be anything more. It wasn't just about them, and the consequences of screwing that up were too severe for everyone.

She hugged a crying Allie to her chest as Jena grabbed a bottle of wine and a glass from the kitchen. But in the back of her mind, she heard Alex whisper.

"Dance with me."

Chapter Two

The car door slamming shut sounded louder than normal in the still desert night. Ollie rolled down the window.

"You got it, or you need help in?"

"I'm good."

His best friend didn't say anything, just lifted an eyebrow. "No more bourbon, Alex."

"Go home. I'm fine."

"Don't wake up your mom. She'll yell at me."

"Good night, Ollie." He started to turn.

"Hey, Alex."

"What?"

Ollie seemed to hesitate but finally said, "She'll forgive you. She has to eventually. Just shake it off."

Right…

Alex waved at Ollie's retreating truck and walked with heavy steps up his parents' front porch.

"I'm not setting myself up just to get knocked down again."

She was never going to forgive him. Ever. Never, ever.

Shit, he was drunk.

He sighed, hearing the steps come down from upstairs as he turned the doorknob. It wasn't locked. Only an idiot with a death wish was going to break into the McCann house. They were the wolf alphas of Cambio

Springs, and no one—not even the most foolhardy Quinn—wanted to test their protective instincts.

"Alex?"

Oh, yay. His father was in the kitchen.

"Hey, Dad."

Robert McCann was in his sixties but didn't look a day over a very healthy fifty. His steel-grey hair was cropped close to his skull, and he still carried the military bearing of the former army sergeant he was. Alex's father hadn't been pleased his son didn't follow him into the service. There had been McCanns serving in the US Army since the Civil War, and Robert didn't let his son forget it. The fact that Alex had made millions in real estate didn't provoke more than a slightly satisfied grunt.

Robert eyed him with suspicion. "Are you drunk?"

Alex leaned against the doorway of the kitchen. His father was making coffee. He didn't need much more sleep than Alex did. Never had. It was a benefit if you were the alpha or the disappointing son of one.

"According to the mostly empty bottle of bourbon Ollie forced me to abandon… yes."

Robert curled his lip but pulled out another mug for coffee.

"That cat giving you problems again?"

"Not talking to you about her."

He refused to talk about Ted with his father. Alex had learned his lesson when he'd been twenty-seven and heartbroken. His father had waited on the porch for Alex to get out of his car, took one look at his haggard face, then told him he knew their relationship would never have worked out anyway, so it was better it ended before kids had become involved.

Alex had spent that weekend at Ollie's, cleaning out the attic and ignoring calls from his mother. He never mentioned Ted's name in his father's presence again.

"You know—"

He glared. "Not. Talking. About. Her."

Robert lifted the corner of his mouth in what might have been a smile. "Fine. I expect you'll figure it out. You have a plan for everything else."

Though he'd never, ever say it publicly, Robert McCann had plenty of doubts about the resort his son planned for his hometown. That was fine. Alex was used to his father doubting him. He'd just work ten times harder to prove him wrong, like he always did.

His father splashed a little milk in Alex's mug. A concession, since the sergeant took his coffee black.

"Your mother got a call tonight from Kathy Crowe."

Alex frowned and tried to focus through the bourbon haze. The coffee helped. "Jena's mom?"

"Joe Russell took off."

"What?" he asked again. "What are you talking about?"

"Took off. Left his family."

"Are you talking about Allie's Joe? Joe Smith?"

Robert nodded. "Never understood why that boy took his woman's name after they married. Russell is a perfectly fine name."

"Joe wanted to fit in. He always did. He *left* her?"

"Yep."

"That *fuc*—"

"Language."

It brought him up short. He was still in his parents' home, and if he had to guess, his mother was listening with her eagle ears. Not *actual* eagle ears. Julia McCann was full human, like many spouses in Cambio Springs, but preternatural hearing must have rubbed off over the years of living in a town full of shapeshifters.

"That ass!" Alex set down his mug, anger and surprise cutting through the bourbon. "Are you kidding me?"

"No. Walked out the door right when Allie and the kids were sitting down to dinner."

Alex was going to kill him.

"Allie's going to need some help." Robert motioned to the kitchen table, and Alex followed him. "She's not technically part of the pack, but—"

"She's one of my best friends, Dad. It doesn't matter that she's a fox."

The other canine shifters tended to be more solitary or roam in family packs. They didn't share the strict hierarchy of the wolves, but since they all shared a common ancestor, they still held a certain level of loyalty.

"I agree. Plus, her mother was a McCann, even if it was distant. She's family."

Alex rubbed his face. "Is Kathy with her?" Allie's mom had died when she was young, leaving her dad to raise his small family of shifters among his wife's people. Jena's mom had been a second mother to the Smith girls.

"I think so. Your mom just found out a few hours ago. They'll get her covered. But if there's a need—"

"It's covered. She's covered. I'll take care of it, Dad."

His father nodded approvingly but didn't say anything while they finished their coffee. It was moments like this, quiet moments, when Alex knew his dad *did* appreciate some of what he'd done. What he was trying to do. They may have different personalities, but their hearts were in the same place. His father would go without before any of his family or pack.

On lonely nights, the knowledge that Alex had the resources to help the people he cared about was sometimes the only thing that kept him warm. The sacrifices were worth it at times like that. He had to remind himself it wasn't all about him. It was about his father and mother. His sister. The wolves who depended on him. His friend with four kids who needed someone to step up when their father stepped out.

"I'm not setting myself up just to get knocked down again."

If he'd really lost Ted forever, it had to mean something.

The next morning, Alex roused himself from his childhood bed, downed as many aspirin as he could get away with, and slipped out the door after a quick conversation with his mom, who was already putting food together for Allie. Then, like every Saturday for the past few months, he headed to his sister's house. The fact that she happened to be home that weekend was only a bonus.

Willow McCann lived at the edge of town, halfway out into the desert and away from as many distractions as she could. The fact that his baby sister was a famous painter with work shown across the Southwest surprised him some days. But then, when he thought about it more, it didn't seem strange at all. In her own quiet way, Willow was the mirror image of their father. She was stubborn as hell. Alex figured one day his little sister had simply decided she wanted everyone to buy her paintings for ridiculous sums of money. Then she quietly set about taking over her tiny corner of the art world until her mission was accomplished. She was like a special ops soldier with a paintbrush.

She had recently taken up ceramics. In a few months, she'd conquer that too. People who didn't know her thought she was shy. She wasn't. Willow just didn't like very many people and found it easier to adopt the mantle of a reclusive artist in their tiny community. It worked for her because it kept most people away.

She was sitting in the shaded lean-to outside her house when Alex pulled up. Some thick vine covered the arbor, lush, green, and dripping with yellow flowers. The road up to her house was covered in a new coat of gravel, and the old place gleamed. It was a small house his grandparents had built, but Willow had improved it.

The desert landscaping was blooming with sparse beauty; colorful murals and tiled mosaics decorated the low garden walls, lending a lush look to the area despite the arid plantings. She'd recovered an old wooden table with a blue-and-green-glass mosaic and added red chairs she'd painted herself. A pot of coffee was sitting on the table along with some sweet rolls he knew she probably only bought for him.

Willow didn't look up but continued sketching in the pad at her left as she drank her coffee.

"Joe left Allie last night," she said. "Took off right in the middle of dinner. What an asshole."

"I heard."

"Apparently she was making meatloaf. And Allie's meatloaf is great. So he's a *stupid* asshole."

"Not gonna disagree with you."

She finally looked up when his chair scraped across the terra-cotta tiles under the arbor. "How did you hear?"

"Kevin called Jena, who came home from the bar. Jena called her mom to help watch the kids so they could go over to Ted's. Kathy called Mom. I knew about it by the time I got home from the Cave." He closed his eyes against the glaring light. "How did you know?"

She shrugged. "Allie called me this morning."

"How's she doing?"

"She's worried about the kids."

Joe was such an asshole.

Alex helped himself to the extra mug his sister had set out and filled it from the bright blue carafe. He didn't say anything. It was one of the benefits of hanging out with his sister. They didn't really need to talk much. Thirty years being related made non-verbal communication a breeze. She passed him the milk and a sweet roll without even looking up from her drawing.

"So," she asked, "has anyone told Ollie?"

Leave it to Willow, asking the one question everyone was thinking and no one wanted to say.

"I haven't."

"Neither have I. I figure Joe deserves at least a day's head start before we set Ollie loose on him. Anything less seems unfair."

Alex snorted. "What makes you think Ollie would track him down? I figure he'd just make sure Joe stayed gone."

Willow didn't say anything for a while. She finally looked up from the sketch and gave him a sad smile. "He would if he thought Allie wanted him back."

"Does she?"

She shook her head. "I don't think so. She sounded sad but... relieved, I guess? I don't think he was an easy guy to live with the past few years."

Alex frowned. "Did we miss something?"

"Allie always puts the best face on stuff. You know that. I think Joe... said a lot of mean shit to her."

"Bad enough."

She nodded. "Bad enough."

They sat in silence for a few more minutes before Alex asked the question he asked every week.

"Please? I promise I'll be quiet."

"No."

"Pretty please?"

"I let you use my house as much as you want when I'm out of town. Don't think I don't see your messes, Alex. You are not moving in with me."

"Mom and Dad are going to drive me crazy."

"And you'd drive *me* crazy if you move in. You're a big boy. Deal."

"I'll be in a mental hospital, and you'll only have yourself to blame."

"You're so full of shit. Why don't you just get your own place? There's not a lot, but there's a few houses in town available. Marcie and Phil are moving. Why not rent their house?"

"Because."

"That is not an answer."

Because...

In the back of his mind, he'd always figured he and Ted would be back together by now and he'd be with her, skipping the awkward "Should we move in together?" conversation because he'd be homeless and she'd take pity on him. His condo in Huntington was already rented out and providing a very nice extra income. Even with as much money as he had tied up in the resort, cost wasn't the issue. If he rented or bought a place without Ted, then he'd be conceding defeat.

Willow picked up her sketchbook again. "Just rent one of Jena's trailers until you and Ted get back together."

Alex stayed silent and glared at her, but she didn't notice.

"You know, she's more likely to think you're actually staying in town if you buy a place."

He still said nothing.

"So stubborn." She sighed. "I can give you tips on groveling once you figure it out."

"You're such a little shit sometimes."

Willow smiled. "I love you too."

By Saturday afternoon, he felt better physically, but he was still pissed about Joe, couldn't get hold of Ollie—no matter how many times he called his house and the bar—and his foreman, Marcus Quinn, had called him to the jobsite to rework the plans he thought they'd already finalized so the guys could get to work right away on Monday.

"I don't get why we have to change the angle of the swimming pool that much."

"Alex, I know you want the bungalows to face the water, but how much do we want to fight nature? If you want the creek to run down this way, then the natural course of the water…"

Alex let his mind drift as Marcus went into details. He knew at the end of the day he'd end up agreeing with him. Marcus Quinn might have been born to a slightly shady clan of reptile shifters—his natural form was a king snake—but that hadn't stopped him from being one of the best contractors around. He'd started with a surveying company but had quickly expanded. He'd gone into partnership with his wife's brother a few years ago, and their business had grown to include landscape and general engineering contracting too.

Like most of the shifters from the Springs, Marcus married away. Josie was a hairdresser from Vegas who seemed to take the knowledge that their three kids would eventually sprout scales in stride. Their oldest was almost ten, and Alex knew they were talking about moving back to the Springs full time.

"So if you want the hot spring to feed into the lake we're digging here"—He pointed at the plans spread out on Alex's tailgate.—"then the slope needs to start here. Which means the swimming pool is going to have to angle southeast a little more. That's going to block some of your afternoon sun, but we're talking about the hottest part of the day. I don't think guests are going to complain much."

"No, you're right." And this was why he'd hired Marcus. The man was bright enough to see the big picture. "Go for it. Can you tweak it before Monday?"

"Yeah, it's minor. And doing that is going to cut back on time too. Because we'll be working with the natural slope."

"Plus, it'll just look better."

"If you're going for a natural landscape, yeah."

"We are."

Marcus rolled up the plans and slid them into a cardboard tube before he tossed them in the cab of his pickup. "It's going to be something, man."

"You think?" Some days, Alex had his doubts.

Marcus slapped his shoulder. "It's gonna be great. This place needs it. Plus, having a resort here is making it a lot easier to convince Josie to leave Vegas."

Alex smiled. "Glad I could help."

"Hey, she needs to work too."

"Does she still have blue hair? Not sure how many of the girls here are into blue hair."

Marcus grinned. "My woman works the blue."

Alex had to admit the man was right. He'd only met Josie once, but she'd made an impression and it hadn't been a bad one.

"Plus," Marcus continued, "she's managing that entire salon now. Doing the hair and all the admin."

"Be good to have you guys in town," he said.

"This place is gonna change a lot." Marcus walked around to the side of his pickup. "For the good, Alex. It's gonna be amazing. Big picture, remember?"

"Yeah. I'll see you Monday."

"See you."

A cloud of dust followed the pickup while Alex sat on his tailgate at the edge of Springs Park, looking over the staked and leveled ground he'd bought from Old Joe Quinn and his own father. Resting at the base of the sandstone cliffs, the seven springs that gave the town its name bubbled steadily, as they had for centuries.

It had been his own ancestor, Robert McCann the first, who began the trek that started east of the Mississippi, in the Great Smoky Mountains, and had led west, gathering others who were looking for a fresh start. Led by Thomas Crowe's vision, they came to the desert, and it was Andrew McCann, the first water witch of Cambio Springs, who found the bubbling mineral waters and the hidden oasis, a fresh spring that provided the travelers drinking water.

The same spring that kept them alive also gave those first settlers the magic that let them shift into the animals that surrounded them. No one knew why. Alex had stopped asking when he figured out none of the grownups had a clue either. It just was.

He walked the perimeter of the property, the wolf in him happy to be checking the boundaries of his new territory. The reception building and office areas would border the existing city park. Placing the buildings there would allow for an attractive entrance to the resort and draw attention to the shops on Main Street, which the city was already cleaning, updating, and landscaping. Walls carefully concealed with palms and bougainvillea would give the resort guests and the town residents the privacy both craved.

It had been a condition of the town council that the residents still be able to use the two largest mineral pools as they always had. Alex, who had grown up playing in Springs Park, agreed. Marcus's plans gave the resort access to draw from the hot mineral water and use the mud pools that were on the edge of the park. Those would be enclosed in the resort property and used for cosmetic treatments and mud baths.

The hot mineral water from the two largest pools would be fed into a man-made grotto, continually renewed by pipes carefully concealed beneath the ground. The runoff from the grotto would feed down into a cooler lake shaded by acacias and palms. Clusters of white bungalows would dot the property, following the traditional clean lines of Southwestern architecture that allowed the landscape and vistas to take center stage. The rock left over from clearing the land would be used to build winding paths interspersed with locally sourced tile. There would be hiking paths and yoga classes. Spa treatments in a beautiful building with views of the mesa. A restaurant that Alex and Jena both hoped would draw raves.

It would be beautiful. It would provide jobs and opportunities for the town to grow.

It might even make Alex some money, if they could stay on schedule.

He wondered what Ted would think of it.

Then he decided not to torture himself. He walked up the hill back to his truck and headed back to his parents' house, deciding to go into the diner to speak to Jena about renting tomorrow.

Chapter Three

"Well, *mamá*, looks like you're all clear."

Little Allie, sitting on the edge of Ted's examining table, let out a sigh of relief. It hadn't been the easiest conversation she'd ever had, broaching the subject of getting tested for STIs, but as Allie's doctor, Ted couldn't ignore the chance that Joe had been cheating on her and might have had unprotected sex that could infect his wife.

It had set Allie off on yet another rant about her husband. She kept strict control around the kids, but when she had a moment alone with either Jena or Ted, the truth came out.

"Well," she said, dark humor coating her voice, "score one for me. One for me and ninety-nine for the asshole."

To say Joe had been emotionally abusive would be an understatement. The bright, confident woman that had charmed the world was a very thin facade over a woman wracked with insecurities planted by a thousand cutting comments and cruel words. Ted berated herself for not looking closer. For not seeing the depression lurking beneath Allie's happy smile.

"You're going to be okay. All this shit? It's just going to make you stronger."

"I don't have a choice, do I? The kids need at least one parent who doesn't check out."

"You need to take care of yourself too. Not just the kids. How are you sleeping?" Ted had slept like shit for a full year after she and Alex broke up.

Allie shrugged. "Okay, I guess."

"Don't miss him?"

"Not… not really. That's sad, isn't it?"

"I don't know. Is it?"

Allie blinked back tears. "Part of me is angry he left us, and the other part of me is glad he's not making me miserable anymore. Then I feel guilty for being glad because the kids are so torn up."

"He wasn't an asshole to them. That seems pretty normal to me. Don't feel guilty."

She sighed and closed her eyes, leaning back on the paper-covered exam table.

"Know what I really want?"

"What?" Ted smiled and began cleaning up her exam room. Allie was her last appointment before lunch.

"I want to have really amazing sex, then shift to my fox and hide in a cozy den for about a month."

Ted blinked. "Um…"

"He stopped touching me months ago," she whispered.

Ted said nothing. It was a special kind of torture to deny their animal natures that way. Foxes, especially, had voracious sexual appetites and were some of the most affectionate shifters in the Springs. So for Joe to deny his wife physical touch was cruel, and he would have known it.

"That's stupid, right?"

Ted shook her head. "No, not stupid."

"I didn't even like him, but I still missed being with him."

"If it was the only thing he gave you, then it's not weird to miss it, Allie."

"I guess so."

"Don't beat yourself up for being a normal woman. And a normal fox." Ted nudged Allie off the table so she could clean up. "But maybe don't go out and sleep with a random at the Cave, either, okay?"

Or Ollie's head will explode.

Allie snorted. Then she broke into a full-out belly laugh. Ted laughed too. Eventually, both women had tears running down their cheeks, and Ted's belly was aching.

"Can you even picture it?" Allie choked out. "I don't think I know *how* to flirt with a man anymore."

"You'll figure it out. If I recall, it came naturally when you were younger."

"Yeah, before four kids and all the stretch marks."

Ted frowned. "You have stretch marks?" It was unusual for shifters to scar at all, but Allie was very fair-skinned. She'd gotten her light blond curls and blue eyes from her mom and had to slather on sunscreen in the desert sun.

"Not many. I can't complain. Human girls have it way worse." Allie looked at her out of the corner of her eye. "You're lucky. You have that gorgeous dark skin. Probably won't get any when you and Alex finally figure things out."

"Shut up, Allie."

"Do you think you'll have puppies or kittens?" Mischief lit her pixie face. "Or do you call 'em cubs?"

"Seriously." Ted was getting annoyed. "I'm not talking about Alex."

"Why not? I'm tired of talking about me. I'd much rather talk about you and Alex avoiding the inevitable."

Ted slammed a drawer. "Why does everyone seem to think we're inevitable except me? You and Jena. Ollie. Alex, especially. Does it even occur to anyone that I...?"

Allie waited, a patient expression on her face. "What?" she finally asked. "You what? Still love him? And he loves you? You guys have always been like that, fighting what everyone around you could see. It's kind of ridiculous."

"It's not ridiculous!"

"No... you're right." Allie's eyes narrowed. "It's not ridiculous. You know what it is? It's *wasteful.*"

Ted's mouth snapped shut.

"It's wasteful, Ted. To have someone who loves you like that and hold them at arm's length. All because you're holding a grudge."

"I'm not holding a grudge!" She was totally holding a grudge.

"I've never had anyone love me the way Alex loves you."

Yes, you do.

It was on the tip of Ted's tongue, but she bit it back. It was too soon for that.

"If I did, I'd grab onto it so fast." Allie was still talking. "And you just throw it away."

"He's never even apologized." Ted tugged off the sweater she kept to combat the air conditioning. "Did you know that? He left me. Strung me along for years, interfered with every relationship I tried to have, and he never even apologized for it."

"Maybe he isn't sorry. He did what he had to do." Allie's eyes narrowed. "At least he takes care of the people who depend on him, unlike some people."

"Fine. He doesn't have to be sorry for leaving me to work in LA. But hurting me the way he did? Never giving me a straight answer?" Ted bit the inside of her lip to keep from crying. "He broke my heart, Allie. More than once. And I know he's got you all convinced that he's back to stay, but he hasn't convinced me. I'll believe it when the resort is finished and he's still here in six months. As far as I'm concerned, this is just another project to him."

Allie's face softened. "You'll figure it out eventually."

"Figure what out?"

"Why he's done all this."

"I know why he's done it." She did. "I know he loves this place. I know it's always been home to him."

"No." Allie's smile was wistful. "You've always been home to him. *You.* Not the town. Not his pack. You."

"Allie—"

"Enough." Allie's quiet sigh stopped her. "I'm tired of fighting. Come on, doc. Let's go to lunch. Jena expected us a half hour ago, and this fox is hungry."

Allie was sitting with Jena's mom, Kathy, and her two youngest kids when Alex walked in. Ted heard the door but didn't turn. Jena looked up, then glanced at Ted. She said, "Hot wolf at seven o'clock, *chica*."

Caleb was sitting next to Ted. "Hey," he said with a frown. "Who's hot?"

Jena leaned over the counter as far as her expanding belly would allow. "You are."

"That's right. Don't forget it." He kissed her. "Hottest man in the world, sitting right here."

Jena's eyes lit up. "You mean you're going to shift into George Clooney later?"

"Jena…"

Ted said, "He doesn't actually do that when you—"

"Of course I don't!" Caleb scowled. "What have you been telling your friends?"

"I don't know what you're talking about."

Ted listened to their banter and tried to ignore the heat at her back.

"Saving this for anyone?"

Why did his voice have to sound sexy when he was tired?

"Nope." She sipped her iced tea and glanced at the clock over the counter, studiously avoiding looking at him. She needed to get back to her office, but she couldn't leave right away. If she did, Alex would think it was because of him. And no one was chasing Ted out of her friend's diner.

"What's good today?" He didn't grab a menu, just leaned toward her and asked. Like a friend. Like they ate lunch together all the time. She half expected him to throw an arm around her back and lean in to kiss her temple like he'd always done when they were together.

It was so easy to imagine it hurt. She had to fix this. They had to at least be friends again. As Jena and Caleb teased each other and the hum of activity grew louder, she turned to him.

"Listen, Alex—"

"Just so you know, I'm done." He lifted his eyes to hers. He was beyond exhausted. Looked like he hadn't slept in a month. "I heard what you said the other night. I'm tired of trying to fix something you obviously don't want anymore."

"What?"

"What we had was… whatever. You know what we had. But now? I— we need to move on, right?"

"Right?"

"Are you asking or agreeing?"

Was he joking? Or just really tired? Ted frowned. He'd been trying to win her back for months, trying to charm her and seduce her. Now he was just… done? Maybe the end was in sight with the resort planning and he was headed back to LA. She should be relieved, right? She was relieved. Alex out of sight was better. Then they could gradually work on being friends again.

He lifted an amused eyebrow. "Asking or agreeing, Ted?"

"Asking you what?"

"If we need to move on. You didn't sound sure."

"No! Of course. I was just surprised. I mean, you've been… you know. And I was just thinking… I mean—"

"What were you thinking?" His voice was hoarse again. "Because that look on your face is making me reconsider the giving-up thing."

"You must be thirsty." She shoved her water at him. "You're probably not drinking enough. You know, even on cool days, dehydration—"

"What were you thinking, Ted?"

She took a breath. "Just that I miss being friends with you. We should be friends again. Real friends. Not you pretending to be my friend to get me into bed, like you have been."

"I had a lot more planned than just the bed."

"Focus." She glared at him. "Allie's going through all this shit with Joe leaving. Jena has the baby coming. The resort is being built. We just… need our friends. All of us."

He looked at her a long time, and Ted had to fight the urge to run her hand along the edge of his jaw. He did look tired. Exhausted. Sometimes when he'd been like that before, he'd lie on her chest and put his face in her neck, breathing in her scent as if just the smell of her would let him rest. She could still feel the stubble where it rasped against her collarbone.

She saw his eyes drift to her neck, like he was remembering too. She turned away and took a drink of water.

"I need to get back to work."

His voice was still rough. "Yeah?"

"The tacos are really good today. I'd have those."

"That sounds good." He stretched his neck and sighed in relief when it popped. "You busy this weekend?"

Hadn't they just talked about being friends? Or was he reconsidering it now?

Shit. She had no idea where his head was.

"I'm around. Why?"

"I was going to ask Jena if I could rent one of her Airstreams. Need to get out of my folks' house."

"I can't blame you for that. I imagine living with the general must be interesting."

The corner of his mouth lifted in a lazy grin. "He was a sergeant, not a general. But yes. My own space would be good."

She nodded toward Kathy. "Talk to Jena's mom. Those are hers to rent out, but I'm pretty sure two are empty right now."

"Think you and the girls would have time to help me move a little stuff? Maybe do a barbecue after? Ollie won't be able to come, but how about you?"

Ted nodded, trying to come off as casual. It was exactly the kind of thing friends did all the time. Just like Sunday dinner at Jena's, which they all went to.

"Sure. I'll talk to Jena and Caleb. You talk to Allie."

"Cool." He rubbed the back of his neck. "Gives me something to look forward to other than work."

"Talk to Kathy. Let me know. You've got my number."

"Mm-hmm." He was trying to suppress a smile when he caught her narrow eyes. "What? You're right. I have your number."

"See you later."

The double meaning didn't occur to her until after she was back at her office.

Sometimes, it was good to be a cat.

Even if that cat was a one-hundred-pound predator who scared the piss out of her more domestic sisters. Ted was between appointments during the slow, hot drag of afternoon when the kids had left school and the sun was high, baking the western windows of her office and making her drowsy.

She'd gone through the rush of morning appointments but wasn't expecting anyone that afternoon. People from the Springs tended to stay indoors when the weather got too hot. Her practice was feast or famine. She was either really, really busy or lonely for days on end. Slowly, word about her clinic was starting to drift to some of the more rural desert residents, which meant she had a few people from outside town who were choosing to come to her instead of driving into Indio or Palm Desert for appointments. When the resort opened, she imagined it would get even busier. But that afternoon?

Snooze city.

Why fight it? Ted slipped out of the scrubs she wore to work and shifted, curling into a sunbeam that crossed the couch in her office, letting a low purr rumble from her throat. She had better instincts as a cat. No one would come into the building without waking her.

And about forty-five minutes later, someone did.

"Will you stop and just—"

Ted lifted her head at the scuffle that sounded out in the waiting room. She only hired a girl to work in the office half days, so after lunch, she was on her own.

"Ted?"

What was Alex doing here? She lifted her head but didn't shift.

"Hey, Ted, are you in—oh, hi."

She let her lion curl her lip.

"Yes, you're very ferocious. Will you shift and come out here? One of my guys is hurt."

A voice came from the waiting room. "I am not that hurt, dammit!"

"Marcus, your forearm has a right angle in the middle of it!" Alex yelled. "You're not shifting until it's been set."

Alex turned back to her. "So… you're not busy, right?"

She just stared at him. If he thought she was shifting with him in the office and the door open, he was nuts.

"Oh!" He shook his head. "Sorry. Yeah, I'll just…" He looked from her toward the waiting room, then back again. "I'll be out here. With Marcus. And I'll leave you. Alone." She heard him mutter something under his breath that sounded like "naked Ted." If she weren't in cat form, she probably wouldn't have heard it.

Alex had loved watching her shift from a cougar back to her human form. Turned him on like a switch. She got up and stalked toward the door, shoving it closed with her nose, but not before she felt the quick slip of Alex's finger along her back.

She didn't shiver. That was just a residual twitch from the shift.

A few seconds later, she was pulling on clothes and listening to the two men muttering in the small exam room.

"Not that bad."

"—file a workman's comp claim."

"What am I going to tell them? 'Healed instantly after turning into a king snake?'"

"If it heals instantly."

Ted shoved open the door. "It will probably heal instantly. Let's just get it set so—oh, whoa!" Her face lit with a smile. "That really *is* at a right angle!"

Marcus said, "Try not to sound so excited, Ted."

"I just rarely see any of us get really hurt! Usually, it's the humans and little kids." She pulled on a pair of gloves and nudged his shoulder so he was sitting on the table. She gingerly lifted the arm, holding on to the wrist and elbow. Marcus didn't even wince. "What did you do to it?"

Shifter bones were strong. For one to break like that…

"One of the guys pulled out an engine with a forklift and dropped it. Caught my arm in the fall."

She made a face. "That'll do it."

Alex said, "I want to know why the engine on that scraper was out to begin with."

"Sid's a whiz with engines, Alex. No need to hire someone off-site when he can just take a look."

"And drop engines on your arm."

"No big deal."

Ted interjected. "Well, it would be a big deal if it had shattered. Luckily, it looks like a clean break. It's swollen, but I don't think you severed anything. Any numbness?"

"I wish."

She felt the skin, but it wasn't overly cool.

"All right. My best guess is the two bones snapped. Nothing is poking through. Doesn't look like excessive internal bleeding or swelling. If you want to make sure, I can take X-rays—"

"Oh, come on," Marcus said. "Really?"

Alex stepped closer from his stance in the corner. "Hey! If she says you need X-rays, you need X-rays."

"Or I'll pull your arm and wrap it. Once it's splinted, then you can shift."

"See?" Marcus looked triumphant. "Knew I liked her."

Shifting when you were hurt could be tricky. If it was a cut or open wound, shifting would sometimes make it worse. Luckily, bones were a bit easier. As long as the bone was in alignment, shifting to your natural form would heal the break when you shifted back. Ted had always theorized it was because their bodies were able to remake their skeletons switching from human to animal.

"I'm warning you, if there's any kind of wonky alignment when you shift back, you're gonna know. I'll have to re-break it, and you'll need X-rays to see what the problem is. But if you want to take the chance, you can. It'll be quicker, but it's up to you."

"Actually," Alex said, "I think it's up to me. Since he was injured at work."

"Bull. Shit," Marcus said. "I'm fine. You know you're not filing a claim on this. It was my own stupidity."

Ted watched them argue. She was putting her money on Marcus, just because Alex looked green every time he caught a glimpse of that broken arm. It really was a miracle the bones hadn't protruded through the skin.

"Okay!" Alex relented, throwing up his hands. "You want to risk it, it's your own arm."

"Good. Hit me, doc."

"Alex, hold his shoulders." Ted walked in front of Marcus, grabbing his wrist with both of hers. "We doing this the old-fashioned way?"

He nodded, so she pulled through Marcus's grunt, bracing herself to straighten the man's heavily muscled arm. She couldn't hear it, but she knew when the bones snapped back into alignment. Sweat broke out on his forehead, but the tight clench of his jaw eased.

"Awesome," he said. "Feels better already."

"Okay. Strip and shift. Let's see if you've got any issues."

Alex and Marcus both gave her a look.

Ted sighed and turned her back to them. "Like either of you have anything I haven't seen before."

Marcus shuffled around, and she could hear Alex helping him get his shirt over his head.

"I just didn't want Alex to see where I tattooed your name on my ass, Ted. He might bite me."

"Fine," Alex said. "I'm out of here. I'll give you guys some privacy." He tried to sound amused, but Ted knew he was squeamish when he wasn't a wolf.

She heard the door shut and asked Marcus, "You ready?"

"One snake, coming up."

The air changed around him as Ted turned back, a shimmer like hot air over asphalt. Within seconds, the large man was gone, and a glossy black snake with pure white rings lay curled at her feet. Marcus was brilliant in his natural form, an abnormally long California king snake who stretched over five feet. Ted loved examining the reptiles because they were so varied. Most mature reptile shifters could turn into anything from a rattlesnake to a large lizard. The biology of it fascinated her. A few of the Quinns were desert tortoises in their natural forms, and as far as she knew, they were more limited in shifting. But most in the clan were scaled reptiles, and they had fun messing with their forms.

She examined the snake carefully, nudging him with her gloved hand to stretch out to his full length, squatting down to make sure no abnormalities presented. After a few minutes, she said, "Okay, looks normal in your natural form. Shift back and tell me how your arm feels."

Another shimmer in the air and Marcus was back. He had black bands tattooed around his forearms, mimicking his animal markings. She'd never noticed those before. *Cool.*

"Come on, Ted." He grabbed his jeans and held them over his crotch. "Give a guy some privacy."

She threw a sheet at him and said, "Forget privacy. Let's see the arm."

He tucked the sheet around his waist and stood, holding his arm out for her.

"All good?"

"Feels fine. Anything look crooked?"

"Nope." She probed along the break, but other than residual swelling, the arm looked good as new. "You got lucky this time."

"That's what she said."

Ted snorted. "Is Josie in town?"

"Nope. Too bad for me. Shifting always makes me..." He smirked. "Well, you know."

"Quinns...," she muttered, picking up his clothes from the floor and throwing them at Marcus before she walked to the door. "Bad boys, every single one of you."

Chapter Four

They started early but were still sweating like dogs before they got Alex's stuff unloaded. He was renting the back trailer from Jena's mom, the thirty-four-foot classic, fully restored and with a brand-new A/C. He would keep most of his stuff from Huntington in storage but was taking advantage of the small sheds Kathy and Tom had built near each rental. It wasn't permanent, but it was good enough. He'd borrowed Kevin, Allie's oldest, and Lowell, Jena's boy, from their moms. The work kept the boys busy and gave Alex the opportunity to see how Kevin was doing with his dad gone.

"Hey guys, two more boxes and then I think we've got it all."

Both of them nodded before they trudged back to the car. At fourteen, Kevin had already been shifting for a year. He'd taken after his mother, so his natural form was a fox. Alex knew the boy probably had a handle on his shifts, but hormones were hormones, and according to Kevin's mother, teenagers were even worse when they turned into an animal at the full moon. Lowell had shifted only a few months before. As Alex watched them both, he realized Kevin had already taken on the weight of leadership over his younger friend. Natural personality, or had Kevin been the de facto man of the house for a lot longer than any of them realized?

"Hey, Lowell?"

"Yeah?"

"Why don't you run to the house and see if the food is ready? Find out how much time we have."

"Okay."

Lowell ran off, leaving Kevin kicking his heels in the dust and looking over a small dent near the rear axle of the trailer.

"You know," the boy said, "I bet Ollie and me could get that out. He's been teaching me how to do body work on his dad's old pickup."

"Yeah?" Alex walked over and looked at the tiny dent. He wouldn't even have noticed it. "You can try if you want to. But ask Miss Kathy first."

"Yeah, sure." Kevin shrugged. "Maybe I'll ask."

Alex sat in one of the folding chairs he'd put up under the shade cover. Kevin took the other one, and Alex handed him a bottle of water from the ice chest between them.

"How you doing?"

"Fine. School's good. Made the honor roll again. Mom's happy."

"Moms like that stuff."

Had he been this hard to talk to at fourteen?

"Hey, Uncle Alex, can you hire kids during the summer? You know, to help out with the construction?"

He shook his head. "Sorry. Have to be sixteen. And you have to have a work permit too. Actually, I'm not sure minors are allowed on the jobsite, but I'll find out if you want me to."

"Nah." He shrugged. "By the time I'm sixteen, it'll all be built, right?"

"Hopefully."

"And you're still gonna stay here?"

"Yep."

"Even afterward?"

Alex nodded, glancing over at Kevin, who was staring out at the main road, watching a car head toward the highway.

"I guess…," the boy started. "I mean, it's not the most exciting place, is it? Dad was always talking about all the stuff he could be doing if Mom was willing to move."

Alex bit his tongue, trying to figure out what to say to the boy.

Kevin continued, his voice a little rougher. "I guess I don't blame him for wanting to get away. The Springs isn't all that exciting."

If Joe Smith were standing in front of him, Alex would strangle him.

"You know, I've been a lot of places, Kev. Some are pretty amazing. Traveling is great. You should definitely go exploring when you're older."

The boy nodded.

"But after you're done exploring, it's good to have a place to come home to," he continued. "And if you ask me, the thing that makes a place exciting is the people. That's why I'm moving back. People like your mom and Jena. Ted and Ollie. Kids like you and Lowell. People are more exciting than places."

"Yeah?"

Alex leaned over and put his hand on Kevin's shoulder, pulling him closer. He spoke in a low, commanding voice, the voice he used on the younger wolves in the pack. Confident. Sure. Maybe a little scary if the pup had messed up. It was the voice his father had used with him, and if Alex knew anything about teenage boys, it worked.

"Kevin, do not ever think that your dad leaving had anything to do with you. That was his failing, not yours."

He sounded like he wanted to speak, but didn't say anything. Alex squeezed his shoulder again, letting his natural authority roll over the boy.

"Do you understand me?"

"Yes, Uncle Alex."

"And do not ever think his actions reflect on you. You are your *mother's* son, and you will be a good man. You're going to mess up sometimes, but in the end, you'll make decisions in life that your mother will be proud of and that I'll respect."

Kevin nodded, sniffing back tears so Alex wouldn't see. He nudged the boy up and out of the seat, saying, "I think there's one more box in the back of my truck. Go get it and put it in the shed."

"Yes, sir."

"Then we'll head to the house and get a beer."

Kevin halted and turned. "Really?"

"Well, I get a beer. You get a root beer."

A hint of a smile crossed Kevin's face. Then he ran back to the truck.

Alex caught Ted watching him from the corner of her eye over and over during dinner. It was Jena, Caleb, and their two boys. Allie and her three boys and one girl. Ted and Alex rounded out the group. They were taking shelter on the back porch while the kids played inside. Five boys under fifteen and one baby sister could make a hell of a lot of noise.

Allie nudged him. "I don't know what you said to Kevin, but thanks."

"Yeah?"

"He seemed a little better after he helped you out this afternoon."

"Good."

"You pull that alpha crap on my kid?"

He knew Allie was teasing, so he said, "Only when he needed his butt kicked. You got a problem with that?"

"Nope." She shook her head before she grinned. "Just be prepared. He might be your shadow from now on. Ollie'll have some competition."

Nope. He wasn't going to say anything. Biting his tongue.

Alex still hadn't spoken more than a few words to his old friend since Allie's husband had left. Had no idea what Ollie was doing with the knowledge that the feelings he'd been carrying for over fifteen years might actually stand a chance with Joe out of the way. He wouldn't say he was happy that Allie's husband left her…

Exactly.

"Might be better if he spends time with Ollie, don't you think?" Ted offered. "After all, Alex works so much. And when—" She broke off, suddenly flustered.

"What?" Alex asked.

"Nothing."

"No, what were you going to say? When what?"

He knew what she had been going to say before she thought twice. In the back of his mind, it twisted and burned. The nerve… Her distrust in his intentions had hurt him. Frustrated him. Now, she was just pissing him off.

At least she had the grace to look embarrassed.

"It's nothing. Forget it."

He didn't want to let go. Months of frustration came to a head. "Tell me."

Jena said, "Hey guys, let's not—"

"No, Jena. I want to hear what Ted was going to say. I'm betting she was going to tell me that I should keep my distance so Kevin doesn't get attached to another guy that leaves."

Allie paled as silence fell over the table, and Alex saw Caleb put a hand on Jena's shoulder.

"Alex," Caleb warned. "Take care."

The embarrassment had left Ted's face. She was just as pissed off as he was. She raised her chin. "I'm just thinking about the kids."

"Hey—" Allie tried to speak up, but Alex cut her off.

"No, you're not. You're thinking about yourself and insulting me, implying I'd *ever* abandon anything that mattered that much."

Caleb stood and ushered Jena and Allie into the house, leaving Ted and Alex alone on the porch.

Her face had paled. "It wouldn't be the first time. Or I guess we didn't matter as much as I thought we did. Good to know."

Her whispered words almost knocked the breath out of him, but the anger was harder, stronger, and it took control of his tongue.

"You're still dredging up history, but as far as I know, the only one in town still waiting for me to leave is you."

"Just because you say—"

"When did I lie to you, Ted?"

A child's shout came from the house. Laughter answered. A reminder of everything he'd given up. The life they could have had.

"I'm not doing this." He stood and left his beer on the table, walking toward the lit trailer in the distance. Ted followed him.

They weren't halfway there before she said, "I'm looking out for my nephew, Alex. The last thing Kevin needs—"

"You are so full of *shit*!" He spun and gripped her arm. "This has nothing to do with Kevin. This is about you and me, so tell me: When did I lie to you? When?"

"You never—"

"I never told you my plans? Maybe that was because you didn't listen."

"That's not true, and you know it."

"Really?" He stood back and crossed his arms. "What did you think I was doing in LA? Following after you like a puppy? Working construction until you graduated?"

"We always planned to come back here. When school was done—"

"That was *your* plan."

"And you never told me different!"

He stepped closer. "Maybe I tried and you didn't listen. Maybe I realized there was only one person whose dreams mattered in our relationship."

She looked like he'd slapped her, and Alex immediately regretted the words, but his blood was boiling and he couldn't stop.

"I gave you everything I could, Ted. Everything. I put up with a hell of a lot of shit that I wouldn't have from anyone else. And half the time, I thought I was invisible. But I never lied. Not once. You just didn't listen."

Her face was pale, but her jaw was set. "Actions speak louder than words."

"And how did my actions lie to you? When we were living together? When we made love? There were two people there, Ted. You can't put that on me."

"No, you can just take off and lie about coming back 'soon.'"

"I didn't lie to you!" He threw his hands up and started walking toward the trailer again. He had to get away from her. Maybe it was all a mistake. Maybe he was an idiot for even looking back. "I have never broken a promise to you. Not once."

"How am I supposed to believe you'll stay? That you won't leave again when the job is done?"

"You left *me*!"

"And you were already gone!"

"I came back."

"Sure you did. But not to stay! I thought you were back five years ago. When you came to me in Palm Springs—" She choked on the words as he turned.

"Ted." Coming to her a year after their breakup had been a mistake. He'd known it even when he was driving to her house. Knew he couldn't offer her what she needed from him. But he'd been weak, and he'd missed her so damned much.

Making love to her had been like coming home. And they'd never talked about it. Alex's guilt fell like a blanket over his anger.

That time, he had been the one to leave, and he couldn't deny it.

"I didn't know what to believe," she said. "You left. Again. And every time I tried to move on, you came back. Every time I met a guy I liked, you were there to mess things up. Just to remind me of what I couldn't have."

"I'm back now."

"And how am I supposed to believe that?"

She stood in the light of the almost-full moon, black eyes flashing, dark hair slipping down around her face.

"You're the most beautiful woman I've ever known in my life."

She took a step back, surprised. "Alex—"

"And the hardest."

"I have to be."

How much of that was his fault?

Alex whispered, "You won't believe a word I say, will you?"

"What does it matter? You said yourself we were done."

"We're not done." He stepped closer, needing to touch her. "We're never done. That was the lie."

"Did it even hurt you?" He almost didn't hear her. Her voice had gone from hard to painfully soft. "Giving me up? You keep telling me I'm the one who left you, but you walked away from that apartment without a backward glance."

It hit him like a punch to the chest. He took a step back. "How could you ask that?"

He'd been wrecked. Broken. A thin covering of man over a broken-hearted kid. It was Ted who had moved on. Ted who'd packed up their apartment and left him behind. She was the one who put up walls.

"You say you never broke a promise, Alex, but you did."

"When—"

"You gave me your heart; then you took it away. And you took mine with it." She blinked rapidly. "So don't tell me I'm hard. I'm just protecting what's left."

Then she turned in the moonlight and walked away.

Hours later, Alex was still awake. Still watching her walk away.

"You walked away from that apartment without a backward glance."

He'd had to. If he had looked back, Alex would have fallen to his knees and begged her to stay. Begged her to give up the residency that brought her back home, even when he knew she needed to go. Being tied to the city had started to affect her health. Her spirit was exhausted. She'd needed to come back. And he'd needed to stay.

"Don't tell me I'm hard. I'm just protecting what's left."

Why didn't he ever hear things when he needed to?

He'd cut her deep. Maybe he'd never realized quite how much. Ted was so good at putting up a strong front that he forgot she needed more from him. She needed to be his *Téa*, not just everyone else's Ted. She'd needed to have a safe place to show that softness, and when they'd been together, she did.

Then he'd taken it away.

So she locked that part of herself down tight. "Protecting what was left." Who could blame her?

He was an idiot.

Why had he let her walk away that night?

He rolled over and banged his head quietly against the headboard. Where was the bourbon when he needed it? Not that getting drunk was a good plan. He'd need to be clearheaded if he had even a sliver of a chance of fixing this.

His phone fell to the floor just as it started ringing.

43

Alex grimaced. No one called for anything good at three eleven in the morning. Squinting, he looked at the screen.

Caleb Gilbert.

Immediate thoughts of Jena and the baby rushed into his head, and he slid his thumb to answer.

"Caleb? What's wrong? Is it Jena?"

"No, Jena's fine, man. We've got another problem."

He shook his head and sat up. "What? What other problem? It's three in the morning."

"Alex, this is shit news, but... Marcus Quinn is dead."

"What?"

"His body was found on your jobsite."

Chapter Five

"Come to the desert, they said. It'll be quiet, they said."

"Seriously, Caleb, shut up."

"All we have are drunk and disorderlies. The occasional vandalism or theft. It'll be so peaceful."

Caleb stood over the body of what used to be Marcus Quinn while Ted took the liver temperature. The body was a mass of vicious bites, and pieces of the face and stomach were missing. Whatever had happened to him first, coyotes had happened second, and it wasn't pretty. They'd eaten around his clothes, tearing pieces of his shirt and dragging it and other parts away from the corpse. It would take hours to collect all the evidence. They weren't even starting until the sun rose.

"Who shifts to a coyote around here?" Caleb asked.

"This isn't shifters," Ted said. "He wasn't killed by coyotes."

"Tell that to the Quinns before we have a riot. Jeremy already has Old Quinn in his truck. Had to escort him home."

"How'd the Quinns find out?"

"Who the hell knows? One of the wolves found the body and called me, but who knows who he told after that?"

She looked up. "Which wolf?"

"Patrick McCann. He's only sixteen. Think he was cutting through here on the way back from his girlfriend's house. Past his curfew."

"That'll teach him to sneak in more make-out time."

"Yeah, no kidding. His dad called me as soon as the kid got home and told him. I asked him to keep things quiet, but…"

"Patrick's dad called Robert McCann about a minute after you, if not before." She looked back down and continued to work. "In case you were wondering. So all the clan leaders know by now."

Caleb's eyes got hard. "I kept my mouth shut when this town took care of Missy the way they did. Jena was bleeding in my arms, and saving her life was more important than the law. But that shit isn't happening again. Not on my watch. This town isn't going to deal out justice by mob."

Ted kept silent. She had her own issues with what had happened to Missy Marquez, but she wasn't going to talk to Caleb about it. It was cat clan business.

Caleb shivered at a gust of wind, clad only in a pair of jeans, a T-shirt, and his hat, of course. Ted had thrown on a jacket as soon as she got the call from him. Nights were cold in the desert, and at crime scenes, there was a lot of standing around. Technically, she was just a consultant. But since all the county's deputy coroner investigators lived in the cities, Ted had been authorized to collect evidence at crime scenes in coordination with the newly formed Cambio Springs Police Department. Most of the time she simply confirmed natural deaths when older people passed at home. As the town's only doctor, the arrangement had worked well. And murders in Cambio Springs were rare.

Or they had been before Missy Marquez had killed Jena's grandmother the year before, fearful of the old woman's influence over the Elders' Council. Crazed at the thought of having to leave the only place she felt safe. That fear had translated into Missy attacking and killing Alma Crowe to eliminate what she saw as the only obstacle to her husband's plans to save Cambio Springs. Missy had been certifiable. And whatever Caleb thought, Ted knew the woman would have killed herself before she'd go to a human prison. It was twisted, but if Missy knew she was going to die, she'd have picked a shifter execution over suicide.

And now, less than a year later, there was another suspicious death.

"Coyotes are scavengers," she said, still kneeling by the body, noting the lack of blood. Not only dead, but mostly bled out when the coyotes had started on him. Interesting. "Marcus was a big guy. He would have been dead before they started eating him."

"Could this have been an accident? Marcus shifted and the coyotes went after him in snake form?"

"It's a possibility. Coyotes will eat snakes if they find them. And if they killed him as a snake, *then* he shifted…"

They all shifted back to human when they died. Born human. Died human. It was only the sticky in-between part that got interesting at times.

Caleb nodded. "They'd have taken advantage of the corpse. Started eating. Makes sense."

"It's possible, but…"

"What are you thinking?"

Ted was thinking that reptile shifters liked the sun, not the cold moonlight. But she said nothing as she looked around Marcus Quinn's mangled body. Caleb had hauled a couple work lights out from behind the trailer at the jobsite, but there still wasn't enough light to take good pictures. She stood and looked at the thermometer.

"I'm estimating he was killed between midnight and two o'clock. Some of that depends on what form he was in when he was attacked."

Quinns were the only residents of Cambio Springs who shifted to a cold-blooded creature, which was one of the reasons Ted had a hard time imagining Marcus would be out in animal form in the middle of the night where coyotes could get him.

"You're saying if he was a snake—"

"Reptile shifters have to warm up a bit when they get back into human form. They do this shivering thing. It's not instant. And even a few degrees could throw off the estimate on time of death. So I'll make my excuses to the county, but between you and me, it's impossible to narrow down death any more than I have."

"Great."

"It's the way it is."

"Ted?" She saw Caleb's eyes narrow and focus. "How likely was it that Marcus Quinn just happened to be hanging out in the desert—in snake form—and got accidentally killed by a pack of coyotes?"

"Honestly?" She looked up at the nearly full moon. *Nearly* full. Not completely. "It's not a moon night, Caleb. He didn't *have* to shift. And it's cool enough at night right now that he wouldn't have shifted unless he had to. Reptiles are different from the rest of us. If it's not warm, they're not comfortable."

Ted looked down at the cheerful man who'd been such a hard worker. A husband. A dad. She hadn't known him well, but from all accounts, he was a bright spot in an otherwise messed-up family. She'd been laughing and joking with the man a couple days before, and now he was nothing more than a pile of meat for the scavengers. Of all the twisted, messed-up

—

"Alex is here," Caleb said.

Ted quickly locked down the protest that wanted to spring to her lips. It was Alex's jobsite. Alex's employee. And Marcus and Alex had been friends.

"Shit," she muttered.

She hadn't been sleeping when she got the call. Thoughts of their fight the night before had filled her mind. Alex's anger. His accusations.

"You're the most beautiful woman I've known in my life, Ted. And the hardest."

It was true. She could be hard. She had to be.

Maybe he hadn't recognized it at the time, but when they'd been together, she'd given everything to Alex. Every worry. Every fear. Every hope. She'd held nothing back. And when he left…

It was as if the foundation of her world crumbled. She'd given him everything, and he'd taken it all with him. It hadn't mattered that she'd been the one to leave LA. He'd left her first. She went home to lick her wounds and piece herself back together. And every time he came and left, the foundation she'd patched up crumbled a little more.

"What are you frowning at?" Caleb asked.

Don't think about it. Think about anything but *that.*

"Maybe I'm frowning because someone I knew has been murdered, and I'm not quite as okay with it as you are."

"Harsh." Caleb's eyes narrowed. He knew she was deflecting. "I called Alex because it's his jobsite. Plus, he and Marcus were friends."

"I don't care that you called him, but if you want my professional opinion, the body was dumped here. There's not enough blood."

"I noticed the same thing, but we'll look more when the sun is up. Hard to search right now, and the body has obviously been dragged."

She couldn't argue with that. The animals hadn't done them any favors.

"Has anyone called Josie?" Ted asked. "She lives in Vegas with the kids, but I think she was coming down next week."

Caleb's face was grim. "Any of Marcus's family live up that way?"

She nodded. "Call Old Quinn. He'll know who to send. Those poor kids."

Ted could hear Alex talking to Jeremy McCann, Caleb's deputy and one of the higher-ranking members of Alex's pack.

Caleb spoke in a quiet voice. "I'm asking for your read on this, Ted. Accidental or criminal?"

She paused but went with her gut. "Criminal. The bite wounds could easily be obscuring the cause of death, but I'm not going to poke around at the body until after I've documented the scene and have him back in my office. I'm betting I find something. Sudden death by natural causes like heart attacks is practically unheard of with our kind. Especially at his age."

"Keep me updated. Let me know what you need."

"The body will go to San Bernardino. I can't do anything about that. If we can't play this off as an animal attack like we did with Alma, then they're going to want to do a full autopsy."

"Will they find anything?"

"I hope not. But honestly? I have no idea."

Caleb nodded before he walked away.

"You have got to be kidding me!"

Alex had clearly lost it by the time Ted was finished examining the body. She heard him shout from yards away. She needed Jeremy to help her bag the body and transport it back to her office, but currently, Jeremy was holding Alex back from throttling Caleb. The chief of police, as always, stood nonchalantly, watching Alex lose his temper in front of the growing crowd of construction workers who had gathered for their morning shift.

They were all shifters, and aggression scented the air. Alex was the future alpha of the Springs, and Ted might not have been a wolf, like many of the work crew, but her lion could scent the rising tension. Workers shifted toward others in their clans. The birds had already disappeared, but wolves drifted to other wolves. Cats to cats. The few bears on-site stood where they were: tall, wary, and waiting. And the reptiles drifted to the edges of the crowd, watching. Always ready to run.

Caleb said, "I have to question her. Just like I have to question you, Alex. And the Quinns."

Ted heard a hiss on the edge of the crowd, and a low growl rumbled from Alex's throat. Caleb may have had a lot of fine qualities, but he could still be clueless about shifter politics. An open challenge like this helped no one. She, as the most dominant cat at the scene, needed to step in.

"Listen, McCann, this is far from my first murder case. Over seventy percent of murders—"

"We don't know that it's murder yet," Ted said in a low voice as she approached the three men. "What are we fighting about?"

Alex's eyes were glowing. "He asks for Josie's number, then tells me she'll have to answer questions about Marcus's death." He was spitting mad, his wolf very close to the surface. "Does she even know her husband is dead yet? Has anyone talked to Joe Quinn? Who's driving up there? If that woman and her kids get a damn phone call—"

"She's not gonna get a phone call!" Caleb threw his hands up and pointed at Jeremy. "You explain it. I'm done with him."

Alex's lip curled up. "If you pull any shit with Josie—"

"Threaten me, McCann." Caleb took a step closer and lifted his chin. "See what happens."

Ted's heart warmed at Alex's protective stance toward Marcus's family, but the two men were seconds from blows being exchanged. And despite current appearances, she knew Alex actually liked Caleb and would regret tearing off one of his limbs in anger.

Probably.

"Whoa, boys." She stepped between the two, then patted Jeremy on his shoulder and gently pushed him away. The poor guy was stuck between the future alpha of his pack and his boss. "Remember, no one wins when testosterone starts flying. Jeremy?"

The young deputy turned to her, an instinctive response to her more dominant animal. Sometimes it annoyed her, but in situations like this, it was useful.

"Yeah?"

"Can you go to my Jeep and grab the bag in back? There's a backboard there too. We need both to get Marcus's body back to my office."

He glanced at Alex, who nodded briefly. Then he ran toward Ted's green Jeep, and Ted stepped between the two glaring men.

"Alex, the chief already talked to Old Quinn. Marcus's sister is on the way to meet Vegas PD. She lives in Henderson, so she's close. They're probably already on their way to Josie's. And Caleb, can we wait to talk about questioning people until we know for sure this is a murder?"

"I'm done talking about any of this with *him*," Caleb bit out. "He's not my boss or my alpha. As far as I'm concerned, he has no role in this investigation. Send your boys home, McCann. This scene is going to take hours to process, and no one gets to work until I say so."

Alex growled low in his throat, but Caleb was already walking away.

Ted stepped in front of him and put her hands on his shoulders. Thoughts of their fight the night before flitted through her mind, but she swept them away. Ignored the tense stares of the men around them.

Alex had lost a friend. He needed calm. He needed comfort. He needed... petting.

"Alex?"

"What?" He was still glaring at Caleb's back, and she could see his eyes glowing gold.

Ted slipped her arms around his waist. He tensed, then wrapped his arms around her.

"I'm sorry about Marcus," she whispered.

His arms tightened, and she felt his cheek against her temple. "Ted, this is… It makes no sense."

She stroked his back, urging him to calm with her touch. "He was a good man."

They stood like that, lion and wolf embracing, until she could sense the tension of the crowd behind him start to dissipate. Low murmurs started as men and women got back to work. She could hear some moving toward vehicles. Hear what sounded like a foreman start to organize the ones that were left. Within a few minutes, the breeze had carried away the scent of adrenaline.

Alex didn't let go. "What the hell happened?" he asked. "Everybody loved that guy."

From what Ted knew, Alex was right. No one in the Springs had a problem with Marcus. Even those who didn't much like Alex and his plans for the resort hadn't shown any resentment to his crew. They were all local boys who were working. And Alex had made sure at least a few were hired from every clan. No one carried a grudge over that.

"I need to know what's going on, Ted."

She knew what he was asking, and she pulled away. "Alex—"

"Whether you want to admit it or not, this *is* my town. You know what being a McCann means. You and I and my father all know what's coming. And you know a lot of people still don't trust Caleb. Old Quinn is already stirring up shit about coyotes or some other canine shifter being responsible for this. Someone even mentioned Joe disappearing, like he might have had something to do with it."

"Did Joe even know Marcus?"

Alex grimaced. "They had words at the Cave a few days before Joe took off. One of the guys told me this morning."

"Shit." The last thing Allie needed was people talking about her kids' dad being a murder suspect.

"I need you to keep me in the loop on this. I need to know where the fires are starting so I can put them out before they get bad."

And have one more excuse to talk to him, despite her bruised heart?

"Why don't you ask Jeremy?"

"I'm already putting him in an awkward position, arguing with his boss like that. You saw him just now. Caleb knows Jeremy looks to me as a higher authority. I don't want to take advantage of that."

Dammit. Why did he have to be such a good guy sometimes? As much as Ted wanted to dislike him, his obvious concern and respect for his pack always softened her. Cats didn't have that. And maybe it went against her animal nature, but part of her longed to be part of something bigger than herself. If there was one thing she envied about the wolves, it was having a pack.

"I can't make any promises," she said.

"Ted, please—"

"But I'll do what I can. I do have some latitude in my own... investigation."

A grateful smile spread over his face. He leaned forward and planted a quick kiss on her forehead. "Thanks, baby."

"Don't—" She lifted a hand and stepped back. "Don't call me baby, Alex."

He winked at her, then turned to walk back to the parking lot where his men were gathered. Jeremy lifted a knowing eyebrow as he passed Alex and headed toward Ted.

"Not a word," she said, grabbing the body bag and walking back toward the body. "Come on, Deputy. Let's do this before it gets hot."

Ted had discovered last year that it was a particular kind of torture to examine someone she'd known in life. She tried to separate herself from it. Tried to view it just as a body.

But inevitably, she'd have a thought like, *Gee, I didn't know Marcus tattooed his kids' names right over his heart.* Then she'd get choked up because half of that tattoo had bite marks in it and the other half would never be seen by those kids he'd loved so much. Kids she could picture, even if she didn't know them well. And their hilarious mom with the sassy blue hair that Marcus had tattooed in a pin-up pose on his shoulder. Josie had everyone rolling in snake jokes the first time she'd ever visited Cambio Springs. Marcus had adored her.

Sometimes life just sucked.

And it especially sucked when she found the evidence she was looking for lodged in one of his ribs. She suspected it had banged around his ribcage for a while, tearing into his internal organs like a lethal pinball. Bleeding would have been extensive. Death would have been quick.

The bullet was heavily deformed from impact, but she carefully bagged it to turn in to the sheriff-coroner's office in San Bernardino. All her pictures and notes would go along with the body, but not before she made copies for her own records. She was tempted to cut into him more but knew that doing that would only compromise the larger investigation. She was a consultant. That was all. And she knew she didn't have the equipment for a full autopsy.

And the county would demand one, especially for a victim like this. A well-loved business owner and family man, living out of state, but with strong ties to the community. The county prosecutor had no idea that in Cambio Springs, justice often took a decidedly vigilante turn.

She heard someone come into the office. From the thump of the boots, she was guessing Caleb. The suspicion was confirmed when he walked right in after a perfunctory knock.

"Hey."

"Hey." She pulled off her gloves and used a spare rag to tug up the zipper on the body bag. "Call the ambulance. He's going to the main office."

"Murder?"

She nodded and held up the small bag with the bullet. Caleb took it, looking it over with a practiced eye. He might not have intended to use his formidable deductive skills when he moved from Albuquerque to the small town in the California desert, but sadly, they hadn't been allowed to get rusty.

"It's a nine."

"Positive?"

"Pretty sure. Send it in. Their ballistics lab will be able to confirm."

"Nine millimeter handguns are common around here."

He sighed and rubbed a hand over his face. "Common everywhere." He pulled out his phone and punched a few numbers while Ted started throwing garbage into the red medical waste bags she'd set out before she started the exam.

"Dev?" Caleb was talking to the sheriff's deputy that covered their area. "Yeah, send them over. ... Uh-huh. ... Yeah, I'll call you when we get the report. Thanks, man."

Dev and the elders in his tribe were some of the few outsiders who knew about the shapeshifters of Cambio Springs. But since they didn't appreciate attention any more than the Springs' shifters did, a tentative alliance had formed.

Ted and Dev had once tried to form a more personal alliance, but Alex had stepped in the middle of that almost immediately. Dev hadn't given up easily, but there was only so much of her shit that he'd been willing to put up with. When Dev figured out he wasn't making any headway, he'd stepped back. He didn't seem all that broken up about it, considering how quickly he'd moved on, but Ted still considered him a friend.

"They'll be here in about fifteen minutes."

Her eyebrows rose. "That's quick."

"Well, I called a while ago. Gave them a heads-up. I had a feeling."

Ted didn't question it. Whether it was his Navajo uncle's *hatałii* blood or just a practiced sixth sense, Caleb Gilbert often had very accurate "feelings" that turned into substantial leads. And now that he'd married a hawk shapeshifter and drank the water of the fresh spring, developing an ability to turn into *other people*, the feeling of "other" her cat sensed in him had only grown stronger. Ted wondered if he even realized it.

She felt her phone buzzing in her pocket. She pulled it out and noticed three calls from her mother and two from Alex.

"Is that McCann?" Caleb asked.

"No." Not this time anyway. "My mom."

"No doubt there'll be an Elders' meeting once this all comes out."

"Your favorite activity, Chief."

Technically, as a city employee, Caleb worked for the Elders' Council that ran the Springs. Seven of the oldest residents of the town, one from each of the seven original families. Her great-uncle was on the council, but her mother would take over eventually, as she was the most dominant in their family. Alex's dad was also a member, even though he wasn't the oldest. But then, Robert McCann had always set his own rules.

"Listen, Ted…"

"Hmm?" She was blinking and trying to remember where she left her keys. It was past three o'clock, and even though her air-conditioning was cranked, she needed a nap.

"I know McCann's going to dig for his own answers. I get that."

"And you're going to try to warn me not to give Alex any information on the investigation."

"I don't think it's a good idea."

Ted stepped around the exam table and set a thick file on top of the body bag that contained the remnants of Marcus Quinn, one of Alex's friends.

"Caleb, I'll tell you the same thing I tell everyone in this town: I don't work for you. I don't work for the Elders' Council. I don't work for the police. I don't even really work for the county. I'm just a consultant."

His eyes narrowed. "I'm not sure what that tells me."

Ted smiled and patted his cheek before she walked past him. "It means you're not the boss of me. But I'm sure you can wait for the ambulance because I'm heading home."

"Please don't involve McCann in this investigation, Ted."

That's right; her keys were on her desk. "They have my number if they have any questions."

"Ted?"

She stretched her shoulders, eager to be home so she could shift and climb. After this day, she needed it.

"Ted?" he called again, even more impatient.

"Good night, Chief. See you when I see you. Tell Jena I said hi."

Chapter Six

Alex was sitting with Josie Quinn, Marcus's widow, drinking coffee in one-hundred-degree heat and listening to Marcus's mom, Delia, weep openly as her sisters tried to console her. Josie took a deep breath and set her coffee down.

"I'm not handling this very well, Alex."

"No one expects you to. You just lost your husband, Jos. I can't imagine—"

"I don't mean that." Her choked voice said otherwise. "Them. All the weeping and carrying on from his mom. His aunts. Like they were so close. Marcus could hardly wait to get out of this house. You know why."

Because his dad was a shifty bastard who yelled at his wife and kids almost as much as he drank. And his mom stood there for years and took it until her old man got drunk and ran himself into a telephone pole on the way back from his girlfriend's house in Blythe.

Alex nodded, then glanced at Josie and Marcus's oldest daughter, who was entertaining her little brothers with a board game by the window air conditioner. He had to hand it to their parents. Josie and Marcus might have been tattooed and dyed from top to bottom, but they let their kids be who they wanted. Their daughter, Kasey, looked like a tiny version of a Disney princess. Completely opposite her mom with her bright blue hair, bird tattoos, and piercings. Still, the sheer amount of love that poured off Josie was mirrored in her daughter's gaze when she happened to look over.

They shared a small, sad smile before Kasey was distracted by the boys again.

"You still moving back?" Alex asked.

"She's ten now. How much longer do I have?"

"Depends. I'd say anywhere from a year and a half to three years. That's about average for girls."

Josie nodded and swiped at the tear that ran down her cheek, marring her thick black liner.

She pursed her red lips and said, "Then we'll be back. Marcus said this was the best place for the kids once they changed."

"It will be. I promise. They won't have to hide who they are from their friends. They'll have people who know what they're feeling. And not everyone is like Marcus's family."

"I know. And he had some good friends here." She glanced toward the kitchen and the dramatic, sobbing women. "Normal ones."

"You let me know what you need. Anything. You know that. We'll figure out a place for you to live. Get you set up. Help moving. Whatever you need. When you're ready. How's the business? Is that going to be enough for you guys?"

"My brother and Marcus were half and half once they expanded. Chris will have to hire someone, but I'm sure they'll be fine. They still have the contract for the resort, right?"

"Of course. The plans were all done. So if your brother—"

"Chris."

"If Chris can come down or send someone else that can do the on-site supervision, I don't see how there could be a problem."

"Chris..." She looked worried. "He doesn't know. About you guys. About the kids."

Alex nodded, hoping to soothe the fear in her eyes. "I'll let everyone know to be careful. If he doesn't need to know, he won't. It's for the best."

"He can be... Well, he's kind of judgmental. I don't know—I mean, he's a good guy—but I'm not sure how he'd react to..." She glanced at the kids. "Scales."

He felt the corner of his mouth tick up. "You know, tortoises are a possibility too."

"Shit, Alex." Josie snorted through tears and slapped his shoulder. "Don't joke about stuff like that. Snakes were bad enough. I don't want my babies carting shells around."

"It's not that bad. Very tough shifters, desert tortoises."

"I hate you a little right now." But she was smiling and looked more like herself again.

"I can handle it. You're not the only woman who hates me."

"Still no luck with your ex, huh?"

He cocked his head. "How—"

"Marcus tells me everything." She caught herself. "Or he did."

He spoke, trying to distract her. "I knew he was a gossip. Never should have had him pass that note for me during study hall."

Josie laughed through her tears. "You guys... He thought the world of you, Alex. I'm sure your girl will come around too."

Alex thought about Ted giving him a hug the day before. Knowing when he was hurting, even if he covered it with anger.

"I haven't given up yet."

"Good." Her eyes glassed over again, and she glanced at her kids. "When you find the right one, it's worth the work."

A loud cry erupted from the kitchen, and she glanced at Marcus's mom over her shoulder. "You know, he sent her money. Every month. Not once did I hear her say thank you. Even though she never stood up for him, he still took care of her."

Alex swallowed the lump in his throat. "He was a good man."

"The best."

The cool wind from the air conditioner picked up, and Alex felt a blessed breeze waft over him. He was still in his work shirt and jeans, having come straight from the job when he got Josie's call that she and the kids had arrived at Marcus's mom's.

"You know the chief of police is going to come by, right?"

"I figured. He a decent guy?"

"Yeah." Alex nodded, even though he'd had his problems with Jena's new husband. "He knows everything about us. Married to one of my friends now, but he's from New Mexico originally. Good detective. Tried to come out here and retire, even though he's young."

"That didn't work out so well, did it?"

"No, but he knows his stuff." He shifted toward her. "You know he's gonna ask a bunch of questions about Marcus, right?"

"Yeah."

"There anything I should know about? Anything that's gonna upset you if he asks?"

She sniffed and shook her head. "Not really? I mean, you know Marcus. He's... Everyone liked him, Alex. He was fair to the guys that worked with him. He was a good dad. A great husband—"

"You know Caleb's going to ask if there were other women."

Josie just started laughing. "As if he'd ever have the nerve to talk to them. As good-looking as Marcus was, he was a total wuss around girls. I had to throw myself at him to get him to make a move." She kept laughing, and Alex had to admit he was relieved. Glad there were no skeletons that Marcus's widow would have to deal with.

"He looked tough, but he was a big softie," she said. "If there was anything that led to this, it might have been that. Him trusting the wrong person or thinking the best of someone he shouldn't. He always wanted to give people the benefit of the doubt, even when they screwed him."

That pricked a memory of something he'd mentioned to Ted. "Do you know Joe Smith?"

She scrunched up her face. "Allie's Joe?"

"Yeah, I heard that he and Marcus got into it at the Cave a while back. Right before Joe took off."

That surprised her. "Allie's husband took off?"

"Yeah."

"That rat!" She glanced quickly at her kids, who were all looking at her. Then she turned back to Alex. "You know, Marcus mentioned that Joe borrowed some money from him and wasn't paying him back. But he mentioned it in passing, like it wasn't a big deal. He did that. He'd loan money to people, but never more than we could afford or anything. I didn't even think about it. I doubt he did, either."

"Caleb's probably going to ask about that."

"I don't know much more than what I told you." Her voice lowered to a whisper. "Do you honestly think Joe had anything to do with this? He doesn't seem like the type."

"I don't think anyone knows what Joe is capable of at this point. Now that he's gone, all the shit is coming out."

"Oh…" She rested her forehead on her hands. "Poor Allie."

Alex rubbed Josie's shoulder and thought that Marcus had been a lucky man to have a woman who'd just lost her own husband but still had room in her heart for a friend. And whoever made Josie lose that man was going to pay, if it was the last thing he did.

It was an hour later when Caleb finally came by. Alex was heading out the door, but Caleb put a hand on his shoulder, stopping him on the front walk.

"Don't put your hands on me, skinwalker." Alex knew it annoyed Caleb to have that term thrown around.

"Do you enjoy pissing me off, McCann?" He hadn't risen to the bait, which left Alex vaguely disappointed. "Because I know you're not stupid."

"I'm helping out a friend. And she's as baffled by this as we are, so don't step over the line in there, or I'll hear about it."

Caleb drew back. "What kind of bastard do you think I am?"

"I think you're a hell of a good detective. That's why I hired you. But when that 'detecting' happens to be about a friend, I don't give a shit about offending you. I'm more concerned about the woman in there who lost her husband."

"And I'll keep that in mind. But you know I have to question her."

Alex nodded. "She can take it. But just saying, her kids are in there, and her mother-in-law's a mess. Josie might be easier to talk to if you get her out of the house."

"Noted."

He started to walk back toward his car, but Caleb called him again.
"McCann."
"Yeah?"
"You're not part of this investigation. You know that, right?"
Alex grinned—the shit-eating grin he knew Caleb hated.
"I am nothing but a humble citizen, Chief."
He could hear Caleb muttering all the way to his car.

Alex was sleeping, but he heard it. Soft padding feet creeping through his trailer.
Big padding feet.
He woke when the bed creaked to find a hundred-pound mountain lion lying half across his legs, staring at him with lazy golden eyes. He shifted to his back and scooted up a little, rubbing the sleep from his eyes.
"Hey, baby."
The lion was silent, but her lip curled up. Alex smiled and reached out, running a finger through the soft hair behind her left ear. The instinctive purr made him smile, but the smile was wiped away when she got up on all fours, leaned down, and hissed in his face, baring vicious two-inch fangs.
A full-grown cougar was a terrifying sight, but it was the silence that had always freaked out Alex more than anything. When wolves hunted, there was panting and crackling as they ran through brush. Little yips and barks to let each other know the movements of the pack. But cats were silent hunters; they could creep up rocks and through brush with little trace, their silence broken only by the occasional blood-curdling scream.
So it was probably stupid that the only thing Alex could think of was getting Ted to shift back to human form just so he could see her naked.
He reached over and grabbed the small bag he had kept in his bedside drawer ever since he moved back to the Springs. The cat lurched back as he opened the bag.
"Oh yeah. You know what this is."

Her eyes glazed over a second before her head dipped down to nuzzle the blanket. Then she shook her head and immediately shifted back to her human form.

Alex grinned. "Still like the catnip, huh?"

"That is so wrong, Alex."

He laughed wickedly, even as Ted grabbed a corner of the sheet to wrap herself in.

"But it's so cute."

"I hate it when you do that!"

"Big scary cougar acting like a kitty cat? How can I resist?"

"That stuff should be regulated." She scrunched up her nose and shook her head, as if still trying to rid her senses of the smell.

Seeing the advantage in her distraction, Alex grabbed Ted and rolled her under him, trapping her hips with his legs. He always slept naked, and it wasn't lost on him that the only thing separating their bodies was a thin cotton sheet.

"My turn to pounce."

"That's not why I came over." She was trying to brush him off, but he could scent her arousal and feel her pulse picking up.

"You're the one who snuck into my trailer naked."

"I wasn't naked. I was wearing fur."

"You're not now."

She shrugged. "I felt like having a run, and I wanted to talk to you. It's quicker this way."

"Definitely quicker." He leaned down to her neck, taking in her scent. "We're both naked. Saves time."

She could shove him off if she wanted to. She was more than strong enough. But she just lay there, staring at him with an inscrutable expression, as if they were in business negotiations, not naked in bed. She had to feel how aroused he was; it wasn't something she could miss with his legs caging her in, but she did nothing. Said nothing.

He let his mouth whisper across her neck, felt her pulse spike. Then he pulled away. "What did you want to talk about, Téa?"

"Why do you keep antagonizing Caleb?"

He lifted an eyebrow. "You want to talk about Caleb Gilbert while you're in bed with me?"

She huffed out a breath. "I'm going to keep you in the loop on this, but it makes it more difficult when you're pissing him off. I do have to work with the guy. And he's married to one of your best friends."

"I wasn't consulted on that." He braced his elbows beside her shoulders and played with a curl of her hair. "I like it when you don't straighten it."

"It's a pain in the ass."

"You didn't straighten it in college."

"I didn't have time in college."

"Hmm." He didn't say anything more. Didn't push things, even though his body wanted him to. It was this he'd missed, as much as anything. Whispering with her in bed. Arguing about things, then kissing the frown from her mouth. He pulled a thick curl from behind her ear and pulled it out to its full length, laying it across her face so the soft strands touched her lips. Then Alex bent down and slowly took the curl between his teeth, letting his lips brush hers as he pulled it away.

Ted let out a soft breath, and her scent bloomed around him. He buried his face in her neck as her hands came to rest at his waist.

His lips trailed up to her ear.

"Kiss me, Téa."

"Alex, we shouldn't—"

"A kiss." He spoke against her lips. "Just... a kiss."

She drew in a breath, and he felt her body relax. Her hips sank into the bed, and her hands spread across the small of his back. His lips rested against hers. Not moving until she opened her mouth and let him in.

A ferocious need tore through him, but he clamped it down and sank into what she offered. Just that. Soft lips pressing and moving against his, then her mouth opened and he tasted her again. Slick tongue licking the inside of his mouth, lapping at him like the cat she was.

His Téa could do amazing things with her tongue.

He smiled as he kissed her, enjoying the familiar rhythm that took over their bodies. They rocked together, hands grasping harder, the friction of the sheets maddening against his skin. Their lips never parted. His hands sank into her hair, tugging her mouth back to his when she pulled away to gasp his name.

"Alex—"

"Shh," he murmured, taking deep breaths, forcing his body away from her and closing his eyes as he rested his cheek against hers. They were flush with desire. She was hot and wet. He could smell it around her. Alex ached to take her like that. Sink into her and sate the need that clawed them both, but he pulled back.

Too much too fast would only come back to bite him. And not in a good way.

"Thank you," he whispered.

I miss you so much.

His wolf growled at him to claim her.

She said nothing, and his heart hurt a little.

Ted didn't *need* him. Not like he needed her. Her life was full. Work she loved. Family. Friends. But cracks had appeared in her walls with the shock of Marcus's death, and he was trying to ease closer without her shutting down. She hadn't clawed at him when he and Caleb almost came to blows. She'd comforted him. Soothed both the man and the wolf with her touch. And so far, she hadn't raised her guard again. It was an advantage he didn't plan to waste, and he didn't think his old friend would mind.

"You know... I'm sorry," he said, still pressing his cheek to hers. His thumb stroked the side of her neck. "For hurting you. Sorry that you didn't know how much it hurt me to lose you. Even if it had to happen, you should have known—"

"I should go."

He closed his eyes. Too much. Slowly, he nodded and rolled to the side, but she didn't get up right away. Just stared at the ceiling while he watched her in profile.

"This place is tiny," she said.

"It's decent for a trailer."

She'd pulled the sheet up to her neck.

"If you're really staying, why didn't you just get a house? There's a few in town that are nice. And you could always fix one up."

Dammit, his sister had been right.

"I like the old places like yours," he said. "There's none of those right now. I can wait."

"For what? Why not just build a new one in the old style?"

"You really want to know?"

She said nothing, but he could feel her tense.

"I didn't want to buy one by myself, Téa. Or build one. Not alone. I always wanted—"

He broke off when he felt her shift. Seconds later, the mountain lion was out the door. He could hear the wind whipping through the trees that shaded the trailer. He listened for a few moments, then stood and walked to the door, looking out into the black night. He didn't see her, of course. He didn't expect to.

Alex sighed. "I wanted *our* house, not mine."

Chapter Seven

Hating someone was easy. Trying to understand their motives was harder.

Never in a million years would Ted have expected Alex to let her go without a fight like he had the night before. He'd have persuaded. Tried to coax her into staying in his bed. Nudged her to have sex because he'd known she wanted it. He wouldn't have had to nudge much. He'd have known that too.

She'd never wanted anyone like she wanted him. It's what made moving on so completely impossible. Shifters were sensual by nature. Physical connection was crucial for Ted, and no one had ever come close to Alex. He could read her body like his own personal map. More than that, he'd never taken advantage of it. Never used her physical need for him against her. No, he was the lover who laughed with her. The one who teased her to the point of madness, then gave himself over completely.

"I didn't want to buy one by myself, Téa. Or build one. Not alone. I always wanted—"

He wanted *their* home. She didn't need to hear him say it because that had been her dream too. Even though they'd never discussed it.

There was a lot they'd left unsaid.

"You're a million miles away."

She blinked and shook her head. "Sorry."

Jena shrugged. "What's on your mind? Work stuff? Friend stuff? Alex stuff?"

She ignored the last one and said, "Marcus stuff. What's Caleb asking Allie about?"

They were sitting in Jena's kitchen. Her dad was working the diner that afternoon, giving Jena a much-needed break from the madness.

"I think he's talking to her about some of the Joe stuff." Jena spoke in a low voice. "There's a lot she didn't know about."

"Like what?"

"Money. He'd borrowed a lot of money from a lot of people. Marcus was only one of them. The more he digs into Marcus's past, the more Joe keeps popping up."

Ted frowned. "How?"

"Joe gambled. It sounds like that was part of the reason he and Allie were so broke all the time. And Marcus knew about it. I guess someone heard him threaten Joe that he'd tell Allie about the gambling when he asked Marcus for money. I guess Marcus used to have a problem and he straightened himself out. The guys at his job said he didn't have much patience for that stuff anymore."

"Well, that gives him motive, I guess."

"It's Joe, though!" Ted could see the stricken look in Jena's face. "Look, he may have turned into a shit husband, but he still loved his kids. He used to be our friend. Used to *adore* Allie."

"And then things got tough and he turned back into the sullen asshole we saw when he was younger. I'm not saying he's a murderer—"

"Good."

"Marcus was shot in the back, Jena."

Jena's mouth dropped open. She hadn't known that. "What?"

"He was shot in the back. Whoever shot him either snuck up on him —which you know would be difficult to do—or Marcus turned his back on him, which means he didn't think his killer was a threat. And people can do stupid things when they're desperate."

"Was Joe desperate?"

Ted glanced at the living room door. She could hear Caleb's low, calming voice and Allie's sniffles.

"Allie was the only thing holding that family together. He worked for her dad. And let's face it; *their* friends were really *her* friends. Everyone loves her. If she found out he was gambling their money instead of buying groceries—"

"She would have freaked. Even if she loved him."

"Allie's a mom. And from what she's told us, he worked pretty hard to kill her love years ago. She was holding it together for the kids and because she was loyal."

Jena said, "But she's not an idiot."

"Not even close. So Marcus telling her about the gambling would probably make him pretty desperate."

Jena rested her forehead on her hands. "Oh shit, Ted. This might get really, really bad."

Ted put her hand on Jena's back but kept her eyes on the doorway where Caleb was comforting Allie. "We'll make it through. No matter what happened. We'll be there for her and the kids."

"Are you working with Alex on this?" Jena asked quietly.

"What?"

"Caleb talks to me. He's not thrilled about Alex poking his nose in all this, even if Marcus was his friend. And Alex can be a hothead. I'd feel better if I knew you guys were working together on this."

Ted snorted. "'Cause I calm him down so much?"

"Hardly, but he listens to you. You're the only one who ever had any chance of changing his mind once he got fixated on something."

"I usually did that by pissing him off. How hard could that be?"

Jena looked up. "Are you working with him or not?"

Ted picked up Jena's left hand and fiddled with the new wedding band that encircled her ring finger. "Do you want to have to lie to him?"

"No."

"Then I have no idea what you're talking about."

Jena's face broke into a reluctant smile. "Right."

"And if Alex and I are hanging out more in the coming days, it's because we're... trying to work on our relationship."

She blinked. "Really?"

"No? I don't know."

"'Cause you didn't sound like you were bullshitting me just then. I mean, a little, but not completely."

Ted paused. "I don't know."

"Really?" Jena scooted back in her chair and grinned. "*Really?*"

"Why are you so excited about that?"

"Because we've all been waiting months for you to stop slamming the door in his face."

"I haven't done that." Exactly.

Jena's expression said Ted was full of shit, so Ted ignored her.

"He apologized."

"For leaving? Or... not coming back with you, I guess?"

"No." Oddly enough, Ted would have resented him apologizing for that. If his motives for staying in LA were important enough to end their relationship, then she didn't want him apologizing for it. "No, he apologized for hurting me. Said I should know how hard it was to give it up."

"Didn't you?"

Ted felt the tears behind her eyes, so she just shrugged.

"Oh, honey."

"I, uh... I didn't want you guys talking about him around me. And we avoided each other so much—"

"He was wrecked, Ted. Every time any of us even mentioned you. *Wrecked.* And his dad was such an ass about it."

"What a surprise." She closed her eyes and took a deep breath. "My mom never liked us together, either. Said if I was going to get married, it should be new blood. Someone who shouldn't challenge my authority. Someone I could control."

"You'd have no respect for a man like that."

"I know." Ted cleared her throat. "She's old-fashioned."

"You and Alex were both hurting. You barely even talked to each other when Lowell died."

Jena's late husband, Lowell, was Alex's cousin. They were close, and losing him must have torn Alex apart. Ted had known it. But she'd been hurt so badly by their breakup that she'd barely had it in her to give Alex a hug, much less talk to him after Lowell's death.

"I was a shit friend to him, Jen. Even if we weren't together anymore —"

"He understood."

He would. She felt a nudge against her walls. This time, the nudge wasn't coming from outside, but in.

"It's hard," she said. "Hard to trust him. Open up again. I feel like we've been at each other's throats for so long it's become a habit."

Jena slid her arm around Ted's shoulders. "You guys had something special. Everyone saw it. Even your families. That's probably why they never supported you. Shifters are clannish jerks, and we don't like sharing loyalty."

"Yeah."

"But open the door a little. Just a crack. At least see if there's something still there you want to explore."

Ted debated, then asked, "Would being naked in his bed last night count as opening a door?"

"*What*?"

Ted had the radio turned up as loud as she could stand. Dropkick Murphys poured out of the wireless speaker attached to her phone, and after she filled out the last of these vaccination reminder cards and mailed them, shipping up to Boston sounded like a brilliant idea. She didn't hear the front door, but she sensed him standing in the doorway. She could feel his eyes on her back.

She let the song finish, completed the last card, then turned the radio down to spin around on her stool. Alex was standing in the doorway, still wearing his hot-as-hell aviators and a dusty grey shirt rolled up to the elbows. Gone were the pressed slacks and the slick hair he'd sported for years when he lived in LA. He looked like a desert boy again. He needed a haircut something awful, and she wished it didn't look so good on him. She also wished his grin didn't stand out quite so brilliantly on his tan face.

"Up," Alex said, tossing his sunglasses on her desk.

"Why?"

He pulled her by the elbows and set her to the side before he sat on the old-fashioned metal stool and rolled to the center of the room.

"My turn on the spinny stool."

She couldn't help laughing. Alex held on to the edge of the seat and spun like a schoolboy, tilting up his head so he didn't get dizzy.

"Tell the truth, Vasquez. You became a doctor so you had a legitimate reason to buy a spinny stool."

"How has no one guessed it before now? You see right through me."

He laughed, then paused, leaned over, and grabbed her around the waist.

"Alex!" she squealed as he pulled her onto his lap.

Ted's instinct was to jump up. Leap away from him. But she remembered Jena's advice.

"Open the door... just a little."

She hooked her legs around Alex's and closed her eyes when he started spinning them faster and faster.

"Hold on."

"You're going to make us both sick."

He just laughed again. Ted felt a smile sneak across her lips.

"You love it," he whispered, sneaking a nip at her earlobe.

She did. Not that she was going to tell him that. But she did let herself laugh. Ted laughed until her sides hurt and her head spun.

"Stop," she gasped after a few more breathless minutes. "Stop, Alex. Please."

He stopped but didn't let her go. He held her around the waist and put his cheek against hers when she let her head fall back to rest on his shoulder.

"I love that you still listen to Dropkick Murphys," he said.

"How could I not? 'The Gang's All Here.'"

"'Rocky Road to Dublin.'"

"'Shipping Up to Boston.'"

He lifted his head and nudged her chin so she was looking at him. His hand slipped down to her hip, his thumb tracing over the edge. "'Rose Tattoo.'"

Ted felt the flush in her cheeks at the memory. He'd been there when she got it.

"I never thanked you for introducing me to them."

"You're welcome. Do I get another kiss today?"

"It was a moment of weakness."

"It was hot. Don't even lie to me that you're not thinking about it."

She resisted the urge to jump up. She wasn't a nervous girl. She needed to *think*, not react.

Her voice was low when she finally said, "I'm thinking about it."

"I'll take that." He nudged her up to standing and then stood himself. "Okay, playtime's over. Are you done with work? I had an errand I thought we could run together."

"I have some charting to do. Then I'm free."

He shoved the stool toward her, then grabbed a chair. "Chart away. I can wait for a few and answer some e-mail. Or is there anything I can help with?"

She looked up, surprised at his offer. "Not really. But thanks. Why don't you go lie down in my office? You look tired."

He shook his head and couldn't hold back his yawn. "If I close my eyes, they won't open again for a while."

"Early days?"

He nodded. "We've got some time to make up. And having Marcus gone makes things harder. Josie's brother is still tied up at their last job. His foreman is good, but he's not Marcus."

"No, I imagine not."

She started to pull out the files she needed, hand-jotted notes attached on sticky papers she used when she saw patients. She was just at the edge of needing to hire a nurse or physician's assistant, and she was hoping one of the Springs kids graduating soon would be able to fill the position. There were two or three that she had her eye on. The trick would be luring them back to town instead of more lucrative opportunities elsewhere. She had to admit the resort opening, along with the new shops and restaurants it could support, would help.

"Why don't you have a nurse?" Alex asked.

"I'll probably hire one in the next year or so. I'm not so busy that I can't get away without one right now. We're a pretty healthy bunch. The human mates are the ones that I see most. Some people still go to see doctors in Indio."

"Are you kidding?"

"Nope. It's taken me a while to build up the practice I have. Which is fine. I get it."

"You came back to the Springs so we'd have our own doctor in town. You were one of the top graduates in your class, you got offers everywhere, and you came back here. Don't they know how lucky they are?"

Ted loved that he sounded outraged on her behalf, but she shrugged. "If you're old and watched me grow up, you probably don't want me doing your prostate exam, right?"

Alex was silent for a minute. "I see your point. You still need to hire someone for your paperwork."

"I have someone a few hours a week. But some of it's unavoidable. All our records have to be electronic now."

"And the insurance stuff?"

She groaned. "I don't want to talk about it."

"The clinic doing okay money-wise?"

He was being nosey as hell, but she could tell he was just worried. He'd never doubted her abilities. Plus, his business brain beat hers any day.

"We'll be fine." She smiled, looking over her shoulder. "I keep expenses pretty low."

He'd closed his eyes, and she knew he didn't want to sleep, so she asked him a question.

"How's construction going? You going to get back on schedule?"

He rubbed his eyes. "Yeah. It'll take a couple weeks and a lot of overtime, but we'll do it. Once the brother-in-law gets here, we'll be in better shape. I hope."

"He in Vegas?"

"No, he was overseeing the new construction on the casino."

"Oh?" Something struck her. "Do the tribes know this guy's connected to Marcus?"

"Probably. I think Marcus is the one who closed the casino deal."

The Colorado River Indian Tribes had a good relationship with the people of Cambio Springs. And most of the leaders were aware of the... unusual nature of the fresh spring, along with the town's secrets.

"So does Marcus's brother-in-law—"

"Chris. Name's Chris Avery."

"Does he know about us?"

"Josie says no."

"But do the guys he's working with over there—the ones who *do* know about us—know that this Chris guy doesn't?

Ted could tell that Alex had the same thought she did because he sat up straighter and his eyes opened wide.

"Shit."

"I think someone better put the word out to Dev. Maybe find out how open they were with him. If the guys over there think he knows about us —"

"Then they might not watch what they say." He nodded, then made a face. "I guess I'll call Dev."

The corner of her mouth lifted. "I'm not sneaking into Dev's trailer at night, so stop making that face."

Lazy pleasure filled his eyes. "Are you going to make a habit of that? Because I'm fine with it."

"You getting rid of the catnip?"

"No."

"Hmmmm." She shook her head ominously. "Not a point in your favor, McCann."

"I'll take my chances."

An hour later, they were bumping in Alex's truck out to Old Joe Quinn's house. He lived over the wash and up in the canyon a bit, but you could hardly call his house deserted. Most of the time, he had four or five shifters from his clan hanging around. Ted hoped they made themselves scarce today. Cats and snakes rarely got along.

"Why are we visiting Old Quinn again?"

"How did you start your clinic, Ted?"

She blinked. "You mean… financially?"

"Uh-huh."

"I got some startup money from my mom. And there was a federal grant I applied for that came through. Mayor Matt helped me with that one, actually."

Alex nodded. "Any business takes capital to start, right? Even if it's a medical clinic. Like that first house I flipped?"

"Your dad helped out and cosigned. I remember."

"Exactly." Alex picked up speed when he drove through the wash. There wasn't a cloud in the sky, but that didn't mean anything. Rain fifty miles away could sweep through a desert wash without warning, taking cars, animals, or people in a flash. "You ever ask yourself where Marcus Quinn—who came from a shit family who never supported him—got the money to start a surveying business that was turning a profit within a few years?"

"Um…" No, she hadn't even thought about it. "A loan?"

"With what collateral? He'd been working for a surveyor. Had some trade school experience. But he owned nothing. A bank wasn't going to loan him money."

"So what's your guess?"

"At first, I thought Old Quinn must have helped him out. But then I started thinking about it."

Ted shook her head. "Old Quinn doesn't have that kind of money. Not until recently with the land sale for the resort."

"You're right," Alex said. "Don't get me wrong. The old guy can make money. I don't ask how, but he does. And he can read people in a heartbeat. But he's also got a lot of people in his clan that don't do shit. And who do you think makes sure all the kids have food and shoes?"

"Old Quinn."

"He's a godfather to over half of them. And it's not just an honorary title."

It wouldn't be. For all their shady dealings, most Quinns were staunch Catholics who took family very seriously. They may give each other black eyes and empty wallets, but no one outside the clan did so without repercussions.

"So where'd he get the money?"

"That's why we're going to visit the old guy. I'm hoping he'll tell me."

"And you think that might have something to do with how Marcus died?"

Alex frowned. "Trust me, Ted. There's very few people that are going to loan money without collateral. And none of them are people you want to cross."

And this was why Caleb Gilbert needed to bend a little and allow Alex into the investigation, even though it wasn't procedure. But that was okay. If Caleb didn't get Alex's insight, Ted would.

"If he borrowed money from someone," she said, "it would have been years ago. He's been in business for longer than he and Josie have been married."

"Sometimes ancient history can still bite you in the ass."

Yes, it could. She was reminded of their hour in her office, chatting about their day. Alex tossing around jokes as she worked. It reminded her of when she was in school. Ancient history to some, but old patterns were easy to fall back into.

"You know," he said, "that was nice back there."

"Back where?"

"In your office."

She smiled that his thoughts had been in line with hers. "Yeah. It was."

"I miss that."

She forced herself to say it, even though it made her feel naked. "Me too."

He just smiled and looked back at the road.

"Ted…" He stopped, as if he'd thought better of saying something. He was even biting his lip. He only did that when he was trying to hold his tongue.

"What?"

Alex took a deep breath. "We were always shit at communicating with each other."

"What do you mean?"

She knew exactly what he meant.

"Physical communication was never a problem. But verbal?"

"Yeah." She relented. "We were."

"You assumed things about my life and my plans. I assumed things about yours—"

"And we both held them back because we didn't want to rock the boat."

"Hey." His voice was softer, and she looked over. "It was a pretty great boat. Hard to risk something like that."

She nodded but didn't say anything more.

He started, "I've been thinking—"

"Don't hurt yourself."

"You just can't help it, can you?"

"Nope."

He grinned. "I've been thinking about what we can do. So our ancient history doesn't come back and bite us in the ass."

The fact that he'd been thinking about it loosened something tight in her heart. "Yeah?"

"Maybe…" He pulled over to the side of the road, just around the corner from the turnoff to Old Quinn's. "Can we try? At least *try* this?"

"Being friends? That hasn't been going so great, Alex."

"We were never just friends. Why do you think we fight so much when we're trying to pretend we are?"

She paused to think. Breathe. Think some more.

They'd gone down that road before with both amazing and explosive results. To try again. To open herself up like that… She didn't want to admit how scared she was. But every week that passed, she had to acknowledge that Alex appeared to be settling. He'd rented out his condo in LA. She hadn't seen his city car in months. Sure, he hadn't bought a house, but she was refusing to think about the reasons right now. Holding on to that excuse just seemed stubborn and immature at this point.

She still worried.

"We're not kids anymore, Alex. We have responsibilities."

"We always did, Ted. Even when we were twenty-two. We can deal with that."

"There's so much stuff in the past."

He took her hand and held it, playing with her fingers. Light. No pressure. Just… there.

"We can't go back. I'm not who I was then. You're not who you were. We've grown up. Hopefully. But… You *know* there's still something there. Something good between us, along with the bad. Something that could be great."

Could it?

It could.

"It's complicated, Alex."

"The good stuff always is." He squeezed her hand. "I'm willing if you are, Téa."

Téa.

He was the only one who called her that. The only one who ever had. A soft name for those times he held her close. Groaned her name in passion. Whispered it in his sleep. For a long time, the memory of it hurt. But now?

She slowly leaned over and kissed him. Light. Just a taste. His firm lips angled over hers when he took the kiss further, but he wouldn't be Alex if he didn't. He was hungry for her, and she liked it. His callused hands were light against her skin. Holding her, but not bruising.

When he finally pulled away, she said, "I'll think about it. I promise."

"Fair enough." He smiled. "Now, let's go ask a shady old man about money."

Chapter Eight

Progress on the Ted front was slow but steady. He'd take that. Her kiss still burned on his lips as he turned the corner to see three of the Quinn boys sitting on Old Quinn's porch, beers in hand and a scattering of empty cans around them.

"Oh, this looks promising," Ted muttered.

"Only one way to honor a loved one," Alex said. "Getting shit-faced in their memory."

"Give them some credit. This might just be a normal afternoon for them."

"I recognize Connor and Marcus's brother, Rory. Who's the other one?"

"Kellan. Another cousin of Marcus's. He's a follower. Not that bright, but loyal."

Alex parked carefully, but a cloud of dust kicked up anyway. Quinn didn't waste his money on gravel for his drive. His home didn't have any pretense of a yard. It was dry brush and cactus. Rocks and scrub and the occasional kids' toy tossed in the dirt. Alex opened the car door and stepped out, standing by the truck as he called to the house.

"Hey, guys. The old man around?"

Connor walked forward. He had a typical Quinn build, whip thin with lean muscles. They were all quick. It was hardly surprising that most of their clan shifted into rattlesnakes or some other deadly reptile. Connor's natural form was a coachwhip, a lean, aggressive snake with the habit of eating its prey live. As a human, he was just as aggressive.

"He's not here," Connor said. "And you're not wanted, McCann." His lip curled at Ted. "Neither are you, pussycat."

Ted didn't react to the provocation. While some of the cats in the Springs did shift to domestics, everyone knew Ted was a mountain lion. She wore her power like other women wore heels. It was one of the sexiest things about her.

Nevertheless, Alex said, "Watch your mouth, Connor. Poking a lion is dumb, even for you."

He heard Rory snort behind him, but the young man quickly covered his smile.

"Why?" Connor turned back to Alex. "You going to kill me and tear me up like some dog did Marcus?"

The other men stood, walking to the edge of Old Quinn's porch, still holding on to their beer.

"Marcus was my friend. And I don't make a habit of shooting my friends in the back."

"Maybe not," a voice called from inside. Alex heard it and sighed when a young woman slinked out onto the porch. "But you don't have a problem *stabbing* them in the back, do you?"

"I'm shocked—shocked—that Maggie's here," Ted muttered. "Who would have expected that?"

Alex eyed her in disgust. Maggie Quinn was attractive and she knew it. And she made everyone else around her aware of it too. The woman used sex like a weapon. Despite that, Maggie didn't have a problem attracting attention when she wanted it.

"I haven't seen Maggie in a few years," he mused. "I didn't miss her."

"You sure know how to show a girl a good time." Ted patted his shoulder. "This afternoon just gets better and better."

Maggie Quinn stepped in front of Connor, two of her sisters flanking her. If there was anyone who could stir up shit even faster than old Connor, it had to be his childhood friend's sister. There were multiple reasons that Sean had fled the Springs when he was eighteen, and one of them was standing on the porch, glaring at Alex.

"Does Maggie know what really happened with you and Sean?"

"Nope."

Quinns were shit to each other, but they valued family loyalty above all else. And Sean had stuck with his family. Through every fight. Every scam. He'd lost a tooth in a bar fight Maggie had provoked. He wasn't one to complain, but he desperately wanted out.

Which was why—when Sean *had* asked him to—Alex had accused his childhood friend of stealing from both the feed store and the diner, giving his friend a perfectly legitimate reason to leave town. No Quinn was going to argue with one of their own running from the law, and no one needed to know the money had been quietly returned with no harm done. The accusation meant Sean got out, but it left Alex on the shit list of most of the Quinn clan.

But then, he'd been on their shit list anyway, just for being a wolf.

"What the hell are you doing here?" Maggie called. "Come to betray another friend? Or have you already done that, McCann?"

"None of the wolves had anything to do with Marcus's death, Maggie. I'm just here to ask the old man some questions."

"That poor girl." Maggie wiped alligator tears from her eyes and put a hand on Rory's shoulder. "Your own niece and nephews, Rory. Fatherless. Not that this dog cares."

Ted said, "She really is a snake, isn't she?"

"Rosy boa. Fitting, isn't it?"

"Kind of."

Whipping her head around as if she'd heard them, Maggie said, "What do you want here, Alex? We're just trying to grieve our cousin and brother in peace."

He resisted rolling his eyes at her drama. Barely. "I want to talk to Old Quinn."

"He's not here."

He glanced at Ted, who nodded silently. "We can wait."

Maggie only sneered. "You're not wanted. This is Quinn land."

Alex and old Joe Quinn got along better than most. He didn't have the soft spot for Alex that he did for Jena, but Alex suspected Old Quinn knew exactly what had happened with Sean because the man wasn't an idiot. And he'd been the one to raise Sean after his dad took off and he couldn't stand being around his mother and sisters anymore.

"Yeah, it's Quinn land," Alex said. "But it's not *your* land, Maggie. It's the old man's. So we'll wait."

She started toward him, clearly unhappy to have her claim challenged. She didn't like her great-uncle, and Alex had to wonder why Maggie was even there. Was a dominance challenge brewing in the snake clan? She might not be strong enough now, but Alex had no question that at some point Maggie Quinn would make her move to take over the Quinn family. And if she was successful, God help everyone in the Springs.

Maggie gave up trying to get a rise out of Alex, and she shifted her attention to Ted.

"And if it isn't the mannish kitten. Are you taking a turn fucking the wolf now?" She cocked her head. "Didn't he have a cute little human just last month? She came out to your sister's house when Willow was gone." Maggie grinned. "Looked nice and loose when she left the next day."

Bitch. Did he explain that his project manager in Palm Desert had come out for a meeting, and they'd had too much to drink after dinner? Lexi was a friend, and nothing had happened, but did he explain her presence to Ted or not let on that Maggie was getting to him?

He shouldn't have worried.

Ted leaned over and said, "That was your friend from Palm Desert, right?" .

"My project manager, but yeah, a friend too. Thank you for not going off on me, mannish kitten."

"Just because I don't flash my boobs around town..." She shook her head with a sigh. "You forget I've been living in the same town as Maggie for three years now. I'm well acquainted with her shit."

He grinned. "You're pretty damn cool, Vasquez."

"I know. Going to get naked now."

He blinked. "You're—what? Why are you getting—"

"Listen to the grass, McCann." Her dark eyebrow arched. "We're surrounded."

It had happened slowly, but the minute he looked around, he saw them. Dozens of rattlesnakes curled up and hissed, surrounding the truck. They'd approached through the dry brush and scrub, blending seamlessly with the land around Old Quinn's house.

"So that's why he doesn't have a yard."

Ted had already slipped off her jeans and T-shirt. Within seconds, a cougar lay sprawled on the roof of his truck.

Alex winced. "Please avoid scratch marks if possible. And are you just going to hang out in natural form until Old Quinn gets back?"

She gave him a lazy stare that told him nothing.

Alex stepped forward, trying to get to the porch, but a sidewinder darted in front of him and whipped his flat head forward, giving it a lethal shake.

No.

Alex growled in the back of his throat. "Call them off, Maggie."

"No." She was gleeful. "Leave. I've told you more than once now."

If she'd been Old Quinn, she'd be justified in attacking. Shapeshifters had strict laws about territory.

But this wasn't her territory. And he was tired of her shit.

Giving her no warning, Alex burst from his clothes as he shifted, snarling as the snakes cowered back from the massive silver-grey timber wolf. He felt the power run through him. Deep. Settled into his natural form, his senses roared. The smell of dust and sweat and alcohol from the porch. The tickling scent of the lion at his back. The sun was brighter. The wind teased his fur.

One rattler came too close and the wolf snapped, baring his teeth at the snake. The snakes, frightening enough as a group, knew that one wrong step by the massive predator would be their end. They slithered back, waiting in a circle, still rattling and twisting around as Alex watched them. If they attacked at once, the sheer power of their venom *could* take him down. But if they did, they'd start a war, and they knew it wasn't a war they were liable to win, no matter their numbers.

Further, the woman commanding them was far from leader of the clan.

Still, she taunted him. "Take off, puppy dog. Or do you need a little more encouragement?" He heard the distinctive rack of the shotgun before he looked up, and Maggie was pointing it right at him, dead between the eyes. "I'm not gonna ask again."

Alex snarled as Ted's scream split the air. From the shadows of a twisted mesquite that grew on the edge of the house, the cougar pounced. Landing with a soft thud, she pinned Maggie Quinn to the porch, knocking the gun from her hands. Her sisters skittered back from the snarling cat, eyes darting everywhere but at their sister.

Alex had never even heard her move from the truck. The snakes continued circling, even more agitated by the scent of violence in the air. One reached out in a half strike, slamming his head into Alex's foreleg, though the teeth didn't sink in.

He bit down his urge to bite. One careless move and there'd be a dead shifter on his conscience. He didn't want that, even if they were threatening him. The problem was they knew it.

Connor, Rory, and Kellan had backed up, scooting away from the mountain lion pinning their cousin. Ted bared her teeth and screamed in Maggie's face again, one paw locked on the shotgun that the woman had pulled, the other pinning Maggie to the ground. Her claws dug into the woman's chest, five deep gouges that welled red with fresh blood.

Adrenaline filled the air, exciting every predator in the vicinity. Alex could feel his hackles rise. The urge to attack the snakes around him swelled.

"Enough!"

He heard the roar coming from the cliffs as Old Quinn walked down the trail, red-faced and wearing a furious expression.

Ted backed off from Maggie and let Quinn pull the young woman up by the throat. He pinned her against the wall.

"You dare, Margaret Quinn?"

"Uncle—"

"You dare pull *my* gun on a clan leader while on *my* land?"

"I asked them to leave! Twice!"

"You're a stupid child, and I have no use for you." His graveled voice rasped in the dry air. "This is not your land, and the territory laws don't protect you. Now I'm telling you to get off *my* land and not come back until I give you leave. That is your only warning."

He tossed her by the neck toward her sisters, who caught her and scrambled off the porch. Connor, Rory, and Kellan stood watching, none of them daring to say a word. Old Quinn stepped out into the yard and yelled at the snakes. "Get! I want all of you gone."

Just as quickly as the rattlers appeared, they left, slinking into the grass and rocks as if they'd never been there at all. Old Quinn glared at the boys on the porch, especially Connor.

"Connor, get out of here."

He had the gall to look hurt. "Why?"

"Because I want you gone!"

Old Quinn didn't have to say it twice. Connor took off without a word. Quinn grunted at Rory and Kellan and pointed at two chairs at the end of the porch.

"Stay there and don't come inside. Rory, don't be an idiot like your cousins. Kellan, listen to Rory."

The boys went to sit immediately while Quinn turned to Ted and said, "If you're not here to give me any kind of fucking exam, then shift and get in the house, doc. We have things to talk about."

Then he glanced over his shoulder and said, "You too, McCann. And I don't want any fur on my couch."

Chuffing out what had to be a laugh, Ted loped back to the truck, ducking behind it to get dressed. Alex shifted and tried to pick up the scraps of clothes that had ripped when he changed. He tossed them in the back of the truck and didn't even flinch when Ted walked past and slapped his ass.

"You still get little freckles on your butt."

"And you still like my ass," he said, trying not to smile. "Cats. Always taking advantage."

"I like the freckles. They're cute."

He couldn't hold back the grin. If they had been alone...

Shifting made him horny. There was no delicate way to put it. After the initial nausea they all went through during puberty, a shift set the blood running. For fight, flight, or sex. It left the body revved up, and very little helped except giving in to whatever urge struck hardest.

He pulled on the spare sweatpants he kept behind his seat and hoped that Old Quinn had something stronger than sweet tea to give him.

Alex was sucking back a beer by the time all three of them sat down in the living room. Old Quinn may have never married or had children, but he was still the head of his family. The Quinn women kept his house for him and kept his kitchen stocked. There was always food and drink to be had, which came in handy when your house was the unofficial hangout of a good third of the town's population.

Quinn eyed them, glancing between Ted and Alex with amused awareness, but Ted's expression said it all.

Back off, old man. This is none of your business.

Nevertheless, the old man smirked. "You here because of Marcus?"

Alex nodded, but it was Ted who spoke.

"Yes, but first, do we have a problem about Maggie?"

"Did you draw blood?"

"Yes."

Quinn cocked his head, never one to let an advantage slip by.

"My clan will have a blood marker on yours, but I'll be cautious about collecting it. I know it was provoked."

Ted didn't look pleased. Alex narrowed his eyes and saw Old Quinn smiling at him as if he'd done him a favor.

Blood markers were inevitable when you had as many predators living together as you did in Cambio Springs. On moon nights, when all the clans shifted, things could get wild. It was one of the reasons snakes usually stayed out of the way when nights got rowdy. Bears, big cats, and wolves could all hold their own, even in a fight where blood was spilled. Birds could fly, and there weren't many of them. But snakes were stealth hunters, better served by isolation and silence than outright attack.

For the cats to owe the snakes a blood marker was significant. The fact that Quinn acknowledged the marker as provoked was... problematic.

While wolves could claim attack on any member of the pack as a provocation, cats were solitary. Provocation would only be acknowledged for immediate family. A child... or a mate. By calling the attack on Maggie provoked, Old Quinn was effectively calling Alex McCann Ted's mate.

And that wasn't lost on Ted.

Alex narrowed his eyes and wondered if Old Quinn had just made his life easier or harder.

Luckily, Ted brushed it off. She nodded and said, "I'll let my mother know."

"Appreciated."

"Maggie's a problem," Alex said.

Old Quinn tugged on the end of his mustache. "You don't have to tell me that, McCann. 'Course you know it'd be better if her brother was around."

Sean hadn't been back in the Springs since high school. The few times Alex had seen him had been in Los Angeles or one of the other cities where the journalist had been on assignment. They emailed regularly, and Alex knew Sean kept in touch with his uncle too.

"You know he's not likely to be back."

"And I know the reasons he stays gone are bullshit."

"They're his reasons, Quinn. I can't—"

"You tell him, Alex. He stays gone after Marcus is dead, and his family and clan are fucked for leadership. Hell, he might actually listen to you." Quinn's voice was soft when he glanced at the porch. "After Sean, Marcus was it. I've got my eye on Rory, but he's young. And he's messed up about his brother right now. All in the older generation are too much of a mess."

The Quinn's last clan leader had been trouble, encouraging the more criminal elements in his family to thrive, and it had left a mark on his parents' generation. Old Quinn started to change directions for his family as soon as his grandfather had died, but that change took time.

"You've got a lot of years left, Quinn."

The old man's voice grew hoarse. "If losing Alma taught me anything, it's that you have to be prepared. We don't have no guarantees here. Tell my nephew to get his ass home. He has responsibilities."

"I'll tell him, Quinn, but you know there's no telling what he'll do."

"Fair enough." He nodded between Alex and Ted. "Speaking of responsibilities, you two thought about what you're going to do to the balance of power here once everyone knows?"

Ted said, "I don't know what you're talking about."

"You're not a good liar, Teodora Vasquez, so don't try to bullshit me."

Alex placed his hand on Ted's knee and felt the tension. She was angry, but he didn't want the old man to sidetrack them. "That's not why we're here, Quinn."

"Just something to keep in mind."

"Fine," Ted said between clenched teeth. "We want to talk about Marcus."

"I bet you do."

Alex scooted forward in his seat, setting his beer on the coffee table. "Ted and I are looking into some things that Chief Gilbert might not think about. Some... alternate areas of investigation."

Now Quinn just looked amused. "You know Gilbert is smart as hell. What do you think you're gonna find that he won't?"

"He may be smart, but he doesn't think like a criminal the way I do."

"You?" Old Quinn hooted. "A criminal?"

"Nothing shadier than real estate deals in Southern California, old man."

Quinn tipped his head toward Alex. "You may have me there, boy."

"Has Gilbert come up here to ask you where Marcus got the money to start his business yet?"

All amusement dropped from Old Quinn's face. "Leave that one alone, Alex."

"Has he?"

"No. But if he does, he has friends in the police department in Vegas who can look into that shit. It's not something you two need to poke around in."

He could feel Ted sit up straighter. "There *was* something sketchy," she said.

Quinn frowned before he took another pull on his beer. "Of course there was something sketchy. You don't start a business with that much capital on account of your smile. I didn't like it, but Marcus did it anyway. And it's something he got out from under as soon as he could. I don't think it has anything to do with who killed him."

Alex asked, "Why not?"

Old Quinn narrowed his eyes. "Because if I did, there'd be seven dead Eye-talians Vegas PD would be investigating right now." He leaned back and flicked his mustache. "Not that they'd get anywhere. Snakebites happen in the desert."

Chapter Nine

Provoked.

Her mother was going to have a fit. Not only was Old Quinn getting a blood marker on their clan, but the Elder was insinuating that Ted had mate privileges with the future McCann alpha. She was never going to hear the end of it.

I'll show you provoked, old man.

She was silent on the drive back, letting Alex navigate his truck over the rocky roads leaving Old Quinn's house. She didn't think about the fact that he was driving. Hadn't even asked if he wanted her to. She drove in the city because he hated traffic and tended to get enraged. He drove in the country because he was better off-road. It was another slip into old patterns that she tried not to think about.

"Your mother going to pitch a fit about the blood marker?"

The fact that he guessed her exact thoughts only ticked her off more.

"Probably not. Blood markers are inevitable, and she knows I'm not a hothead."

"And it was *provoked*…" She could hear the mischief in his voice.

"Stop. Just… stop."

"You know I won't."

She sighed. "Try."

Alex didn't just stop talking; he pulled the car over.

"Is she?" he asked.

Ted was lost. "Is she what?"

"Your mother. Is she going to throw a fit?"

He wasn't just asking about the marker. It was all of it. Her and Alex.

"You two thought about what you're going to do to the balance of power here once everyone knows?"

She hated that Old Quinn was right. There was more than one reason most shifters looked away from the Springs for mates. It wasn't that inter-clan pairings didn't happen. They did. Jena's late husband had been a wolf, even though he'd never shifted. Ted had cousins who were in different clans because their parents weren't cats. Children from such unions had a fifty-fifty chance of being either animal.

But among the leadership...

Ted was one of the most dominant cats. Alex was the future alpha. None of their elders had liked their relationship in college, and all of them had been quietly relieved when it ended. Despite the fact that she had no interest in leading her clan—and had told her mother so repeatedly—she couldn't ignore the implications of being in a relationship with Alex.

"I don't know," she admitted.

"Ted—"

"It doesn't matter," she said. "I'm an adult. And at the end of the day, she wants me to be happy. She's not a horrible person, Alex."

"No, but she'd sure like it if I were submissive to you."

"Yes." There was no use denying something he knew already.

He silently stared at her hand where it rested on the console between them. He reached over and twined their fingers together.

"Not going to happen, Téa." His voice wasn't arrogant. If anything, it was a little sad. "I'm the head of my clan. Dominance is in my blood. You know that, right?"

His firm touch eased the knot of worry in her chest. If he'd wavered, she might have doubted. But Alex was a man who knew who he was. And what his animal was capable of.

"I know, Alex."

"Being submissive... There's not a damn thing wrong with it. It's a necessary balance for some. But it's not me. And it never will be."

She wasn't interested in challenging him. Ever. But he didn't need to know that.

Plus, her cat wanted to play.

Ted twisted her hand around and clasped her fingers around his wrist. "You sure about that? Ever?" She squeezed her fingers tight around his skin. "Because that's just… unimaginative, Alex."

The heavy atmosphere in the car couldn't last through his rueful grin. "I'm not sure we're talking about the same thing anymore."

"Are you complaining?"

"No." He pulled away his wrist and put the car in gear. "But she's going to cause problems if we get back together—"

"Which I'm still deciding."

He turned his head and cocked an arrogant eyebrow at her. "Sure you are."

"Conceited."

"Stubborn," he said. "And my dad won't be thrilled either. The benefit is they've got all the same arguments they always had, and we have the same answers, plus a few new ones."

Ted started to play devil's advocate on their hypothetical relationship.

"We can't belong to both clans."

"Of course not," Alex said. "You'll stay in your clan; I'll stay in mine. We're people first, not animals."

"Our loyalties will be divided."

"Only if there are problems. Plus, our relationship will give us a greater incentive to work together."

"Oh." She smiled. "Good one."

"I just thought of it."

"Our children might be *wolves*." Her eyes widened in mock horror. "Poor things."

"Even worse, they could be *cats*."

She smiled. It was an old argument, and one that had never been an issue for either of them. As long as their children shifted, that was all that was important. Cambio Springs children who didn't shift always died young. Cat or wolf, she didn't care what form her children took, as long as they were healthy.

Her children?

There she went, jumping to the same conclusions she had in her twenties. She went from considering a relationship with Alex to imagining their children, all in the space of a car ride. She needed to think about it. Consider whether letting him back into her life was—

"Hey," he asked, "want to go to the Cave for dinner? I don't feel like cooking."

"Are you asking me on a date? A real, honest-to-goodness date?"

"Yep."

She didn't allow herself to second-guess it.

"You're on."

They picked a booth in the corner of the Cave, out of the way of the local crowd, most of whom gave them either speculative looks or outright smiles. Ted saw Josie on the other side of the room, eating with her two kids and a brown-haired man she guessed was her brother. He was nothing like Ted would have imagined.

While Marcus's widow had bright blue hair and colorful, swirling tattoos, her brother looked like he'd walked out of the L. L. Bean catalogue. They were about as opposite as two siblings could be in appearance. Luckily, Ted saw his arm around his niece's shoulder as he tried to pry a smile out of one of Josie's younger boys. Maybe he wasn't as stuffy as he looked.

"You met him before?" she asked Alex, right after Tracey took their drink orders.

He shook his head.

"Should we?"

"Yeah. You mind?"

"Nope." She hadn't seen Josie since she'd done the preliminary exam on her husband's body. She tried to rid her mind of that image and focus on the man Marcus had been. Laughing. Generous. Whatever shadows had been in Marcus Quinn's background, he'd been nuts about his family.

Josie looked up as they approached. "Hey, Alex. Ted." Her eyes widened a little. "You guys just came in?" *Together?*

It was the unspoken question in Josie's voice and the quirk at the corner of her mouth that had Ted smiling. "Yeah. How are you doing?"

"I'll be better after I get my burger." She nodded at the man across from her. "Alex, this is my brother, Chris Avery."

"We've spoken on the phone, but it's nice to meet you in person, Chris." Alex held out his hand, which the other man grasped firmly. "I'm sorry it wasn't for better reasons."

Chris nodded but didn't smile. Then again, he'd just lost his brother-in-law.

"I'll be out on the job first thing tomorrow. Just got into town tonight."

"No problem. Priorities." He tugged the ponytail of Marcus and Josie's oldest. "Kasey, did you find the library?"

The little girl nodded. "Your mom's real nice."

"*Really* nice, sweetie," Josie quickly corrected. "Not real."

Alex smiled. "I think she's nice too."

Chris cleared his throat. "Good to know a town this small has a library."

"We try. It's a fine place to grow up."

The other man's smile was tight. "I'm sure you think so."

Ted could hear Alex grinding his teeth to keep silent at the insult. She took his right hand in hers and felt his tension ratchet down.

Josie's smile was brittle as she looked at her brother. "Chris, we talked about this."

"Marcus *just...*" He glanced at his niece and nephews. "We'll talk about this later."

Ted put a hand out. "I'm Dr. Teodora Vasquez, Mr. Avery."

"Nice to meet you." He took it, obviously still stewing. "You the vet?"

She cocked her head. "MD. Family practice." She smiled at Kasey. "I see a monkey every now and then, but they're usually little brothers."

Kasey giggled, breaking the tension at the table. Ted tugged on Alex's hand to lead him away. "We won't take up your dinnertime," she said. "Just wanted to say hi, Josie. You've got my number if you need anything?"

She nodded, and Ted and Alex were just turning when Tracey walked up with a huge tray of burgers. She let Alex's hand drop to squeeze by.

"Hey, you two." Tracey set down the tray and mumbled to Ted as she passed, "He's a peach, huh?"

"No kidding."

Before they could say any more, she felt Alex's hand on the small of her back, and he ushered her to the booth where their drinks were waiting for them. They sat down across from each other and both took a drink before they said anything else. The day had been hot, and though the sun had gone down, Ted still felt the dust of the afternoon on her neck. She swiped at it and grimaced.

"I could use a shower, too," Alex said, watching her.

"Do you think he knows?"

"Who?"

"Josie's brother."

"About us? I don't know." He drank again. "Maybe. Was it odd that he asked if you were a vet?"

"I don't know," she said. "It's not as uncommon as you'd think for people to assume I'm a vet. Don't know why."

"Your animal magnetism," he said with a wink. "Gets me every time."

"He doesn't like them living here."

"Would you? If your brother-in-law had just been murdered, would you want your sister moving to the town out in the middle of the desert where it happened? And where she'd have no family around?"

"No," she said. "I'd want them close. No matter what town they were moving to. After a loss like that, I'd want my sister close."

Alex shrugged. "It's probably that."

"Yep. Could be." They both fell silent, and Ted picked up a menu, even though she knew what she wanted. She set it down after a minute. "I just feel like there's something…"

"What?"

"More." She glanced across the restaurant where Josie and her brother were ushering the kids out of the booth and gathering their things. "I feel like there's something else."

"Maybe he knows," Alex said. "Knows about us and doesn't like it. He doesn't strike me as the most open-minded individual."

"But is that enough for murder?"

Alex's eyes narrowed. "Possibly. But Josie said Marcus and Chris were full partners in the business too. If he was involved, it might be prejudice against shifters, or…"

"Or it could be something way more old-fashioned."

"Money?"

Ted lifted one shoulder. "It's a classic motive for a reason."

"It is." Alex nodded at someone over her shoulder, and Ted turned to look. It was Ollie, hulking behind the bar and polishing glasses during a lull. Ted hadn't seen him in over a week, and she wanted to pick his brain about more than one thing.

"Be right back." She hopped to her feet.

"Ted…" Alex's voice was a warning. "Don't meddle."

"It's cute how you think I'm going to listen to you. Order me a burger, will you? You know how I like them."

Ted ignored his sigh as she walked over and parked her butt on the barstool right in front of Ollie.

He was a distant cousin on his father's side, but more than that, he was one of her best friends.

"Hey," she said, trying to get him to look at her.

"Don't ask." Ollie didn't look up.

"About what?"

"Don't ask whatever question you have about how I'm doing, or have I seen her, or what I'm going to do about everything. I don't want to talk about it."

"Brooder."

He looked up then, and he was annoyed. "You think you're funny, but you're not. Keep pushing, Ted. See what happens."

"I know what I *want* to happen—"

She blinked when he slammed a glass down so hard it cracked. Without missing a beat, he tossed it in the trashcan behind him, not even looking as it fell in. Then he leaned forward, and Ted was reminded that Ollie wasn't just an easygoing barman. He was a predator. Quiet... until you pushed him too hard.

"Don't." His voice was barely audible.

"Okay."

At her quiet acquiescence, she saw his face soften.

"I know you want everyone to be happy, sweetheart, but it's not as simple as that."

"Can it be?"

His mouth opened, but he didn't speak for a few moments.

"It's not simple. It never was. What we want and what's best isn't always the same thing."

"Ollie—"

"Too soon," he growled. "It's too soon."

"For what?"

"For everything I want."

"Allie—"

"Isn't ready. Not for this. Not for me. She's in shock. She doesn't need... *me*. Not the me I want to be. She needs her friends."

"You are her friend."

A defeated look flickered in his eyes, but he quickly looked away and started cleaning glasses again. "I'm not a friend she needs right now."

Because he'd never wanted to just be her friend. He'd always wanted more. Ollie had hung on for years, never settling down with anyone else, his heart already owned by the girl he'd never have.

"How do you stand it?"

He glanced up. "What?"

"Waiting. Not having what you want so much."

The bear's eyes flickered over to where Alex was sitting. "Why don't you ask your date? He knows as well as I do. Maybe better."

"We were nothing like—"

"You ever wonder, Ted—" Ollie interrupted her with his quiet voice. "—which guy has it harder? The guy who knows he'll become an alcoholic given a chance, so he never takes a drink? Or the guy who tastes it—fills himself up to the top and still can't get enough—then leaves it behind, knowing it's the only real choice he has?"

She swallowed the lump in her throat. "You comparing me to whiskey, Ollie?"

"No comparison, sweetheart. The right woman's more addicting than whiskey." The corner of his mouth tipped up. "And tastes a hell of a lot better too."

The next day, Ted sat in her office, spinning idly on her stool, remembering the rest of her date with Alex while she waited for the medical examiner to call her from San Bernardino.

They'd eaten their dinner. Joked around. He'd driven her home and given her another bone-melting kiss at her front door. Then he'd left and she'd all but collapsed from exhaustion. Work, the fight out at Old Quinn's, shifting. And running through the day was the delicate sparring with Alex as her heart balanced on the edge of pushing him away and falling for him all over again.

If it had been a date with any other man, she'd be ecstatic. She'd be on the phone with Jena, crowing about the hot, funny guy who'd taken her to dinner, kissed her like it was his mission in life, and starred in some very vivid dreams.

But like Ollie had said the night before, it wasn't simple. For her and Alex, it never had been.

Oh, they'd fooled themselves for years when they were living in LA. When home and family responsibilities had seemed so far away. But they weren't playing house anymore, and the phone call she'd forced herself to make to her mother that morning only drove the point home.

Lena Vasquez hadn't thrown a fit like Alex had predicted. It had been worse. She'd been completely silent as Ted related the story of how the blood marker had been drawn and Old Quinn's acknowledgement that Ted had been "provoked."

Lena hadn't said a word.

"We'll speak of this later. We both need to get to work."

Her mother was the principal of Cambio Springs Elementary School and ruled the children of the town with the same loving—and very firm—hand that had raised Ted. Her father had been the jovial softie of the family until he'd been taken by a heart attack when Ted was only a freshman in college.

Like most of the female cats, Lena had married a man who catered to and cared for her. A strong man who always put his wife and daughter first. The fact that her daughter had formed a relationship with a shifter who had a host of responsibilities other than Ted was something Lena had never liked.

The phone rang, startling her out of her slow spin. She grabbed for the phone.

"Hello?"

"Ted?"

She smiled at the friendly voice of Larry Carlisle, her favorite of the three forensic pathologists who worked in the San Bernardino County Sheriff-Coroner's office. Larry was an amiable guy, despite the death and destruction he regularly saw. He was old enough to be her father but had always treated her like a colleague.

"Hey, Larry," she said, nerves twisting her gut. Larry might have been friendly, but he had sharp eyes and a perceptive mind. If there was anything unusual about Marcus's body—anything unique to his shifting nature—Larry would have caught it. "You have the results back on Marcus Quinn?"

Far from the near-instant results shown on television shows, autopsies and toxicology screens took days, more often weeks, to get results. If the coroner's office and lab was backed up, it could take far longer.

"Autopsy's done, and it's what we both expected. Gunshot wound killed him. No question of that. Pretty massive internal bleeding. I can send you a copy of the report if you'd like."

"That'd be great, thanks." Larry didn't question her interest in the case. He knew Cambio Springs was a small town and she'd known the victim. "Anything... unusual?"

"Nothing unexpected. Except... well, there was one thing, but it doesn't appear to have anything to do with cause of death. It's just kind of weird."

She sat up straight. "What was it?"

"He'd had a recent break in his arm, not unusual for someone in a physical job like he had. The bone was healed, but it was the tissue damage that was odd."

"How?"

"If I looked at the tissue, I'd say the bone broke maybe a week before death. The bruising. The muscle tissue. But the fracture was *healed*. He must have been in a cast for weeks, but there was no loss of muscle. It's... odd."

"Yeah, weird." There was no use denying it. She tried to distract him instead. "Tox?"

"We've got preliminary, but not final. Did the victim have any history of drug use that you know of? Current prescriptions?"

"His wife said he was healthy as a horse, and she hasn't held back anything that we're aware of."

"There were a few things that seemed off in his initial screen, so I'm requesting some additional tests."

"Care to share?"

"Nothing solid right now, but I'll let you know. May be nothing."

"Let me know. As far as I know, he wasn't taking anything."

"He was a big guy."

"Yeah."

Was Larry implying that Marcus had been given something to make him vulnerable? It was something to think about. If he'd been drugged, that changed the whole scenario of someone sneaking up on him or him turning his back on someone he trusted. Then again, drugs worked very differently on shifter metabolisms.

She started spinning again. "Anything else?"

"For tox? The final report isn't finished. They'll have it by the end of the week. But they sent over a preliminary when Chief Gilbert prodded them, so I thought I'd pass along the results."

"You call him already?"

"E-mail."

She nodded, though she was alone in the room. "I'll talk to him later today."

"Let him know I'm available if he has any questions you can't field."

"Appreciate it."

"You got it." He hesitated. "Things are getting more interesting up in your neck of the woods. There was that animal attack last year. Now this..."

"Yeah." She started shuffling papers and making noise, trying to sound busier than she actually was. "Hey, Larry, I've got to go. Thanks again for the info."

"Anytime. And Ted?"

"Yeah?"

"Hope things calm down."

"Me too, Larry. Thanks."

Chapter Ten

Alex walked Chris Avery through the jobsite, introducing him to the foreman he didn't know, going over the updated plans that Marcus had drawn. Chris nodded along but kept quiet for the most part. They started at the bottom of the hill and walked up, slowly going over each grade and contour of what would make up the Cambio Springs Spa and Resort.

Walking the land, he could see it begin to form in his mind. The subtle dip of the earth enhanced just enough to provide a sense of isolation so the resort guests would focus on the sweeping walls of the canyon and the vivid blue sky. The sound of trickling water would fill the air, carried on the dry wind. The water carefully recycled and used to water the palms and succulents that would create an isolated oasis.

It was what the town had always been to him. His oasis and his home. His love for Cambio Springs wasn't only born of familiarity. As much as he enjoyed the ocean and the morning mist that drifted from the Pacific, he needed the dry wind and sucking heat of the desert. He felt lazy in the water-laden air near the coast. In the Springs, he was strong and lean. His wolf stretched and pawed, content that nothing would confine him. The sky was big enough for his eyes. The landscape vast enough for his energy.

"So…" Chris Avery interrupted his thoughts when they reached the trailer that served as the main office. "You really think people are gonna come all the way out here for vacation?"

"No." Alex smiled at the man's surprise. "They're going to sneak out here for a very exclusive break from life. They're going to rest. Maybe work. Breathe clean air and soak in the water. This place will never be Vegas."

The human looked around with poorly concealed disdain. "You can say that again."

"I'd never want it to be like that circus." Alex ignored the disparagement. It was fine by him if the man finished the job and never set foot in the Springs again. In fact, he'd prefer it. "Our clientele are going to want exclusive. Quiet. Privacy. That's the market we're aiming for."

"And you think you can attract that kind of attention?"

"Yep." Alex sat down and stretched out his legs, grabbing a bottle of water from the small ice chest by his desk and passing it to Chris before he opened another for himself. "I already have."

The other man didn't hide his skepticism. "Oh yeah?"

He waited for Alex to explain, but the wolf just grinned. Marcus's brother-in-law didn't need to know that Ollie had been quietly passing the word around to the many musicians he knew. Some of the biggest acts in rock and roll had once cut their teeth at the Cave, going out of their way to hang on the wall with the greats who had played before. And if Ollie put the word out that there was a place near the Cave that catered to those looking for quiet and privacy, the word would get around. A few of his associates had even asked if there would be recording facilities on the premises.

Alex was considering it, but Chris didn't need to know any of that. He just needed to finish the surveying and land-moving work that Marcus had started, then get the hell out of Alex's town.

"Well, good luck," Chris said when it was obvious no other answer would be forthcoming. "As long as the bills get paid, Crescent Construction is happy to work."

"Appreciated. Your guys are good."

"Yeah, they should be," Chris said quietly, glancing out the window at the group of guys walking past. "We don't hire guys who don't know their stuff. Or who can't speak the language, if you know what I mean."

Alex bristled at the comment, noting that the guys who'd just passed the window were joking loudly in the mix of English and Spanish so common in the California desert.

"No, I don't know what you mean, Avery."

Chris shrugged. "I'm just saying I see a lot of local guys working around here. That's good. Good that you're more interested in quality work than just getting cheap labor."

"And what does quality work have to do with speaking the 'right language?'"

The man blinked, as if just realizing his words could cause offense. Then he smiled an "aw, shucks" grin and said, "Hey, no big thing, man. I saw your girlfriend the other day. Sweet."

"I wouldn't call her that to her face."

The other man smiled and nodded. "I get it."

Alex crossed his arms. "You get what, exactly?"

Chris's friendly demeanor changed, and he sat up straighter. "No need to make a big deal about it, McCann."

"It's gonna be a big deal if you can't work with my crew. See, we have all kinds of 'quality' workers in the Springs, and they speak all kinds of languages. And not all of them use the boys' bathroom, either. You gonna have a problem with that?"

"Nah." His eyes narrowed. "I hear what you're saying."

"Good."

"After all, the customer is always right."

Alex could tell by the squint of Avery's eyes that he'd just made an enemy. Then again, mosquitos were annoying, too, but they didn't keep him from getting the job done.

"Glad to hear I'm always right. You need anything else before you get to work?"

"I got your number," Avery said. "I'll let you know after I meet with Sid."

"I'll let you get to that, then."

The man took the unspoken invitation and stood to leave. "Later."

Much later if Alex had anything to say about it.

He had no patience for idiotic prejudice. Racism was only one of the things the founders of the Springs had been trying to flee. White, black, Mexican, Cherokee. They'd all traveled in the same caravan, looking for a place where hard work and character meant more than the color of their skin. Cambio Springs may have had rivalries between animal clans, but racism was seen by pretty much everyone as plain stupid. What the hell did it matter what color your skin was if you had the same fur under the full moon?

As Alex watched Marcus's brother-in-law walk to his truck where his foreman was waiting, he had to wonder. If Chris Avery was a racist, what else could he be prejudiced about? And how would he react if he knew just how different their little town was?

He'd called Ted to see if she wanted to meet for lunch, but she'd been swamped with a sudden rash of strep throat among the town's third grade population. Who knew passing suckers around at recess would have that result? Apparently, not the many eight-year-olds with fevers. Luckily, she hadn't said no to Alex dropping off a sandwich. He decided to kill two birds with one stone while he was at the diner since he needed to talk to Jena about the restaurant at the resort.

Jena was poking and prodding at the plans he'd spread out in the booth, a small frown creasing her forehead.

"This is the main building?"

"Yep." He pointed to the top of the hill. "It'll have the reception area, the restaurant, a small cafe—"

"You might want to think about a juice bar instead," Jena interrupted. "I don't know how many people are going to want caffeine, you know?"

"Juice and tea? Stuff like that?"

"It's a spa, right? Juice. Tea. Healthy stuff that people can grab when they're done soaking. Or stuff to take down to the water."

"Good idea."

She arched her back and her belly rubbed against the edge of the table. "That's my job."

"How you feeling?"

"Good, mostly." She frowned again, still looking at the plans. "So where's the restaurant?"

"Here. One side will have a fitness center and the cafe—or juice bar, I guess." He penciled in notes as he talked. "The other will have the restaurant and bar."

Jena grinned. "Can't be too healthy, can we?"

"Wine's healthy. Mostly."

He went over the rest of the plans quickly, making notes at her suggestions and coaxing her cooperation about room service when she balked at the many bungalows that would dot the property. When he offered to give her delivery guy his own custom golf cart, she relented.

"Talk to me about Ted," Jena said when he was rolling up the plans.

"What about Ted?" He shuffled the papers around and tried to dodge the question.

"Oh, come on… you're picking up her lunch. You're taking her to dinner at the Cave." Jena raised a suspicious eyebrow. "So what's what?"

"I don't know."

"Come on."

"I don't." He smiled ruefully. "Wish I did. We're trying out more than friends. I think. She's…"

"What?"

"She's Ted, you know? She's tough."

Jena said, "She has to be. And be honest. You'd have lost interest years ago if she wasn't a challenge."

"You think that's why she's making me jump through hoops? She's afraid I'll get bored?"

"How many girls threw themselves at you on a regular basis the last ten years or so?"

"I refuse to answer that without counsel."

Jena cracked a smile. "She always saw that, you know. All the girls. Even when you were together."

Alex frowned. "You're saying Ted wondered about me and other women?"

"Not while you were together. We all know you're loyal as hell. I think…"

"What?"

"Maybe she's worried you want someone who caters to you. She's not that woman, Alex. She never will be."

He sat back, almost offended, even though he knew Jena meant well. "What am I? Five years old?"

"What kind of women did you date the last few years?"

"Not as many as she thinks."

She rolled her eyes. "What kind?"

The kind he could call when it was convenient for him. The kind that would drop everything and come running if he needed a date for a business function. The kind who…

"Shit," he said.

Jena rested her chin in her hand. "You're a busy guy. But if you think the word about your girlfriends didn't trickle back to town, you don't know the gossip network."

As if he needed another strike against him. He was already battling Ted's belief that he was going to take off when the resort was done. And their massive communication problem. Family disapproval. And now he realized he may have inadvertently sent the message that he was looking for what could only be referred to as "arm candy."

"That's not… I mean, those girls were never serious. They weren't…"

"Hey." Jena's voice was quieter. "When you think ten years from now, how do you see your life?"

"Me and her." His voice was rough. "It's always been me and her."

"Then you just have to make her see that."

He frowned and looked away. Out to the window where a dust devil swirled in the parking lot.

"What is it?" Jena asked.

"I don't think I know how."

Jena winced. "Hurt to admit that?"

"Don't rub it in."

She smiled. "Normally, I'd tell you to be upfront and honest, but you've done that and it hasn't cracked her. So in this case, I'm going to advise you to *not* be the Alex she thinks she knows."

"Oh?" The corner of his mouth turned up in amusement. "And which Alex should I be?"

She leaned closer. "Charm her. You can sell anything to anyone, Alex. Sell her on *you*. Tempt her. Romance her. Reign in your alpha wolf-ness and take a little time with her. She works so much we can barely get her out of her scrubs these days."

Charm Ted? The idea had merit. But...

"She'll be pissed if she thinks I'm playing her."

"You're not playing her. You're charming her," Jena said with a smile. "And besides, you like it when she's pissed off."

He stewed all the way over to Ted's office, parking next to her Jeep and noticing the lack of cars in the lot. Apparently, the strep rush was over. At least until all the brothers and sisters got sick. He walked into an empty waiting room with the door to Ted's office hanging open. He set the sandwich down on the receptionist's desk and walked in.

She was sleeping on her couch, sitting up, her head thrown to the side as dust danced in the sunlight streaming through the window. Bonnie Raitt's "You" was playing softly from the speaker on her desk, and her breathing was slow and easy.

Ted was nocturnal, and it wasn't just her cat. She'd always been more productive at night, speeding through studying or writing at lightning speed. She caught up on sleep in the afternoons. Then she was raring to go when she woke. He couldn't count the times he'd come home from work when they'd lived together to find her just waking up. Afternoons with Ted were meant to be spent rolling in bed. His blood rushed south at the memory.

Romance her, huh? Tempt her? Well, that couldn't be much of a hardship.

Being patient? That might be a bit harder.

He lowered himself to her side, then leaned over and brushed his lips over hers. Her mouth was slightly parted as her eyes fluttered open.

"Ted," he whispered.

"Hey." Her smile was slight and sleepy.

He kissed her again, just a brush across her lips, but her mouth moved against his in a lazy caress. Her tongue peeked out and caught the edge of his lip. He moved closer, cupping her face in his hands as her arms came around his waist.

"Hey, yourself," he said as he lowered his mouth to hers. It was soft and slow. Lazy like the afternoon sun and the song on the radio. Her mouth tasted like mint and coffee as he parted her lips with his tongue. She opened to him, stealing his breath when the hands at his back slid up and curled around his neck. She pulled him closer, her tongue meeting his before it drew back and she nipped at his lip.

Alex shifted, easing her onto his lap to straddle him as his hands slid from her face, fingertips trailing down, flirting with the sides of her breasts before he curled them back and pressed on the small of her back, pulling her closer. She arched back at the pressure. He took advantage and trailed his lips down her neck to lick along her collar, biting at the graceful bone that lay under her burnished skin.

"Sexy," he muttered, biting the other side, sucking at the hollow at the base of her throat. "This right here? So damn sexy."

"It's just… a clavicle," she said, her hands gripping his hair.

"It's a sexy clavicle."

"Alex—"

"Do you know—" He couldn't keep his lips away from her mouth. Her sexy, smart-assed, swollen lips that could curl in a smile or a sneer. He didn't care which it was as long as it was directed at him. He drank from her lips and rocked against her. "Do you know how much I missed you? Missed this?"

Her grip grew tighter. "No."

"I did."

"Spent the last few years pining, huh?"

He could hear the bite of sarcasm in her voice. How did he romance the woman who resisted romance? Who analyzed every detail? Luckily, pretty much everything about her turned him on. He ignored her tone and continued trailing soft kisses along her jawline as her hands tangled in his hair.

"I love it that you call me on everything."

"I annoy you because I don't buy your bull."

The rebuke might have been more effective if she hadn't panted it out.

He grinned into her neck and kept talking. "I like it. I like that you call me on my shit. Don't ever stop."

Her voice was rough. "Alex—"

"I like that you interrupt me calling you sexy to tell me the scientific name of what I'm kissing." He nipped her throat. "It's hot."

"Most people find it annoying."

"It's annoying too."

Her mouth dropped open in protest, but he kissed her, teasing her taste into his mouth before she could speak. Then he grabbed her hips and flipped them over so she lay under him on the large couch, big enough that she'd be able to sleep on it in lion form. He kissed her breathless as her leg curled around the back of his thighs. He rocked into her, imagining he could hear her purr.

"You annoy me," he said. "I annoy you. It's only fair."

Her cheeks were flushed, her mouth swollen. "The door. It's open. We should—"

"You challenge me." Another kiss. "Keep me sharp." More kisses along her neck. "Do you understand?"

"Understand what?"

He met her eyes, letting the smile grow over his face. She was under him. Kissed to distraction with lips red from his attention. Charming Ted was going to be more fun than he'd anticipated. He could scent her arousal filling the warm air, but he didn't push for more.

Patience, McCann.

His lips lowered to hers again as he teased another kiss from her. Then he said against her mouth, "We're perfect for each other."

That left her silent. Perfect was never anything anyone would have labeled them. Ever.

Not their families. Not even their friends.

"We're not perfect," she said.

"Says who?"

"Says everyone. You and I—"

"I know you," he whispered. "I *know* you. And you and I?" He bent his head and brushed another whisper-soft kiss across her mouth. "We're perfect."

"You're delusional." But she wrapped her leg around him more tightly, her body pulling him close.

"I'm not delusional," he said. "I just have vision."

Her mouth turned up at the corner. "So you admit you're hallucinating?"

"I'm not hallucinating this." His hips rocked against hers, and this time he didn't imagine it. She definitely purred.

And then she cursed because the knock at the clinic door was loud, and when the chief of police yelled out, "Hey, Ted!" it wasn't something either of them could ignore.

Chapter Eleven

Caleb shifted his weight from right to left as Ted looked through the final toxicology report the chief had added to Marcus Quinn's file. They both pointedly ignored the restless wolf shifter in Ted's office. She was half-grateful, half-annoyed that they'd been interrupted. When she said slow, she'd meant it, but Alex had a way of making her question what exactly "slow" entailed.

"The pathologist said he was ordering more tests when I talked to him the other day." Ted closed the file and handed it back to Caleb. "I'm grateful he didn't make any mention of the abnormal bone healing in the overall report. The tox is surprising."

"Marcus was *roofied*?" Caleb asked.

"Larry mentioned seeing something off in the initial tox. Maybe he just got a hunch. He's like that. Must have ordered them to test for it. You have to test for benzodiazepines specifically."

"It's a date rape drug, Ted."

"It's also very easy to give to someone you don't want to rape, but do want to incapacitate. Marcus's reflexes would have been slowed and his ability to shift hampered. I'm guessing he wouldn't have gone out cold, but he'd be easy to manage."

"Past experience?"

"Not Rohypnol specifically, thank God, but the Springs is like anywhere else. Teenagers are stupid and experiment. In my experience, shifters using narcotics either lose control of a shift and can't shift back, or more often, they can't shift in the first place."

"How much would it take?"

She shrugged. "I honestly don't know. I could ask Larry if you want. It would depend on size and weight. Marcus was a big guy. On the other hand, most of us rarely take any drugs, even painkillers, so we tend to be lightweights. When I prescribe something, I use the dosage for normal humans and just ask people to be very careful monitoring their use."

Caleb kept studying the paper, even though Ted sensed he wasn't actually reading.

"Easily available," he muttered.

"And easily masked. Still, it's hard to imagine someone slipping him something. He'd have trusted whoever gave it to him."

"Yes," Caleb said. "Add that bit to the fact that he was shot in the back, and the idea of a crime of passion or opportunity is starting to look unlikely."

"It was premeditated."

"Most likely. Nothing about this reads as a crime of passion. We still need to find out if he had any history of drug use. I'll ask around with his buddies. Hit Josie up again. Though she was pretty certain, and she seems sharp."

"And that would be your area, Chief—" She patted his shoulder. "—not mine."

"Yep." A shuffling from the other room caused Caleb's eyes to narrow. "Are you talking to McCann about this?" he asked quietly.

"Why would you think that?"

"'Cause it took you more than a couple minutes to answer the door just now. I know the wolf's here. And something tells me you weren't playing Scrabble."

"Shows how much you know," Alex said from the doorway. "Ted and I are known for our Scrabble games. They're epic."

Apparently making out put Alex in a teasing mood, so she decided to play along. "It's true. We used to sell tickets in college."

Caleb sighed and rubbed his forehead. "You know, I think I liked it better when you two were at each other's throats."

"Who says we aren't now?" The wolf's smirk gave away more than Ted liked. She lifted her hand to her neck in an unconscious gesture, remembering Alex's lips there and his tendency to mark his territory when he was younger.

Caleb noticed.

"Great." He looked at Ted. "Wonderful. Confidentiality, remember? He is not privy to the details of this case."

"Independent consultant, remember?" she answered. "You're not the boss of me."

"Fine." He tucked the file under his arm and turned to go. "I'm out of here. Stay out of trouble, Ted. I don't want to explain to my cranky pregnant wife why her best friend is in jail."

She gave Caleb a few minutes to leave before she spoke to Alex. "You had to imply we were necking?"

"I think he guessed that himself. Fairly sure there's a hickey on your neck."

"You little shit." She pushed past him into the hallway that led to the bathroom. Looking in the mirror, she saw a little redness from Alex's stubble, but no hickey. "Ass," she muttered under her breath.

He slid in behind her and put his arms around her waist. "You like my ass and the freckles on it."

"Alex—"

"Stop fighting this, Ted. Just think about how much fun it'll be tormenting me with all the added ammunition you'll have being my girlfriend again."

She fought the rush of her blood urging her to give in. He was tempting enough as it was, but when he let out his playful side, she caved. She always had. And it would be so easy...

Ted tried to play off how much his attention was affecting her. "Is that supposed to convince me of something?"

"That you can't live without me? That I complete you? That I'm the wind beneath your—"

She slapped a hand over his mouth. "Please stop before the clichés go any further."

He nipped at her fingers until she took her hand away. "Are you sure? I was just about to start on the cat ones."

"Like curiosity?"

"Mmmm." He leaned down and his tongue flicked her earlobe. "I like curious cats."

She cocked her head as an idea struck her. Alex took that opportunity to let his lips wander over the stubble burn he'd left on her neck.

"I like cuddly cats, too," he murmured as his hand trailed from her waist down her hip, slowly sliding toward the part of her that was not arguing with Alex's attempts at seduction. "And if we're talking about cats, I especially like—"

She slapped another hand over his mouth before he made all logic flee. "How about cats who want to take you to Vegas?"

"Mmnph?" He was frowning when he pulled his mouth from behind her palm. "A boy has dreams, you know. I don't want Fat Elvis performing the ceremony, and you didn't even ask with a ring."

"Not that, you idiot." She was trying not to laugh, but it was hard.

"You mean there are other reasons to go to Vegas? Do you have a secret desire to be a showgirl? Because I'm okay with that, but I prefer a private performance."

She slowly turned and pushed him away. "One. Track. Mind. Do you remember what Old Quinn said the other day?"

"About Marcus and the mob?"

"Yep. I've been thinking about that. Old Quinn may have written them off, but things like that have a way of coming back to haunt people. I'm not so sure Marcus's killer wasn't someone holding a grudge. I wouldn't put it past someone in the mob to lie low until Marcus wasn't expecting retaliation. Do you think we can look at the public records and see if any names appear on his business license application? Maybe loan stuff?"

Alex thought for a moment. "I have an assistant in LA who is the public records queen. She lives to dig up details on my competitors. Jolene is good and very discreet."

"Jolene, huh?"

He grinned. "She's old enough to be my mom, but her sources are golden. She knows everyone, and most everyone loves her or owes her a favor. If there's a record of any name other than Marcus's in his business history, she could find it."

"Can you ask her?"

"I'll call her this afternoon. And once we find it?"

She shrugged. "Vegas?"

Alex grinned. "Vegas, baby."

"So you're going to Sin City with the man you may or may not still be in love with—"

"Who said love? I didn't say that," Ted said.

Allie waved a dismissive hand. "And you're trying to be… what? Dating? You guys have already lived together. Do you need to date a person when you've already…" Allie scrunched up her face in confusion. "This is complicated. I'm going to have to learn all this stuff again, aren't I?"

"What, dating?"

"Yes."

"Unless you plan on taking Joe back, yeah."

Allie shuddered. "Never going to happen."

"Have you even heard from him?"

"Nope. It's like he dropped off the face of the earth."

Ted grimaced. Allie was well and done with Joe, but their father's absence would be hard on her kids.

The fabled Jolene had found a name within hours, and Alex had called Ted and confirmed Vegas was the right direction, so their weekend was a go. They decided to leave on Thursday to beat the abysmal Friday traffic.

Ted had asked Allie over because her friend had borrowed the suitcase she wanted to take for the weekend. Plus she just felt the need to check in on her.

Jena was naturally distracted the longer she went in her pregnancy. Cambio Springs was approaching the full moon. The urge to shift would be all but irresistible for any shifters other than pregnant women, who could miscarry if they shifted. Not being able to shift made expecting moms more than a little cranky at the best of times. During a full moon, they were practically unbearable.

The moon brought a shifter's animal nature to the front of their mind. Tempers were more easily riled. Instincts were harder to suppress. Ted had the urge to ask Allie if she'd seen any lone bears sniffing around her house, but she resisted. Ollie would kill her if he thought she'd brought it up. She didn't know what the man was thinking, and she didn't have the energy to figure out anyone's love life but her own.

It was then that Ted realized she'd be with Alex McCann in Las Vegas during the first night of the full moon.

Because she was an idiot.

"I don't know what Alex and I are doing." She scowled at her suitcase, annoyed with the oversight. "Other than making out occasionally."

Allie sighed. "I miss kissing."

"And we're going to Vegas because we're looking into something about Marcus. He lived there for years. If someone wanted to kill him, the motive is more likely going to be in Vegas than here."

That was the whole reason. It wasn't because she wanted to see what it was like to be with him away from their families and responsibilities. To see if it could be as good as she remembered to just *be* with him.

Allie looked nervous. "But why don't you let Caleb investigate? That is his job. And he can work with the police there, right?"

"Yes, he can. And he will. But Caleb won't let Alex get involved. And like it or not, Alex McCann is the future leader of this town."

After talking it over with her mother that morning, she realized it was the one thing they agreed on regarding the McCanns. They were good leaders. The cats were loners. They didn't want the responsibility that lay in town leadership. They wanted the stability and respect that came with being the second-largest clan, but they didn't have the interest to lead more than themselves. If they occasionally antagonized the wolves, that was just an entertaining side benefit. Both her mother and Ted agreed that having the wolves wield a steady hand over the various canines, birds, reptiles, and bears was a good long-term strategy. And if the McCanns wanted to pretend they had authority over the cats… well, they could think what they liked as long as they didn't interfere.

"People in Cambio Springs need to see Alex taking part in solving this murder. Especially the Quinns. It's better for everyone if they can see him doing something. It promotes stability. Caleb is a smart guy, but he's new. He doesn't get that."

"Yeah, that makes sense."

"Plus, Alex's instincts are gold."

"They are. He told me years ago that Joe and I were a bad idea."

"He did?"

Allie nodded, but Ted decided not to pursue it.

She continued, "I also know that Alex has friends in Las Vegas. Friends who might be considered… somewhat shady."

Allie's blue eyes widened. "Really?"

Ted shrugged. "Despite being the golden boy of the Springs, Alex knows how to get his hands dirty when he needs to."

"But will you get to roll around in the mud with him?" Allie grinned. "That's the real question."

"Troublemaker."

When Alex picked her up in his truck on Thursday afternoon, he was annoyed. She could see it in the set of his shoulders.

"Something wrong?"

He frowned and shrugged, closing the door behind her as he tossed her bag in the back of the crew cab. Ted rolled her eyes. Hours in the car with Alex in a bad mood was going to be barrels of fun.

Ten minutes of loaded silence was all she was willing to take.

"Tell me what's got you pissed off or turn the truck around and take me home. I'm not putting up with this shit."

Anger flared in his eyes. "Seriously, Ted, leave it. I'll be fine with a little quiet."

"You're full of it, brooder."

He tore off his glasses and looked at her. "What?"

"Brooder. You brood, Alex. Like a little kid, sometimes."

"I do not." He put his glasses back on, but his mouth settled into a pout. Ted tried not to laugh at the petulant expression.

"Caleb?" she guessed.

"Whatever."

Not Caleb.

"Marcus's brother-in-law?"

"An asshole, but at least he's an efficient one."

She paused. "Your dad."

The clench of his jaw told her she'd hit the bull's-eye. Alex said nothing, but his knuckles were white.

"You can tell me what he said, you know. He's probably as thrilled about us as my mother is."

"Oh?" His voice came out in a low growl. "And what does your mother say?"

"Probably the same thing your dad says. We're too old for childish rebellion. Our relationship will never work. I need to find someone more appropriate for my future role in life."

She wasn't prepared for the sudden swerve off the road and the slam of the brakes. Alex put the truck in park and reached over, grabbing her over the center console and bringing her lips to his, branding her with a ferocious kiss that threatened to make her head swim. Color flashed behind her eyes. She could feel her cat clawing her skin. She wanted to run. Wanted to give in to the animal who recognized her mate. Scent. Touch. Everything was too close to the surface. She could taste the bite of blood at the corner of her mouth where he'd nipped her. Alex sucked her lower lip into his mouth, tempting then soothing with a stroke of his tongue before he nipped her again.

She pushed him away. "Stop."

"Why?" He barely sounded human. "Do I not fit your 'future role in life,' whatever that means?"

"You know what she means, just like I know your father has told you the same thing. I know he doesn't want you mated to a cat."

"I don't give a shit what he wants. I'm not him. And his choices don't affect mine."

"You trying to convince me or yourself, Alex?"

He said nothing. Just stared at her for a minute before he put the car in drive again and started back toward the highway. But she could feel the roiling temper and the tantalizing sensual energy that filled the air. If she could come from scent alone, she would have. He was that tempting.

And they were still two nights away from the full moon. Yay.

"You really want to start the weekend like this?" She finally managed to steady her voice. "We have work to do. We're not here to—"

"What? Give in to this heat? Like we should have months ago?"

"Scratch the itch so we could concentrate on more important things? That's not why I suggested going to Las Vegas."

"I know it's not. Acting like this isn't important is just going to piss me off. Can you ignore it?"

She took a deep breath and tried to overlook the burning need in her body. "Let's just get there. Did you look up the name your assistant gave you?"

"Didn't need to."

Good to know his natural arrogance hadn't taken a serious hit. Maybe it was fed by his libido.

"So who is it?"

"The name's Frank Di Stefano. And you know him."

"I do?"

"We went to a party at a house he rented in Malibu. He wanted to throw his son a big party for his twenty-fifth birthday."

"Wait… Cam? Your friend Cameron's party?"

"Yep." Alex's jaw was tight, and this time it wasn't from his own father, but his friend's. "Cam's dad is the one who helped finance Marcus Quinn's business."

Ted fell silent. Because Cameron Di Stefano's dad didn't just help Marcus start his business. He'd had a hand in Alex's as well.

Chapter Twelve

Stupid, stupid, stupid. He had Ted to himself for a whole weekend, and he'd started out pissing her off because his father had annoyed him.

What happened to romance? He had to get his head on straight. The fact that they'd be together in the days leading up to the full moon would be challenging enough for their different animals.

"You're being selfish, Alex. She's not the right mate for you, and you know it. She'll never be the woman our clan needs. She's a cat. A dominant one. Do you want to be fighting for dominance in your own relationship?"

The problem was he and his dad saw things from entirely different angles. Alex's mom was fantastic, and she'd relished her maternal role. She'd been a great partner for his father.

But Alex wasn't his father.

He didn't want someone who always looked to him for leadership. He had enough of that with all the wolves in his pack. When he was at home, he wanted someone who challenged him. Who questioned him in a way his mother would never question his father. He wasn't being charming when he told Ted she kept him sharp.

He would be a better alpha with her influence. He just needed to make his father see that. He could rebel, but it would affect the pack. Affect the whole town. A power struggle between the alpha and his heir wasn't what the Springs needed with all the other changes taking place.

"Alex." Her voice was unexpectedly tentative. "Are you worried because Cam's dad—"

"It's not that, Ted." He reached across and took her hand, grateful that she closed her fingers around his palm. "I always knew Cam's family was a bit shady—"

"A bit?"

He grinned. How did Ted being a smartass always pull him out of a bad mood?

"We never had a full partnership; it's not something I'm worried about. It was only two houses we financed together, and it was years ago. We went our separate ways, but we're still friendly."

"Does he still live in LA?"

"Cam? No. In fact, we're staying in his hotel once we get into the city."

"We are?" Her eyes narrowed. "I knew I should have been in charge of the hotel reservations."

She probably should have been, if she wanted to keep her distance. As it was, he'd reserved a very nice suite at Cam's boutique hotel on the Strip. All the location with none of the noise. Alex hated the sound of slot machines. He'd already called Cam's secretary, hoping to set up a dinner. Plus he'd have Ted in the same suite for the whole weekend. To say he planned to turn up his charm offensive was an understatement.

Ted turned up the radio and leaned back to take a quick nap, and Alex smiled. She hadn't pulled her hand from his.

They pulled into the hotel a few hours later. Alex felt conspicuous driving his dusty pickup truck under the sleek striped awning, but he'd left his Lexus in LA. He had no need for it in the Springs and nowhere to park it at the moment.

"Ted." He squeezed the hand that still rested in his palm.

"Mmm?"

"We're here."

She blinked awake and immediately went to pick up her purse before she looked around.

"Oh. Wow. This is… nicer than I expected."

"There's got to be a few advantages to running myself ragged with work."

"Right." She sniffed and rubbed her eyes. "Right. Well, I hope I brought the right clothes."

He got out of the truck and walked around, taking perverse pleasure in tossing the keys to the valet, who eyed the truck with unconcealed disdain. Alex opened Ted's door before the bellhop could reach it and leaned toward her, his voice whispering low in her ear.

"Their job is to please you, not the other way round. Never forget that."

It was Thursday, but the chic hotel was still buzzing with energy. Bellhops took their bags and gestured toward the front desk, but Alex walked immediately toward the concierge desk, keeping Ted's hand in his so she wouldn't bolt. He smiled in relief when he saw the familiar face.

"Romano?"

The impeccably dressed man turned from speaking with a young member of the staff. He was only in his late twenties but carried himself with a confident calm that Alex hoped to see in his own hotel manager when he got to that point. Romano was a cousin of some kind. Italian by way of Milan, as opposed to Cam, who was Italian by way of Brooklyn.

"Mr. McCann!" Romano said. "What a pleasure to see you again. Does Cam know you're in town?"

"Not sure. I called Stephanie on my way here. It was a last-minute trip. Good to be back, Romano."

"You are most welcome."

The hotel was one of his favorites, despite the ridiculously young crowd that flocked to the luxurious lounge and European-style pool. It held none of the faux arrogance of the larger resorts. The walls were covered in rich art and old mirrors. Bronze nudes stood in discreet niches, demure in a way the average guest would never be. Cam had done a hell of a job with his first solo venture, and according to rumor, the hotel turned a good profit, even as new as it was. Alex couldn't wait to pick his old friend's brain about work.

He glanced at Ted. She looked silently around at the lobby of the hotel, taking it all in with a jaded eye, unimpressed with the glittering birds who checked in at the front desk. Smiling a private smile that told him a million witty remarks were circling until they were alone. He put an arm around her waist, eager to get to their room. Alex wanted to spoil her, and he hoped she'd let him, if only for the weekend.

Romano turned his charm toward the woman at his side. "And you've brought such a beautiful friend to visit. Welcome to Las Vegas."

"Thank you," Ted said with a smile.

"Romano, this is Dr. Teodora Vasquez, a good friend of mine."

"If you need anything at all, please let me know." He handed Ted a simple card that Alex knew would have his personal line on it. "You asked for the family suite when you booked? Or the master?"

"The family suite was free. Stephanie said she'd arrange it."

"Excellent." A few taps on his tablet computer must have brought up the information. "Everything is in order." He pulled a thin wallet from a drawer at the top of his desk that Alex knew would hold two key cards to the most private suite not reserved for the hotel owner. "If you'll follow me, Dr. Vasquez, Mr. McCann?"

Romano led them through the lobby, where all eyes were on the dusty couple who warranted the attention of the manager.

"Seriously, man, we've eaten dinner together at Cam's. When are you going to call me Alex?"

"When I'm not at work, Mr. McCann."

Alex shook his head and smiled. "Is Cam on the property?"

"I believe so, but he was in meetings most of this afternoon, so he's probably catching up. I'll make sure to let him know you've checked in." He ushered them to the door and handed over the key. "I'll have your bags brought immediately. The fridge is stocked with the usual, but would you like anything else to eat or drink?"

He could see Ted repressing her eye roll. "I think we'll manage. Thanks."

"Of course. Please make yourself at home."

Alex was already waving the key in front of the lock as Romano walked away.

Ted said, "Please tell me the family suite has more than one room."

"Of course!" He held open the door as she walked through. "It has three. Of course, there's only one bedroom."

"I knew it."

Alex could tell she wasn't really mad. He grabbed her around the waist and nipped at her neck before she could go exploring. "Seeing as you already make a habit of sneaking into my bed, I didn't figure you'd mind."

"Charming..." she murmured, but he didn't know if she was talking about him or the room.

It was pure luxury, from the leather sofas and the solid antiques to the red drapes and—

"Are those mirrors?" Ted asked, looking up. "On the ceiling?"

"Well..." He kissed her neck again. "It's classy, but it's still Vegas."

They were waiting in the lobby for Cam a few hours later. His old friend had called just an hour after they'd arrived at the hotel, asking them to meet him and a date for dinner. The simple black dress that Ted brought was perfect. She'd done her hair in the loose curls he loved and brushed on some makeup, which she rarely wore at home. It made her dark eyes even more dramatic. The only jewelry she wore was a pair of deep turquoise earrings. The pop of color against her gold skin and dark hair was eye-catching. Despite her earlier reservations, more than one man turned to look as they walked through the lobby. But then, Ted had never needed elaborate outfits to catch a man's attention.

"We're meeting Cam and his dad? Or just Cam?" she asked.

"Cam and a date. Don't know who it is. But the new restaurant here is supposed to be good."

"It'll be nice to see him. It's been... ten years since the last time?"

"Or more. I haven't seen him in over a year, even though I called him when I knew I'd be opening the resort in the Springs."

Cam had asked him to visit Las Vegas at the time, but he hadn't been able to. So Alex was more than happy to meet for dinner, glad to catch up with his old friend and hopefully find out if meeting Cam's dad was also an option.

The old man and his son appeared to keep their businesses separate, from what Jolene could find out. Even though Frank Di Stefano had transitioned most of his business into legitimate enterprises, a few shadows still lingered. Shadows he didn't want near his only child. Still, if Alex and Ted wanted any information from Frank, then Cam would need to be convinced. Cam trusted him… to a point. But the information they were after had to do with the distinctly shadowy portion of his father's business. He'd be cautious, but Alex was expecting that.

"Alex!"

He turned and saw his old friend. Cam had taken after his French mother's side, so he looked far more California golden boy than East Coast mob scion. That, too, was something Alex suspected Frank Di Stefano liked. Going legitimate was a generations-long process, and the cleaner he could keep Cameron Di Stefano, the better things looked to investors.

"Alex." Cam stepped forward and gripped Alex's hand. "How the hell are you? I heard you moved out to the desert, huh? Leaving the field open for me?"

Cam and Alex had competed—in a friendly way—for almost everything. Contracts. Property. Women.

The other man's eyes went to Ted, surveying her in an appreciative way. He ignored the blinking blonde at his side, who Alex would bet money on being an "actress/model" so common on the arms of wealthy men in Southern California. He ought to know. They'd been his type when he hadn't wanted anything serious.

"Ted, you're far more beautiful than even my exceptional memory could recall," Cam said as he leaned over and kissed Ted's hand. "And still obviously far above this man's league."

"Don't even think about it," Alex said.

"Thinking's over, man. I'm on to the planning stage already. Keep up."

Luckily, Ted laughed. She gave Cam's hand a polite squeeze but then linked her arm with Alex. "Nice to see you too, Cam. Who's your friend?"

Cam looked over his shoulder. "Ah. This is Laura—en. Lauren." He held out his hand and the girl stepped forward, not appearing to notice that Cam had forgotten her name.

Alex felt a kick of embarrassment, knowing he'd done the same thing more than once with the women he'd dated after Ted had left. They'd been interchangeable to him, a social necessity with no emotional connection. He felt a stab of disgust at the man he'd been, but it only made him pull Ted closer. Those days were over. Ted was his future.

It was a startling realization to have among the shiny facade of Las Vegas, but Alex knew at that moment that nothing else in his life was as *real* as his relationship with Ted. At her side, he was the man he wanted to be. Anything less than that was unacceptable now. Anyone other than Ted would be a lie.

His hand tightened on her waist and she turned to him. "What is it?"

"Tell you later," he whispered, brushing his lips across her temple.

They followed Cam into the restaurant and toward a corner booth draped with a set of heavy curtains that had been pulled back. A private room where the owner could still enjoy the buzz of the busy restaurant and the curious patrons could also see him. A smart setup in the image-centric city that also would afford them privacy if they wished.

The chef greeted them after the sommelier brought out a selection of wines. The cuisine was Italian, with an American bend, and Alex was looking forward to it. One of the things he did miss about Southern California was the food. Though the Blackbird Diner was a great restaurant, it did get more than a little monotonous.

He heard Ted take a deep breath. "Smells so good," she said with a smile. "I need to remember to come up here more often, just to eat at the restaurants."

"I was just thinking the same thing. Come up here for a quick weekend away. It'd be fun."

"Yeah." There was a light blush on the arch of her cheek. "That would be fun."

With Ted, organizing expense reports would be fun.

Maybe that was stretching it.

"So, Alex…" Cam broke into his thoughts about what he'd do with Ted later. "Tell me about this resort. Sounds like an interesting opportunity."

They spent most of the dinner talking about Alex's plans for the Cambio Springs Resort and Spa, which was great for Alex since Cam had been in the hotel business longer than he had and offered a lot of insight. But it had to have been boring for Ted. He was grateful she chimed in with questions or comments now and then. It made him wonder how much she'd actually been paying attention to the project, even though she claimed to not care about it one way or another. Cam hung on her every word, obviously charmed. "Laura-en" just smiled a lot.

By the time dessert was offered, they'd covered construction woes, budget oversights, staffing problems, and the unpredictable vagaries of desert weather, but Alex had no idea how to politely broach the topic of a meeting with Frank Di Stefano about Marcus Quinn's murder. Luckily, Ted came to the rescue.

Ted turned to Lauren and said, "So, Lauren, did you know, as well as being an MD, I'm also the sheriff-coroner's consultant for Cambio Springs? I deal with the dead bodies. What do you do professionally?"

The color drained from the woman's face, and she put a hand on her throat. Cam stifled a smile and put an arm around her shoulder. "Lauren, sweetie, could you go see if Romano has any of those cigars that I like? He'll know the one's you're talking about."

She nodded, clearly happy to have a reason to escape. "Of course, Cam. I'll be—"

"No rush."

There was a flicker in her eyes that told Alex the girl knew she was being dismissed. As soon as she left the table, Cam turned to Ted. "So, gorgeous, why'd you want to scare away my date? Since Alex is still here, it's not for the reasons I'm hoping."

"No, but it does have to do with a dead body."

Cam's eyes darkened and flickered to Alex. "What's going on, man?"

"Cameron, we need to talk to you about someone... someone your dad had business with a few years ago."

His friend's eyes grew sharp and slid to Ted, then back to Alex. He read Cam's sign without needing a word.

"Ted," he said quietly.

"Not on your life, Alex."

He gripped her hand under the table and glanced at Cam. "A minute."

Alex pulled Ted up from the table and led her to a quiet hallway near the kitchen. Her face was set in stone.

"Don't even think about cutting me out on this," she said.

"You need to go."

"Do I need to remind you that technically this is my investigation? Technically, I'm the only one that has any, admittedly dubious, jurisdiction in this case. Nothing he says—"

"Nothing he says is going to be repeated in court." And he sure as hell wasn't going to put her in the position of feeling like she had to report someone or violate oaths he knew she'd taken, personally or professionally. He knew what had happened to Missy messed her up. No way was he going to ask her to step into that grey zone for him. And definitely not for Cam.

But she didn't give up.

"Alex—"

"You need to go." And he had to get back to the table. The mere fact he was even having this conversation with Ted was probably causing Cam to doubt whether he could trust either of them.

Her eyes were on fire when she tore her hand from his and walked from the dining room, not sparing a glance at Cam as she passed their table. She swept out of the restaurant, five feet eight inches of pissed-off female in three-inch heels. Alex closed his eyes and took a deep breath, knowing he didn't have time to deal with her until later. He walked back to the table to see Cam watching the door. Then he turned to Alex and tried to suppress his smile.

"See I didn't do you any favors there."

"Yeah, she's not real happy with me right now."

Cam's voice got serious. "This isn't about a boys' club."

"I know that."

"That said, she makes a hell of a sight walking away, man."

He closed his eyes and shook his head. "Cam, if you have any respect for me, please do not jerk me around. And please tell me you can help me out here."

Cam poured more wine into both glasses and said, "My dad and I keep stuff separate, Alex."

"I know that, Cam."

"That said, family's family. And I am not, and have never been, clueless about shit."

"I know that too."

He paused, took a sip of wine, and considered Alex a few more minutes.

"My old man taught me not to trust anyone outside my family. He also said if I had to trust a friend, you'd be a good one."

That surprised Alex, and he didn't try to hide it. "That means something, coming from a man who probably doesn't trust many."

"Or any."

"Yeah. Or any."

"Know why he said that, Alex?"

"No."

"He said it was because you knew what it was to keep a secret. Not a little one. A big one."

A cold lump settled in Alex's gut. Cam's dad had probably said that years ago. That meant Frank Di Stefano knew—maybe not the details of Cambio Springs' secrets, but that there was a secret at all. It was enough because Cameron Di Stefano was a very smart guy. He used that knowledge when he needed it.

Tit for tat. You keep my secrets; I'll keep yours.

"You get me, Alex?"

"I get you."

"Good. Now lay it out for me with as few names as possible, and I'll see what I can do."

Chapter Thirteen

Ted hadn't made it five steps into the lobby before she was intercepted by Romano, who fell into step behind her.

"Dr. Vasquez, may I be of assistance?"

She slowed, despite her rage. "I need a key to my room."

"Of course." He held a hand out, gesturing toward the corner where his desk sat. "It will only be a moment."

She'd left her purse at the table. Left Alex at the table. Seriously considered leaving him completely, but not before she got her things from their room. Their gorgeous room with the massive bed she'd been intending to share with Alex that night.

Well, that wasn't happening. Not after she'd been dismissed a few moments after Cam's arm candy. She wasn't a woman to make a scene, so arguing with Alex at the restaurant wasn't going to happen.

And neither was anything else.

As Romano had promised, it was only a few minutes and she was in her room again. Her suite. She didn't want to know how much it cost a night, and she didn't care. If Alex thought he could bring her to Vegas, dazzle her with fancy rooms and fancy meals, then treat her like one of his LA women, he was grossly mistaken. She'd known she made a mistake trusting him.

Romano was still standing in her room when she grabbed her suitcase.

"Is there anything else I can help with, Dr. Vasquez?"

"No—yes." She couldn't stay here. She was furious. And with her temper running high—partly from Alex's actions but also from the effect of the moon—she was as likely to tear into him as listen. "I need a rental car, please."

For the first time, the man hesitated at a request. Ted stopped packing and looked at him.

"A rental car, please."

His face was impassive, but his voice came more softly. "Dr. Vasquez… Teodora, are you certain you want to leave the hotel?"

"Yes," she answered immediately, surprised by his concern.

"Perhaps another room—"

"Why are you arguing with me on this?" Ted felt her cat clawing under her skin.

He said nothing for a few minutes, then took a step back and shut the door to the hallway, giving them privacy. She squared her shoulders and slid her rings off, wary of the possible threat. Romano only stepped a few feet into the room and stopped, hanging his hands in his pockets in the only casual gesture she'd ever seen the man make. It hadn't escaped her notice that she was alone in a hotel room with a strange man, even if he was handsome and wearing a designer suit. She kept him in the corner of her eye as she went back to packing.

"Mr. McCann told you I'd been to eat with him at Cam's house," Romano started.

"I remember."

"It's happened more than once."

"Okay…" She had no idea where he was going with this, but she stopped stuffing shoes in her bag and looked at him.

"I'm Cam's employee, but I'm also family. So when Alex treats me as a friend, please know I consider him the same."

"Ah." It was becoming clearer. Alex's buddy was trying to convince her to hang out. Well, that was understandable, even if it was useless. She turned back to her suitcase.

"Ted, don't leave."

"Romano, you seem like a nice enough guy, but you have no idea what happened tonight, so—"

"Cam called me minutes after you left the restaurant to make sure you were taken care of and had everything you need."

"I was your next stop after Lauren, huh?"

"Cam didn't mention Lauren, and I wouldn't expect him to."

There was a soft knock at the door, which Romano turned to answer. He cracked the door open. Then a small hand slid her purse through the door. He took it, closed the door, and set the black clutch on the table in the hallway.

Ted said nothing, trying to think through the implications of a man with possible mob connections telling a family member that she should be "taken care of."

She looked up. "Romano—"

"I keep having to interrupt you, and I do apologize for that, but if you could let me explain one thing, I would be grateful. And then I will call a rental car for you if you still wish it."

Fair enough. She stood and crossed her arms. "Go for it."

He took another step forward but did not change his relaxed stance. "You can tell a lot about a man from the way he conducts himself when he's had a little too much scotch."

Well, that wasn't what she'd been expecting.

"Cam is…" Romano smiled. "Cam. He's a very funny drunk. Very appreciative of the few people he considers friends, Alex among them. Very generous. Tells a great joke."

"I can see that."

"Alex is not a funny drunk."

Ted said nothing. Because when they'd been together, he had been. He'd been funny and affectionate. Sweet and a little crazy. The first time he'd told her he loved her, there'd been bourbon involved. Of course, he'd repeated the same thing the next morning when he woke her up with his mouth. He hadn't forgotten. He'd whispered it in her ear as they made love.

It was a stark reminder that he wasn't that man anymore. He was a different man. Years had passed. Life happened. And the young man you fell in love with at twenty-two could turn into a man who sent you from the table when a conversation turned uncomfortable.

She cleared her throat. "So what kind of drunk is Alex?"

"Quiet."

Yeah.

Yeah, she could see that.

"Romano—"

"I keep having to interrupt you. Perhaps I need to be more succinct." He took another step toward her, but Ted's cat had calmed. This man was no threat to anything except her temper, which was slowly subsiding. "One of the few times Alex talked to me on a night that there had been more than a little wine poured, he spoke of you. And there was a… well of regret when he did."

"Romano—"

"He missed you," the man said quietly. "Deeply. He admires you. You are his ideal in the best possible way."

"He sent me from the table," she said quietly. "Cam sent Lauren away; then Alex sent me away. As if I were…"

"You are not Lauren, nor will you ever be. I don't know what happened tonight, but I do know the man who's talking to Cam right now does not want you leaving him. He looked happy today. Happy in a way I have not seen since I've known him. So… please don't make me call a rental car. Be angry if you're angry." Romano smiled a devastatingly handsome grin. "He probably deserves it. But don't leave."

Ted thought for a moment. "You don't have to call a rental car."

"Thank you."

"But give me a few hours, and I might need your help stealing his keys from the valet."

He gave a slight bow and said, "I'll await your call, Dr. Vasquez."

She smiled at him before he slipped from the room.

Ted heard Alex's footsteps an hour later. Heard him hesitate at the door.

Good.

Ted was still pissed at him, but she wasn't a dramatic teenager, running off in a huff. She'd calmed down. He'd have a chance to explain. Then she'd decide if she was stealing his truck and leaving him in Sin City with the Laura-ens of the world.

She was sitting on the couch, dressed in the black yoga pants she'd brought to lounge in, along with a black camisole. She'd been trying to read on her tablet, but her mind kept slipping to what Cam and Alex might be talking about. Part of her reaction was a consequence of the nearly full moon. She knew it. Alex probably knew it too. Moods were volatile around moon nights, and Ted knew from years of living with the swings it was the absolute worst time to fight about anything. If she and Alex escaped this without claw marks, it'd be a miracle.

The door clicked open and she saw him walk in, hands in his pockets. His stance was a deliberate attempt to remain casual, but she could see the tension in his shoulders.

"You're still here."

"Romano calmed me down. I'm keeping his number in case I need to steal your car later."

"Romano?" He stepped closer.

"How was your chat with Cam?"

"Cam worries about exposing his father. Doesn't trust many people. But it went okay. Let's go back to Romano calming you down."

She lifted her eyes from her tablet. His tone of voice scraped across her nerves. "Why?"

"Because I want to know."

"Well, I'd like to know what, specifically, you and Cam talked about. Why don't we start with that?"

He pulled off his black jacket. "Why don't we get to that part after you tell me what the hell Romano did to calm you down, why his scent is all over this room, and what you're doing out of your dress, Ted?"

Her eyes popped open. "You're joking."

"No."

"You *must* be joking."

"I'm not joking, Ted. Now what the hell—"

"Where do you get off accusing me of something like that, Alex?" She sprang to her feet and barely resisted snarling. "I was about five minutes from walking out of this room because you acted like a jerk at dinner, and you—"

He stepped into her space. "You know why I wanted to speak to Cam alone. He doesn't know you. He doesn't trust—"

"And *that's* why you dismissed me?" She sneered. "That's why? Maybe you should have delayed your conversation until you two could have a private drink. Maybe you could have simply met for coffee. Maybe you could have told me ahead of time and I could have faked a damn headache, Alex! What you shouldn't have done was send me out of the restaurant, following Cam's fuck buddy!"

He leaned down and yelled, "Why the hell was Romano here?"

"Be glad he was because someone needed to remind me why I love you, *asshole!*"

Alex's hand shot out and grabbed the nape of her neck, pulling her head up as his mouth slammed down on hers. Her back arched as he gripped her hair, pulling it back and twisting the long strands in his fist. She gasped when he let her mouth go, only to dive to her neck, kissing, biting her with sharp nips she knew would leave a mark.

Her body was on fire, and his hunger consumed her.

She turned her head but couldn't move an inch because his left arm had welded her torso to his. Her arms twisted around his neck and pulled him closer as Alex's teeth sank into the soft curve where her neck met her shoulder.

Burn, burn, burn.

She closed her eyes and felt it. The curling heat spread from her middle, filling her limbs with a strange weight. She wasn't a weak woman, but she had the feeling she would fall if he didn't hold her up.

Alex walked her backward and she started tearing at the buttons on his shirt.

"Téa?" he panted.

"Yes." There it was. She felt the buttons start to pop, and his shirt was gone, falling to the floor like so much ash. He let go of her to yank it off as he continued to walk them backward to the bed.

"Mmm…" He pulled his mouth from her neck and claimed her mouth again, drinking her in deep gulps as their breath mingled and their lips danced. Touching. Teasing. He caught her lower lip with his teeth. She licked at his tongue.

"Need—"

"I know."

He fell on top of her, bracing himself with his forearms for a second before his mouth was on her again. She struggled to unbuckle his belt, then sucked in a deep breath, back arching as Alex pulled down the top of her camisole, baring her breasts to the cold of the air-conditioned room. They didn't remain uncovered for long because he was on them.

His mouth descended to her left breast, taking it in his mouth as his teeth scraped the edge of her nipple before he pulled, sucking the tip in his mouth as his fingers teased the other. Her back arched off the bed at the sensation. Raw hunger seared through her and she needed—*needed* more.

"Alex!"

"Shhh." He took one more deep pull, so hard he probably left a mark before his mouth was on her again. Twisting farther up the bed, Alex quickly unbuckled his belt. Then struggled with his pants while Ted pulled off her top.

Alex growled, on her in seconds, but this time his burning skin hit hers, and she wrapped her arms around him, digging her nails into his shoulders as he lifted her in his arms, bringing her up to straddle his lap. He fisted a hand in her hair again, and she let him, baring her neck to his teeth.

Only with him. Only ever with him.

He laid her back on the pillows, chest heaving. His cheeks were red with hunger, and his jaw clenched as his eyes narrowed on her pants. He reached down and ripped them off, along with her panties.

She lay there bared to him. His eyes drank her in. Every inch. Their eyes met, and Ted's heart almost stopped.

Alex. Her mouth moved to form his name, but she couldn't say it. Couldn't say anything. The sheer hunger in his gaze leveled her.

And she needed him. Needed his touch. His hands. His mouth. More than she'd ever needed anything in her life.

She was his.

He closed his eyes and sucked in a deep breath, tasting the weight of the air around them. Then he bowed between her legs and put his mouth to her.

She cried out at his kiss. His tongue. His teeth on the soft inside of her thigh. He devoured her. She was lost, her eyes closing as she slipped closer to the edge, but then he was gone. She opened her eyes to see him watching her, crouched over her like the predator he was. His eyes never left hers as he bent his head to her skin.

"Alex."

"Watch." His voice was feral.

He kept her eyes when his teeth closed over the flesh of her belly. He kept them when his tongue licked up her ribs. He watched her as his teeth scraped over her breast again. Then his lips touched hers. Not kissing. His breath caressed hers as their gazes locked and he surged inside.

Ted gasped and her eyes fluttered, but he growled out, "Eyes!" as his hips nudged deeper.

They made love with eyes locked on each other, Alex braced over her. Her legs wrapped around him. And when she came, he watched her face and the flush on his cheeks grew dark. It was hard and raw and fast. It was everything and nothing like it had been before.

She saw him start to fall over the edge.

"Eyes," she said, and his gaze sharpened on her.

"Téa…"

"Yes," she whispered, arching back to bare her neck to him, eyes still locked with his.

"Baby."

"Let go."

And he did. His mouth touched hers as he came with a groan. When he finally stopped moving, he let her eyes go and buried his face in her neck.

"I love you, too," he whispered.

Her arms moved around him, long strokes up and down his back as she felt the tension seep away. The waxing moon, nearly full, shone through the high arched windows. Her cat stretched beneath her skin, soothed by the fierce lovemaking and the weight of her mate's body.

Alex moved to her side, pulling her with him, chest to chest, he lifted her thigh to lie over his and locked her to him. His left arm came around her waist and pulled her close, and she rested her head on the hard curve of his bicep. It was surprisingly comfortable.

"Alex," she whispered, "I need—"

"Shhh." He kissed her temple. "Leave it. Just stay here. Stay with me."

She hesitated for only a moment before her body relaxed into his. "Okay."

"Sleep, Téa."

She thought she'd still be wired, but with his hand playing in the curls of her hair, her arms wrapped around the massive burn of his body, she felt herself start to slip away.

Within minutes, she was asleep.

She woke later to feel a warm washcloth cleaning her up.

"Alex?"

"Shhh, Téa. Go back to sleep." He tugged the cool sheets over her and walked back to the bathroom, his body outlined in the light that glowed over the sink. Then he turned off the light, and the room was pitch black except for the moonlight that still shone.

She'd had sex with Alex. Fighting, then sex. And right in the middle of that, she'd told him she loved him.

If *that* wasn't a familiar pattern, she didn't know what was.

She awaited the anxiety she'd expected. Looked for the fear, but he'd worked it out of her. His hunger had burned so hot there wasn't room for any doubt. She was exhausted, physically and emotionally. Any second-guessing could wait for the next day.

Or maybe the day after.

He came back and slipped beneath the covers with her, pulling her into his arms again, sliding her leg over his thigh so they were tangled together.

She pressed her face into his chest, her eyes barely open. "We didn't use a condom," she whispered, "but I'm on the pill."

His hand didn't stop playing with her hair. "I've only ever *not* used one with you."

"Me too," she murmured. Then her eyes closed completely.

Her mind drifted, but her body was content. The cat in her had stopped prowling hours ago, the minute Alex had pulled her into his arms and taken her. She was sated. Safe. A drowsy voice came to her through the haze of sleep, but it barely registered.

"It's only ever been you."

Chapter Fourteen

"Did you really think something happened between me and the concierge?"

"Did you really think I put you in the same category as Cam's girl?"

She was quiet for a minute. They were curled up in bed together, the sunlight touching the shear drapes that hid them from the rest of the world. He'd pulled her back to his chest and rested his stubbled chin on her shoulder as they dozed.

"No. I don't think you put me in the same category as 'Laura-en.' My boobs aren't nearly fake enough."

He chuckled against her back. "Your boobs are great. That's why Romano was checking them out when he met you." He was. Asshole. Even if he was an asshole that kept Ted in Vegas and not driving down the road, pissed out of her mind the night before a full moon.

"Seriously? Romano?" Ted reached down and grabbed both of his hands from around her waist, crossing them over her chest so he cupped her breasts. "Feel better now? Marked your territory, alpha boy?"

He gave them a squeeze. Then another. "I feel a little better. And don't pretend you didn't mark some territory yourself. I have the scratches on my back to prove it."

"There's bite marks on your neck too."

"Some on you too, baby."

"Don't call me baby."

At that, his arms tightened, and when he spoke, his voice was raw. "I missed mornings with you."

She said nothing, but grabbed his hands and squeezed them in her own.

Alex took a deep breath and asked the question that had haunted him all morning. "Are we back? I need to know. You told me you love me, but —"

"Love was never the problem, was it?"

"No."

She turned in his arms and looked at him, bringing her hands up to stroke his cheeks. He nuzzled into her hand and scraped his chin across her palm, content to let her pet him. But he turned his eyes to hers, locking into her as he had the night before.

"You want the job?" she asked softly.

"What?"

"The job. Taking my back. Putting up with my crazy family and their bullshit. Putting up with me when I'm a raging bitch because you know I can be. Not giving up when I'm stubborn. When I'm angry." She paused, but just like when they'd made love, his eyes never left hers. "Sticking with me," she continued. "Making the Springs home, all the messy—"

"I want the job."

No questions. No hesitation. The tightness that had creeped up on him when he woke eased away even as she blinked in surprise.

"Alex—"

"Best job in the world."

"But—"

"No buts. I've got just as much baggage as you do. Maybe more, considering my pack. So Teodora Vasquez, if you're willing to take me on…" He rolled over and trapped her under him. "Then I'll take you on. Are we back?"

He could read her answer in her eyes.

"*Querido*," she whispered.

Querido. Dearest.

They were back.

Holy shit, they were back.

She smiled, a soft, sweet smile that made him want to take her again. The night before had been intense and fast and hot as hell, but he needed to drink deep. He'd missed her for too long. Missed their mornings together, when they would talk about random stuff. Some of it serious. Some of it silly. Talk and pet and kiss.

He bent down, working soft lips from her jawline up to her mouth. Then he held it, suspended in the sunlight that crossed their skin.

They were back.

A soft growl left his throat as the wolf inside stretched in approval.

"That said"—Ted broke from him.—"we still have shit to talk about. So no growling."

He laughed and rolled her back into the pillows with him, settling her on his chest so he could play with her hair.

"Fine," he said. "As long as the shit we need to talk about is *how* we're going to be together, not *if* we're going to be together."

"Deal."

He kissed her again. Longer. Sweeter. Just a lick of his tongue against her lower lip. "Deal."

"Mmm," she hummed in quiet contentment.

"You know, Jena told me I needed to charm you."

"Oh, really?"

"Romance you."

Her shoulders started to shake. "Was the 'Did you hop in bed with the concierge?' argument part of the charm and romance strategy? If so, that wasn't very effective."

"No. I think I just figured charm and romance wasn't working, so I'd go with pissing you off."

"It's probably not a healthy sign that it actually worked for you, is it?"

"It's us," he said. "What can I say, Ted? It's just... us."

They drove out to the Di Stefanos' house in Alex's truck, and the dusty, scratched Ford looked just as out of place in the luxurious gated community as it had on the Las Vegas strip. He pulled in behind Cam's Jaguar and walked around to help Ted out of the cab. He'd asked Cam the night before if he should bring her or if it was just going to cause another fight. Cam had laughed and said to bring her.

Alex didn't know if that was because Cam and his dad wanted to see Ted, or if Cam just thought Alex and Ted's fights were fun to watch.

"So we're meeting his dad. That's all you got out of him?"

"That was an hour-long negotiation, Ted. Cam doesn't like crossing wires."

"Crossing wires?"

"He has family life and business life. And they don't often meet."

She nodded and took his hand. "And you're business life."

"And a little bit family life, since I've known him a long time."

"I can see the conflict."

"His dad's very old school, so if he asks to speak to me alone—"

"I got it." As they made their way up the walkway, she turned and tugged on his collar. "I won't go off half-cocked."

He smiled. "It's not that you're a woman; it's that you're sort of like a cop."

She laughed and started walking again. "Me? A cop?"

"In their minds? Yeah."

By the time they reached the front door, it was already opening, and Cam stood there, tan and smiling in a golf shirt with a drink in his hand.

"Alex. Ted. Just in time for drinks."

"Hey, Cam." Putting his hand on the small of Ted's back, Alex ushered her into the house. He saw her chest rise as she took a deep breath. Testing the scent of the room. Scanning for threats. Her sense of smell in human skin had always been better than his. She had to focus her attention, but when she did, it was almost as good as her natural form.

The corner of his mouth turned up as Cam shut the door. Alex bent to tuck a curl of her hair behind an ear and whisper, "Anything I should know?"

She smiled at him and put her mouth to his ear, giving the impression to anyone else that they were flirting. "Five men, two women by scent. But the air-conditioning is blasting, so that's messing me up."

"Got it." Alex was guessing that the two women were Cam's mom and younger sister. If Constance and Yvette were there, Alex and Ted had nothing to worry about. Frank and Cam were both intensely, almost obsessively, protective of the women in their family. Most likely because Frank's sister, according to Jolene's research, had been murdered at sixteen by a business rival of Cam's grandfather.

They stopped in a huge living room with a view of the golf course behind Frank and Yvette's house. Massive double-pane plate glass windows looked over the ninth green, and in the distance, Alex saw a group teeing off at the tenth. He felt a moment of longing for his clubs before he focused on the people sitting in the room.

"Alex!" Frank said with a huge smile. "How long has it been? My God, look at you. You're an adult, just like my kids. What's the world coming to?"

"Frank, good to see you again." He held out his hand and shook Frank's.

Frank Di Stefano was clearly on the way to building a solidly legitimate reputation. The dark tan and stylish clothes spoke of a healthy professional in late middle age. Successful. Active. The house on the golf course, along with the distinct lack of the typical "wise guy" accent, were only part of his carefully constructed identity. His wife was Catholic, but not from Jersey, where he'd been born. His children went to private schools on the West Coast. And his house looked like a page from *Architectural Digest*.

Yvette Di Stefano rose and came to Frank's side.

"Alex. So good to see you. I hope your family is well."

"They are, Yvette. Thank you." He nodded to Cam's sister Constance, who stood silently but politely behind her parents. "Connie."

"Hey, Alex."

Stylish, trim, and still holding on to a hint of a French accent, Yvette gave Alex a quick kiss on the cheek before she held out a graceful hand to Ted. "You must be Dr. Vasquez. Welcome. It's very nice to meet you."

"Thank you. Please, call me Ted."

"Ted?" Yvette's laugh sounded like bells.

She grinned. "My mother was out of it when my dad named me after his grandmother. So my name is actually Teodora. Ted was the nickname that stuck."

"I think that's delightful."

Alex pinched her waist and said, "I think it fits."

"It does," Cam said. "Have no idea why, but it does."

"Are we still talking about my name?" She gave Cam an arch look. "Or are you going to get me a drink?"

"You're still pissed about last night, aren't you?"

"Cam!" Yvette said. "Language, please."

Ted just grinned. "I am. So vodka tonic or it's gonna get ugly, Di Stefano."

Cam laughed as he sauntered to a marble-topped bar in the corner while the rest of them sat near the windows.

"Ted"—Yvette nodded at her.—"it's so nice to meet Alex's *girlfriend*. You seem like such an interesting, *accomplished* woman. Cam said you're a medical doctor?"

Cam called from the bar, "Mom. Don't."

"I am. Family practice." Ted gave him a confused glance, but Alex only tried to hide his grin. "Strep throat. Colds. Exciting stuff like that."

"That's wonderful." Yvette turned to Alex. "Your parents must be thrilled you've found such a bright girlfriend."

Now Ted was the one trying to hide an incredulous snort as Cam walked over.

"Ma, really?" he said.

"How did you meet?" Yvette asked Alex.

"We grew up together. Then we both went to college in LA." He squeezed Ted's shoulder, catching her attention as he smiled. "We lost touch for a while. Finally back where we need to be."

Ted smiled, ignoring the drink Cam held out to her. "Yeah," she said softly.

Alex cleared his throat and looked back at Yvette, who clearly thought theirs was the most romantic story she'd ever heard. Then her expression sharpened as she glanced at her son.

"Imagine!" she said. "Not meeting a woman at a bar—"

"Mom."

"Or a dance club—"

"Seriously, Ma—"

"But finding a woman who clearly has goals beyond finding a new purse."

Cam gave up and sighed, leaning back in his seat as he took a deep breath and let his mother speak.

Ted grinned at him. "This is making me feel so much better about last night."

"Glad I could entertain you, Ted," Cam mumbled.

Alex smiled and leaned back, his arm around Ted's shoulders. Judging by the expression on both Frank's and Connie's face, this was not an unknown topic of discussion.

"Connie," Alex broke in, trying to save his friend the grief. "What are you up to lately?"

She smiled. "Managing a gallery in Santa Fe, actually. Just here for a visit. We got some of your sister's new canvases in last week. They're stunning."

"I'll have to tell Willow. She'll love that."

"And your new place?" Frank asked. "Cam's told me a bit about it. Sounds like a challenge."

"It is." He turned and caught Ted smiling at him. "But I do love a challenge."

Lunch was fantastic. Conversation was polite but warm. More than one joking reference to Cam's love life was made while Alex held Ted's hand under the table and played with the seam of her pants. If only she'd worn a skirt…

After lunch, Yvette very diplomatically went to "sort the kitchen," taking Connie with her. That left Frank, Cam, Alex and Ted sitting with glasses of wine in the living room, which had suddenly gone very quiet.

Alex saw Cam looking at his father. "Dad?"

"She stays," Frank said quietly, his eyes level on Ted.

Alex leaned forward and said, "Frank—"

"You're a smart girl, aren't you, Ted?" Frank spoke directly to her.

The room fell silent, and Alex squeezed Ted's hand.

"Wouldn't exactly call myself a girl," she said.

The man shrugged, and in it, Alex saw an edge of the wise guy Frank hid so well.

"You're the same age as my kid," he said. "You're a girl. Not intended as a slight." He took a sip of his wine, then looked at Alex. "You live in an interesting place, Alex."

His breath was deliberately even. He didn't allow his expression to change to anything except casual amusement.

"Not that interesting, really. Just home."

"Lot of people depending on your resort project going smoothly."

Alex paused. "I took a hit when Marcus Quinn died. He was a good man."

"Yeah." Frank took another sip of wine. "I knew Marcus. He *was* a good man. And a good businessman. Took care of his family. Honest with his investors." Frank's quick glance told Alex he knew *they* knew the Di Stefanos had financed Marcus Quinn's operation. "A tragedy, what happened to him."

"Not a tragedy," Ted said softly. "A crime."

Frank's eyes swung back to her. "Yeah. A crime."

Cam leaned forward. "Listen, Ted, maybe you could—"

"She stays," Frank said as a muscle jerked in Cam's jaw. "Don't you worry about Teodora, Cameron. She won't be a problem."

Ted said nothing, staring at Frank with a cool smile on her face.

"Frank," Alex said, mirroring her posture. "I don't much appreciate threats against my woman."

"Not a threat, Alex."

And Alex realized it wasn't. If anything, Frank was sizing Ted up as he would a competitor.

"She's a good match for you, Alex," Frank said. "Got the same eyes."

Ted said, "How's that?"

"Secret eyes, Teodora." Frank gave her a slow smile. "You know how to keep a secret, don't you?"

"Yes."

"You know what my business is?"

Alex heard Cam suck in a breath.

"I know what you do." Ted glanced at Cam. "And what you're trying to do."

Frank's face softened. "Do you?"

"It's admirable."

"Takes time."

"Do you have it?"

The corner of Frank's mouth turned up. "I'll make it."

Then, showing a business savvy that Alex had no idea she possessed, Ted leaned forward and asked, "What do you want from me, Mr. Di Stefano? Not Alex. Me."

"You're a doctor."

"I am."

Of course… Alex closed his eyes.

Frank shrugged again. "A good doctor—a discreet one—is hard to find sometimes."

"First, do no harm, Mr. Di Stefano."

"Ask no questions, and I'll tell no lies."

Ted leaned back and into Alex. He wrapped a hand around her shoulder and squeezed, hoping she realized he'd back her play, whatever that play was.

Bad guys played rough, and gunshot wounds—or anything that indicated a crime had occurred—had to be reported, making medical care something of a problem for Frank Di Stefano's men, particularly if they had to be out in the desert where even emergency medical clinics were scarce. They had interests. Quiet relationships with farmers and truckers. People who lived or moved with regularity through the corridor between Las Vegas, Los Angeles, and Mexico. Interests that Frank needed to watch over, along with his people.

Ted took a deep breath. "How often?"

"Less and less all the time. But occasionally…"

She pursed her lips. "It's a small town. Off the beaten track. Discretion is possible."

Fuck. She was making the deal and she didn't even know what Frank Di Stefano was offering. But Alex knew the old man had something, so Ted had probably figured that out as well. He wasn't going to all this trouble to recruit an asset just to piss her off when he gave them useless information.

Ted continued. "It's also a place with a lot of families. Kids. And it needs to stay safe. Anyone who might… come to me for help needs to understand that."

"I understand, and they will too." Frank glanced at Alex, and the man's eyes held steady. "I respect people who take care of their own."

The coldly political side of him knew this was a good deal. Moral implications aside, Frank Di Stefano clearly knew that Cambio Springs had a secret. What that secret was, he might not know, but the Springs was already on his radar. Giving the crime boss an interest to protect, and possibly deflect attention from, was a smart move.

The fact that it laid the woman he was in love with open to possible cooperation with criminals was the part that churned his gut.

Ted took a deep breath and made her decision. "I'll give you my number."

"That would be much appreciated, Teodora."

"And I'll leave it with Yvette, too," she said. "The next time you're nearby, you should call. Our turn for lunch."

Fuck, but she was smart. Yvette liked Ted, and reminding Frank of that was a good call.

The old man's mouth twitched. "Once that spa's running, she might be a permanent resident."

"Might be a while with Marcus gone," Alex said, bringing them back to the reason they were there.

"Yes, Marcus," Frank said, glancing at Cam.

Cam stood and smiled at both of them. "You'll have to excuse me for a moment; I just remembered I have a call to make."

Keep Cam protected. Alex smiled. Oh yes, Frank Di Stefano had very clear priorities.

Frank watched Cam walk out of the room. Then he lowered his voice, and Alex could hear the East Coast edge again.

"Marcus was a good guy. He one of yours?" Frank was looking at Ted.

She glanced at Alex and nodded. "He grew up in our town. His family's not that great, but Marcus was always a good guy."

"Hard worker," Frank said. "That man worked his ass off. That's the reason I fronted him. I knew he'd be able to pay me back. Banks don't take that shit into consideration, but a man can tell."

Alex asked, "So it was a straight loan?"

"It was." Frank nodded. "No funny business. Nothing going through or coming out." He raised his shoulders. "Not saying I didn't see the possibilities, with his crews moving all over the desert like they did, but Marcus was a family guy, and I respected that."

"How long did he take to pay you back?" Ted asked.

"A while. I'm not a charity. But he paid regular and he paid in full over five years ago. Went through a bad period a while back after his woman lost a baby..." Frank shook his head. "Too much drinking. Too much time at the tables. It's a hard thing. He got behind in his payments, and I had to have a word. But he straightened out. Since then, no business with him, though Cam's given him some work with his businesses. I see him around town. He's asked my advice on a few things. We were friendly."

"So nothing shady on his end?"

Frank shook his head. "Nothing. Quinn was straight. He might have understood grey, but he kept his business clean, which is not always easy to do in this town. And he was damn good. Growing. Opened an office in

Barstow but kept the one here because of the wife's family. When I heard he was killed, *that* surprised me."

Ted crossed her arms. "So if that *did* surprise you, what *didn't* surprise you?"

Alex turned to her and muttered, "I love how smart you are." Then he turned back. "Sorry, Frank."

Frank was amused. "No worries. Don't ever stop doing that shit, and you'll be a happy man. Married to Yvette forty years and not a day goes by I don't tell that woman what a gift she is."

"That's sweet, Frank," Ted said with a smile. "But seriously, what didn't surprise you? There was something, right?"

"The partner. Chris Avery. You know him?" Frank asked Alex.

"Marcus's brother-in-law. Yeah, I know him. He's finishing up the project since Marcus is gone."

Frank turned to Ted, who seemed to be his new favorite person. "You know how I said a man knows? Even if banks don't? On paper, Avery looked clean. Knew Marcus wanted to expand, came to him with a business plan. Marcus had lunch with me to look it over. Asked my advice. And on paper? Good plan. Clear. Partnership agreement was clean. Smart deal."

"But he wasn't," Alex said quietly.

Frank shook his head. "Something in my gut, Alex. Just like I knew Marcus Quinn was a man who'd pay me back the money I loaned him, something else told me that Chris Avery was trouble. I met the man. I wished I hadn't given that business plan my approval. I kept waiting for the day I heard he stole something or paid someone off. Something that would give Quinn problems. I didn't, but there was something about the guy I didn't like."

"Murder?"

Frank pursed his lips. "Hard to say. Like I said, it was a surprise. But I've heard whispers that Quinn was having money problems, so I'm not sure what that's about."

"Can you ask around?" Ted asked. "See if the whispers get louder?"

"Are you going to answer your phone at three in the morning if it's an emergency?"

"I already do that, Frank. I don't ignore calls."

"Then I'll ask around." Frank looked at Alex. "But if you're right, bad news. Josie's a good woman. If her brother was involved in her man's death…" Frank shook his head. "Very bad business, Alex."

"We'll take care of it," Ted said. "And her."

The smile he gave her wasn't just a smile; it was a grin.

"Don't make me curious, Teodora. I might just drive out to the desert and look for what's behind those secret eyes."

Chapter Fifteen

The full moon painted stripes across his back as he lay between her legs. Ted felt like hours had passed, and he still hadn't come up for air. She was going to break through her skin if he didn't go faster.

"Alex, please."

"Shh." The whisper stroked the inside of her thigh.

"I can't. Come here."

"No." His voice was inches away from the wolf, a low growl that sounded barely human. She gripped his hair tighter and felt the rumble of appreciation in his chest.

Sex was one of the few ways shifters could distract themselves during a moon night. And since Alex and Ted were miles away from home in an unknown hotel, both of them had decided to resist the change. It was difficult. Almost painful. But they were some of the strongest shifters in their clans, and they could take it.

Plus it wasn't like they hadn't used this means of distraction before.

Alex was just maddeningly patient when it came to this particular task. She caught the edge of her release and held on, not letting the hint of pain distract her as Alex's fingers dug harder into her hips. He would leave bruises, but she didn't care. She'd left her fair share on him tonight too.

"There it is, baby."

"Yes." Her back arched off the bed when she came, and before she could catch her breath, he was on her. In her. Pushing her knee up and out to drive deeper as he gritted his teeth and lost himself in their connection.

She reached down. Felt them joined.

"Beautiful," she breathed out.

He rose over her, his eyes wild when she met them.

"Beautiful," she whispered again, reaching out to wrap her hand around his wrist where it was planted at her side.

"*Téa*," he groaned when he finally came, then fell over her, chest heaving.

Round four and they'd just hit midnight. Alex rolled to her side and shoved his face into her neck, letting out a harsh breath. Her arms came up around his damp shoulders, held him as he caught his breath.

"Not enough," he panted.

"Shhh." She soothed him, alternating long strokes along his back with hard digs into the muscles at his back. "I see office work hasn't softened you up," she said, trying to distract him.

"Hope not."

He was built like a rock. Different but familiar. The young man's body had hardened into what it was now. Thicker at the shoulders but still trim at the waist. There was nothing soft about Alex, and she found she liked exploring him. Liked seeing the beginnings of wrinkles around his eyes. Liked the stray silver in his hair. He'd grow more handsome with age. She wondered what he thought of the changes in her body but figured he didn't mind anything considering they hadn't left the bed in about four hours.

Her fingers trailed over his bicep, massaged the triceps before moving to his neck. He shifted farther into her, hips still between her legs, his arms around her back as soft lips marked lazy pathways at her neck. Ted sighed in pleasure and let him explore.

It was an intensely vulnerable position between shifters. Ted had never let anyone put their mouth at her throat except Alex.

That, she supposed, said it all.

"You still love me?" he asked.

"Yes."

"Even though I pissed you off at dinner?"

"You can't pay for everything, Alex."

"I can try."

"I'm a grown woman."

He pulled his head back, then kissed her mouth, touching his tongue to hers before he pulled back and grinned.

"Thank God for that."

She could see it again, the heat building in his eyes. She had a voracious sexual appetite, but it was nothing compared to Alex on a moon night.

"Ready?" he asked.

"Don't get lazy, McCann."

"Mmm…" He lowered his mouth to her breasts. Slow kisses that made her toes curl. "Wolves don't get lazy. Cats do."

"I can keep up."

"You keep up," he said, the growl coloring his voice again. "But it's my job to make you purr."

Late Sunday afternoon, they drove back to Cambio Springs, brainstorming about what they'd learned in Las Vegas.

"I think it was Avery," he said.

"Marcus was a smart guy. If there was something funny in the company—"

"Josie told me the day after Marcus was killed that if there was anything that might have killed him, it would be him thinking the best of someone. Trusting the wrong person. Something like that."

Ted fell silent. Yeah, she could see that. Marcus was a nice guy, but he'd had a bad childhood, so he knew that marked a person. And he'd turned his life around in a bad spot, so he probably thought others could do the same. Plus, he was a born optimist.

"Do you not think it was Avery?" Alex asked.

"I don't *not* think it. I just don't think we should leap to conclusions when we don't know much."

"We know more."

"Yeah. I'm glad we went," she said. "I think it was worth the drive."

"Me too." He turned to her, smiled, and grabbed her hand to pull it into his lap. She knew he wasn't talking about Marcus's murder, and he was right. That was worth way more than a drive.

"So..."

"Hmm?"

"How are we going to tell everyone?"

"Tell them what?" He frowned. "About Avery?"

"No, about us."

Alex chuckled. "It's Sunday, Ted."

"So?"

"We're going to Jena's for dinner. We walk up holding hands, no one's going to wonder a thing. By Monday afternoon, everyone in town will know. No announcement necessary. Done."

"I was talking more about our parents."

"Oh." His smile fell. "I should have dragged you to Fat Elvis when I had the chance and just been done with it."

Her head swung around and she pulled her hand from his. "What?"

"Oh, come on."

"Come on, what? Did you just joke about getting married a day—a *day*—after we got back together?"

"It's almost two days now, and I wasn't joking."

"Oh, *that* makes all the difference!"

Alex said nothing for a few seconds. Then he burst into laughter.

"Why are you laughing?"

"Why are you pissed off?"

"Because—"

"Baby, where do you think this is heading?"

Ted said nothing because obviously it was heading where he said it was heading. She just wasn't going to say it out loud. Yet. Alex's laughter fell off and he reached over to grab her hand again. She didn't try to stop it. She knew they were both headed in the same direction. Knew that what they had would be solid, not just because they loved each other, but because they would *make* it solid.

Still, two days.

"You could have dragged me there, but I would not have married you at the Fat Elvis chapel, Alex."

They were on a completely deserted stretch of the highway, but he still pulled over. "And I wouldn't have taken you there." The humor had fled his voice. "I would never take the woman I love to get married by Fat Elvis."

"Alex—"

"I would have found Young Elvis." The corner of his mouth twitched. "Or maybe Frank Sinatra."

Ted couldn't help it; she smiled.

"Class, Ted. All the way. Young Elvis or Frank. Maybe Liberace, but never Fat Elvis."

"Stop." She started laughing. "We're not getting married in Vegas!"

He leaned over and planted a hard kiss on her mouth. "Good to know you're not going to fight me on the marriage thing, though."

Then he put the car back in drive and turned up the radio before she could say a word.

Ted had called Jena on the road and told her they'd be there for dinner. They stopped at the market in town and grabbed some drinks and tub of macaroni salad since Caleb was grilling hamburgers. Everyone knew they'd be there, so it wasn't surprising that the door opened as soon as they pulled up. What was surprising was the carefully controlled—yet obviously angry—expression on Caleb Gilbert's face.

"Great," Alex muttered.

"Why's he pissed?"

"You really think he buys that we went off for a weekend away on a moon night so we could explore our future together?"

"Oh."

"Yeah." He parked and asked her, "I don't suppose you're going to stay in the truck."

"I'm glad you realize that." Ted popped open the door and left the drinks and salad in the car. "Hey, Caleb," she called out.

Caleb ignored her, which pissed her off. He walked straight to Alex, and his voice was low when he spoke.

"Jena's best friend," he said.

"Chief, you're going to need to—"

"The woman who saved her life."

"Caleb—"

"Saved *my* life the day she saved Jena." He tipped up his head a bit to meet Alex's eyes. "The woman *you're* in love with—" His voice was rising. Furious. "—and you take her to meet—"

"Step back, Caleb." Alex's voice was controlled, but Ted could see his shoulders tense with anger. Caleb, whether he realized it or not, was challenging him in a very dangerous way.

"—a fucking mob boss, McCann! She walked into the house of a known criminal. And not a minor one. A major one!"

Ted's lip curled up, and she lunged toward them, grabbing the front of Caleb's shirt and shoving him back.

"You don't speak about me like I'm not here, Caleb Gilbert. You want to see the lion come out, keep talking."

Her eyes flashed to his. She saw fear behind the anger, knew the emotion that was working him, but she didn't care. The chief of police wanted to treat her like a defenseless female. He'd learned differently that moment.

She felt Alex's hand at her back. "Ted, not here."

"You don't get it, Caleb, so I'm going to clue you in. Alex—" She grabbed his hand. "—would never put me in danger because Alex knows what I'm capable of. It was *my* idea to go up there and poke into Marcus's connections. *My* idea. And I'm going to clue you into something else. You need him involved in this investigation."

Caleb's eyes narrowed, and he crossed his arms over his chest.

"Open your eyes. Who do you think people look to in this town? This is not Albuquerque, Caleb. It's not Indio. Hell, it's not even Parker. We do not do things the way humans do. You may think it's weird or old-fashioned, but that's the way it needs to happen or this place would be a zoo." She stepped closer. "He's not going to be the alpha of the biggest clan in this town because he's the biggest and the baddest or he has the most money. He's the alpha because people respect him. Know him. Trust him. And they'll follow him. And *also* because he's the biggest, the baddest, and if you saw him in a fight, you'd probably piss yourself the way everyone else does. *That* is who took me to Las Vegas. *That* is who walked me into Frank Di Stefano's house. *That* is who has my back."

She felt Alex pulling her back, wrapping his arms around her waist. Her back hit his chest and she took a deep breath.

Alex said, "You need to stop being stubborn about this, Caleb."

"I'm not going through another Missy, Alex. Not having a mob take over and ignore the law."

"You won't."

"I was brought here to do a job, not be the lackey of a council that expects me to follow commands while they do whatever the hell they want."

"Don't you get it?" Alex leaned forward over her shoulder. "I want the same thing. I know things need to change, but it's not going to happen if we're fighting each other."

"Alex—"

"We want the same thing, dammit."

"Then don't go behind my back, disrespect me, and treat me like an idiot."

Ted blinked. "How have we treated you like an idiot?"

"You think I didn't know Marcus Quinn was connected to the Di Stefano family? Did you think I wouldn't be looking that direction? That I wouldn't be looking into those payoff rumors?"

"No!" Ted shouted. "Because you didn't tell us!"

"You—" He pointed at Ted. "—are a doctor! And you—" He pointed at Alex. "—are a real estate developer! So no, I didn't tell the town doctor and real estate developer what I was doing on a murder investigation!"

Alex finally spoke. "We're not just that, and you know it. Like it or not, Chief, we're the ones who are going to have to pull this town into the twenty-first century, and we can't do that without being involved. People here need that. They still don't trust you, and I know you hate that, but it's true. They need to see Ted involved because she's the fiercest cat in her clan and she's all about protecting her own. They need to see me because I'm *me*. So let's stop fighting, go inside, eat hamburgers like we're friends, and talk after dinner."

Ted turned to him and said, "They need to see you because you're you?"

"Baby—"

"Could you get any more arrogant?"

"You know I can." He gave her a slow grin. "And according to you, I'm the biggest and the baddest—"

"Okay, let's go inside." She spun and walked toward the house, leaving Caleb and Alex to shake off their testosterone. Maybe they'd punch each other, and then she wouldn't have to do it. Until then, she needed a beer.

When they walked into the house ten minutes later, no one was bleeding, and the only scratches on her man were the ones she'd left there the night before. Belatedly, she noticed Caleb had more than a few similar scratches, and she had to hide her smile. Not being able to shift was a bitch. And Jena was going on seven months. She couldn't even imagine, though she supposed she'd have to try once she and Alex started—

Ted sucked in a breath as the whirl of predinner activity spun around her.

Too fast. Too. Damn. Fast.

"Hey." Alex slid down next to her and put an arm around her shoulders. "Grab me a beer?" He must have noticed her frozen expression. "What's wrong?"

"Nothing."

"Ted."

"Nothing. I'm fine. Just... processing."

He put a finger on her chin and tilted her face toward his. "All right?"

Her voice dropped to a whisper. "You trust me a lot."

"Yep."

"Trust *this* a lot. You and me."

His eyes were soft on hers. "Yeah."

"How?"

He paused. Thought. "Because we had it. And we lost it. And losing it was bad. I don't think either of us ever wants to go back there, Ted."

"No."

"No." He pressed his lips to her forehead and hugged her shoulders tighter as Ted heard sniffing. She looked up to see Jena watching her with fat tears rolling down her cheeks. Allie had a smile, but Ted could see the sadness behind it, so she decided to poke at Jena.

"You crying at Hallmark commercials, too?"

"Shut up, Ted." She threw a wet hand towel at the both of them. "Get up so the kids can set the table, or I'll make you guys do it."

"Yes, Mom."

Then Jena narrowed her eyes on Alex. "You and my husband sort things out?"

"I think so."

"Good."

"Meeting on Wednesday night," Alex said. "Here. No kids."

Jena said, "My mom and dad will cover."

"Allie," Ted asked, "you think you can find someone to watch yours?"

"My sister's in town," Allie said. "She's offered to give me a break; I just haven't taken it. So probably."

"Good," Alex said, glancing at Caleb as he came through the door with Jena's boy, Bear, hanging on his back. "We need to get on the same page. For everyone's sake."

Chapter Sixteen

Alex watched the steady flow of activity outside the trailer at the jobsite. Graders rumbled between the constant sound of trucks backing out and rolling in. Chris Avery stood at the top of the hill, pointing out something on a clipboard to Alex's new foreman, Levi Campbell. Alex had lured Ollie's cousin back to town after Marcus died, knowing the man was looking for something closer to home before his wife had their second son. He'd moved from Dallas the week before and was proving to be as much of an asset as Marcus had been, if not more. Everyone liked Marcus, but Levi, with his huge Campbell build and steady disposition, inspired confidence and not a little bit of fear.

Things were getting back on track for the resort, and already some of the families that had moved away were back. They had four new families in the McCann pack alone. The resort was months away from being finished, but the town was preparing. The Blackbird Diner had gotten a new paint job. Shirley's Mercantile had new flowers out in front. Lou Marquez had painted a fresh mural on the garage doors of his body shop on Main Street, and Alex had heard Harry Green, the owner of Desert Fountain Drug Store, talk about restoring the old lunch counter and soda fountain that used to do business before Alex was born.

It was happening. His town was coming back to life. And it'd keep happening if he had to hunt and kill Marcus Quinn's murderer himself.

Alex could kid himself that it was for his pack, but he knew, deep down, the driving need to keep the Springs safe was a purely selfish need.

It was home. He loved it here. Plus, Ted needed Cambio Springs to be happy. He needed Ted. And that was that.

His eyes narrowed on the man he suspected had put that in jeopardy.

Chris Avery.

He'd quietly checked around, but it appeared Avery was being cool. On the job early. Back home with his sister at night, helping her set up the house she'd just rented off Spring Street. He hadn't breathed another bigoted comment in Alex's presence, and according to the men he'd talked to, Avery had been nothing but professional.

He didn't joke around. Took his lunch in his own truck. He didn't go out for a beer with the guys. Didn't go to the Cave unless it was for lunch with Josie and the kids. Didn't hang anywhere in town, but had been seen heading toward the river on weekends. Meeting friends at the casino? Possibly. He'd have to have a word with Devin Moon and find out what all was going on over there. He'd been putting it off because Dev still pissed him off just by existing, but he figured, with Ted back in his bed, he could deal.

He got out of his head and back into the paperwork he'd been shuffling on his desk. He needed to set up a proper office in town. He had one in Palm Desert, but he could move it up here and let Cambio Springs be his base of operations in the desert. Sure, it was out of the way, but he didn't give a damn. Once the resort was in, he'd have a great place to wine and dine clients, and a showpiece of a property they could walk through. He'd set up his office in LA to be mostly self-sufficient. A few visits a month were all that was needed, unless a deal got complicated.

"Nicely done, McCann," he muttered as he compared the estimates on the roofing tile.

He heard the telltale rattle in the corner of his office just a moment before the diamondback slid from the shadows and the heat-on-asphalt shimmer filled the corner of the room. The snake shifted to a tall man with shaggy black hair and Quinn-blue eyes. He stretched out in the chair in front of Alex's desk in a movement so smooth he might have still been in natural form.

"Talking to yourself already, Alex?" the man said, naked as a jaybird and clearly not bothered by it. "I would have given you a few more years before senility crept in, but then you've always been kind of an old man."

A grin split Alex's face. "Sean Quinn."

"As you live and breathe, cuz."

They weren't cousins. It had been a private joke between them because Sean always figured Alex had a Quinn somewhere back in his family to be as devious as he was. Over time, "cuz" had stuck. Sean Quinn, of course, had not.

It had been five years since Alex had seen him, but he looked the same. Tall and lean, Sean had the typical Quinn build but had added more muscle. He traveled the world and purposefully put himself in situations where knowing how to take care of himself was important. Not all situations could be diffused with a Quinn's easy charm and quick wit. And growing up in the family he had made him a scrapper. Ollie may have had the bulk, but it had always been Sean Alex would pick to back him up in a fight.

"Why the hell are you here, and where are your clothes?"

Sean shrugged. "In my car. I didn't feel like announcing my presence quite yet."

"The old man know you're back?"

"If he checks his e-mail, he'll be expecting me."

"So that's about fifty-fifty, then."

"Yep."

Alex reached down and grabbed the pair of sweatpants he kept in a gym bag behind his desk. "Put some pants on so I don't go blind, asshole."

He grinned but caught the pants Alex threw. "You're not going to ask me why I'm in town?"

Sean stood and put on the sweats as Alex walked over and drew the blind on his office window. If Sean wanted to slip under the Cambio Springs radar for a bit, he wasn't going to argue.

"If I ask, will you take off?"

"Nope. But I might not give you an honest answer."

Typical Sean. He'd lie to you if it suited his mood, but he'd be upfront about it. Which had always made him oddly trustworthy. Alex knew when it came to the important stuff—the really important stuff—there was no one he could trust more.

He sat back behind his desk as Sean walked to the fridge, shivering as he passed in front of the window-mounted air conditioner.

"Too cold for you?"

"Just shifting chills. Give me a minute and some water."

He drank deep from the bottle he'd grabbed from the fridge, then sat back down again.

"So?" Alex said.

"So I'm back because my sister's a bitch and I missed you guys. Not necessarily in that order."

Somehow, Old Quinn's word had gotten back to his oldest grandson. Whether Sean was back to stay, Alex wouldn't even ask.

"Good to see you."

"I was in Thailand. Came back to the U.S. when Jena e-mailed me about Marcus."

"I'm sorry, man. I know you guys were close when you were young."

"I headed back to the Springs when Joe Russell showed up at my place in Laguna."

Alex leaned forward. "What the hell? Joe Smith was at your house?"

Sean blinked. "Keep forgetting he took Allie's name when they got married."

"He said it was for their kids."

"It was for himself because he knew he was a shithead and wanted to pretend to fit in with a decent family. See that worked out well."

"What was he doing at your place, Sean?"

He shrugged. "You all know I'm out of the country most of the time. That place is, at best, a crash pad. Joe was crashing. Why didn't anyone tell me he and Allie split?"

Sean looked pissed, but then he'd always been protective of Allie. They all had. Jena and Ted radiated tough. Allie was the kind of woman you wanted to take care of, even though Alex suspected the well of quiet strength she drew from was far deeper than she ever let on.

"He took off over dinner, Sean. Walked in and told her he didn't want to be married anymore. Left her and the kids, and we haven't seen or heard of him since you slithered in just now."

His friend sat back, eyes blinking in confusion. "What the hell?"

"I know."

"I knew he was an idiot, but I had no idea how much. Is Allie okay?"

"She will be. I think she's relieved, more than anything. Kids are having a harder time."

"They would be." Sean shook his head. "Was it Ollie who beat his ass?"

"What?"

"Ollie. I was never sure whether he'd beat Joe up or throw a party when they split—because honestly, cuz, you could see that one coming a mile away. So was it Ollie? Or you?"

"We didn't beat him up."

"Jena's new man?"

"As far as I know, Joe left the Springs as ugly as he came in, but no one I know laid a hand on him. By the time Allie told us, he was long gone."

Sean frowned. "He was beat up, Alex. *Beat up.* I think he'd been at my place at least a week, and he still had bruises on his face. Lip was cut up. Looked like someone had tried to wring his neck."

"When was this?"

"Few weeks… maybe a month. I don't know how long he was there exactly. And I didn't come straight here. I had some shit to do in the city, wanted to get stuff taken care of before I headed home."

"Where did Joe go?"

Sean shrugged. "Hell if I know. He was there one night after I showed up, and he spilled about leaving Allie. Then he took off. He knew how pissed I was. Went to the store for beer, and he was gone when I got back."

Alex put the timeline together in his head. A few weeks. Maybe a month…

"If Joe showed up at your place a month ago, he could have gotten those bruises from Marcus."

Sean lowered the water bottle he'd been about to drink from. "What?"

"Joe owed Marcus some money. They had words. Joe left Allie before Marcus died, but he might have been hanging around. Might have holed up somewhere… We need to get together with Caleb on this shit. I think he's been trying to track Joe."

"Are you saying the police think Joe had something to do with Marcus's death?"

It churned his gut, just like he knew it churned Sean's. Joe had been an asshole, but no one wanted to think that someone who'd been a friend could have done something so wrong. Taken the life of a good man with a family.

"It's possible, Sean."

"No."

"If he was desperate—"

"What would he be desperate about?" Sean was almost yelling. "He was already leaving town. So he owed Marcus money. It's not like Marcus was the Russian mob. He'd let that shit go, Alex. You know he would."

"I know he would. I'm not saying Marcus—"

"This was not about money. Not money between Joe and Marcus, anyway."

"Then what was it about, Sean? Because, honest to God, I've been wracking my brain to figure out why the hell someone would kill Marcus Quinn. The man was liked—no, loved—by most of the people around here. He was one of the few people in your family that everyone trusted. No offense."

"None taken. But Alex…"

They both sat silent for a few minutes, Sean sipping a water bottle, Alex tapping a pencil eraser on his desk.

Finally, Sean said, "I want to see Allie. The kids."

"They'll be home or at her dad's store. Not sure what her schedule is today."

"Has Ollie…?"

"Nope."

Sean shook his head. "Not surprising. Jena okay? I can never tell from her e-mails because she always talks about everyone else."

"Big as a house and her husband pisses me off regularly, but he's a good guy. Thinks the sun rises and sets on her and those boys. He's good."

"He really do that freaky shit about shifting into other people?"

"Not often, but he can."

"Weird. As. Hell." Then Sean's mouth tipped up in the corners. "And you're back in town permanently. You and Ted killed each other yet?"

"We're living together."

Sean burst into laughter.

Alex grinned. "Practically, anyway. We'll get the formalities taken care of soon enough."

"You don't drag your feet, cuz."

"No," he said quietly, the smile falling from his face. "I dragged my feet too long."

"You both did what you had to do." Sean's face was serious too. "Sucks. But you know I'm right."

"I do and I don't," he said. "Wasted seven years, man. Could have had her. We might have had our own kids by now. Seven years."

Sean looked at him in silence, then looked to the window and nodded toward it. "All this, Alex. What you're doing... It wouldn't be possible if you'd moved back with her."

"I know."

"So does she. And she knows it's important."

"I hope so."

Sean smiled. "She's Ted. She knows. Even if it pisses her off."

He nodded, not wanting to say more. "Good to have you back, Sean."

"Good to be back, cuz."

Alex grinned. "Now I know you're lying."

"Hey, handsome," Ted said as she sidled up to Alex at the bar. He'd called her and told her to grab Jena and Allie after all the kids were in bed, but he didn't tell her why. Just told her to meet him at the Cave. "Good to see you."

"You too." He pulled her to him for a quick kiss. Sean was hiding in the hallway, waiting to surprise the girls, but Ollie knew he was there.

The bear was behind the bar, trying very hard not to look at Allie, who was cute as a button in a pair of nice jeans and a bright yellow top. Alex was glad to see her dressed up a little. She'd hardly left the house in the past month.

And from what Alex could see, she was looking anywhere but at the big man standing behind the bar.

Interesting.

"How was work?" Ted asked.

"Hot. Dusty. Grading is almost done, though. So that's good news."

"Awesome," she said with a grin. "Your place or mine tonight?"

"Are you still the one with an actual house and a bedroom that doesn't rock?"

"Yes."

"Then your place it is."

"You're making breakfast."

"I can do that." He put his arm around her waist and pulled her between his legs, letting his lips meet hers in a long, lingering kiss. He heard a few whistles sound around the bar, but he didn't care. Everyone in town knew she was his by now. He was more than happy to give them a show.

"Alex," she said as she backed away. A flush stained her cheeks. "Seriously?"

"I waited seven years to be able to kiss you like that in front of God and everyone, Ted. I have the urge to indulge."

Jena was grinning at him over Ted's shoulder. "I love it. Love. It."

Ted said, "That's because you're a sappy pregnant woman."

"Yes, I am. And my husband's working tonight, so I have no one to kiss, and I'll have to live vicariously through you."

"Hey, Ollie." Alex heard Allie's voice on his other side. "How's it going? Been a while."

Ollie didn't look up from pulling a pint. "What are you drinking, Allie?"

"I…" Allie's eyes darted to Ollie, then away.

Alex tried not to listen. Tried to distract Jena and Ted too. But all of them kept glancing at Allie's pale face and Ollie's impassive expression. It was almost painful how uncomfortable it was. He saw Ollie take a deep breath, then look at the woman he'd been silently in love with for fifteen years.

"Allie girl," he said in a low voice, "what do you need?"

They were staring at each other, and Alex could have sworn every single eye in the bar was on them.

She was holding her breath; Ollie was holding her eyes.

Alex heard Jena whisper, "Come on…"

Then Sean Quinn jumped out from the hallway, wrapped his arms around Allie's waist, and bent to plant a kiss on her cheek.

"Miss me?"

Allie yelped and turned in his arms. "Sean?"

"Hey, honey." He dipped down and picked her up, swinging her around in an embrace as Jena and Ted ran to them both.

"Sean!"

"What are you doing here?" Jena asked with a laugh.

"Hell," he said, grinning. "I missed my girls."

Feminine laughter filled the air, and in it, Allie's laugh rang loudest. Alex glanced over his shoulder to see Ollie looking away, pulling another pint, but his jaw had gone granite. Alex looked at Sean, who was also glancing at Ollie with a devious expression on his face. He shook his head and looked away.

Only Sean Quinn would poke at a bear and think it was a game. Alex just hoped Sean knew what he was doing. Ollie was as mellow as they came. Until he wasn't. It took a lot, but when that bear let loose, even the biggest predators ran.

It was an hour later when Caleb Gilbert sauntered into the bar. He must have been off duty because he went behind the bar while Ollie was pulling another draft and grabbed a longneck from the case. Then he walked back and sat next to Alex, watching the girls as Sean spun them around the dance floor.

"So," Caleb said, "that's the prodigal friend?"

"Yep."

"Any particular reason he's back?"

"Other than to charm our women?" Alex asked.

Caleb smiled, clearly enjoying watching his wife dancing, even if she was a little less graceful spinning around the dance floor while carrying his baby.

"They love him," Caleb said.

"He's a lovable guy."

Caleb raised an eyebrow at him. "Jealous, McCann?"

"Nope." He glanced at Ollie. "*I'm* not."

Caleb caught his meaning. "Ah. Well, it'll be… interesting having him back."

Ollie didn't say anything, but Alex heard a glass come down on the bar and crack. Just as quickly, he heard it crash in the trashcan.

"Dang it, Ollie! I just ordered a whole bunch more of those glasses," Tracey shouted. "Take it easy, will you?"

Ollie's eyes leveled on Tracey. "This my bar?"

She said nothing, clearly still pissed and just as clearly not willing to say another word to him.

"Table six needs you," Ollie said. "Get to it."

Tracey stomped off, her order pad in one hand, still glaring at her boss.

Caleb muttered, "Not like him."

"I know," Alex said just as quietly.

"When that snaps—"

"Trust me. I know." Alex changed the subject. "Joe was at Sean's place in Laguna. A few weeks ago. Sean said he was beat up pretty bad."

"Oh?" Caleb glanced at Ollie. "Did Joe say who messed him up?"

"No. He took off pretty quick after Sean showed up."

"Joe Smith…" Caleb said. "I'm discovering a lot more about Joe Smith —or Russell, which is what he uses to check into cheap hotels—than I expected."

"Is that so?"

"Tomorrow night, McCann." Caleb downed the rest of his beer, then stood. "We'll get into it tomorrow night. I had a shit day. But I've had a cold beer, my woman is here and laughing, and I saw her eyeing my boots. That means I need to dance with her."

Alex watched Caleb swing over to Jena, and within minutes, his arms were wrapped around her and he was smiling like the cat who drank all the cream, then came back for seconds.

Speaking of cats…

Alex's eyes slid to Ted, and he decided Caleb Gilbert wasn't an idiot. A shit day could be solved by cold beer and dancing with a good woman. He had no idea what the boot thing was about, and he didn't want to know. He just finished his Coors and walked over to dance with Ted.

Chapter Seventeen

"Téa…"

"We need to get to Jena's."

"They can wait."

His mouth was hard on hers, but his hands were soft. He was holding her down as she straddled his hips, and both hands were already up her shirt. One hand trailed teasingly along her spine while the other slid along the hem of her jeans.

Tease. He could be *such* a tease. How had she forgotten that?

"We're going to be late," she panted.

"I haven't seen you all day."

"So come back here after."

A low growl rumbled in his throat, and she saw the gold light his eyes when he pulled his mouth away from hers.

"They don't get you until I do," he said in a low, hard voice.

Ted felt her hackles rise. "Cool it."

"Not until you understand me."

"Alex, do not pull the alpha wolf, macho bull—"

"It has nothing to do with being an alpha and everything to do with you being mine."

The hackles were done rising. They were up, and Ted felt like baring claws. But before she could open her mouth, he put a hand over it and leaned close, his eyes intent on hers.

"You're mine. And I'm yours. Understand this, baby; for the rest of our lives, we're going to have your family and my pack tugging at us. Your patients. My employees. We have responsibilities we can't escape. But you are my *mate*."

Seeing as he wasn't grunting or pounding his chest, Ted pulled his hand away, but she didn't speak. She cocked an expectant eyebrow at him as he continued.

"For the rest of our lives, there will be something or someone who needs our attention. Always. But this?" He pulled her closer and squeezed his hands at her hips. "This is priority. You have a busy day; I come to you and give you what you need. I have a busy day; you do the same. But you and me comes before everything else. Get that?"

"Alex, I—"

"I can hear the 'but' in your voice, Ted, but this is not something that's negotiable with me. We don't get that from each other; we drift. We drift; we lose our connection. That is not acceptable."

She took a deep breath and said, "There are—"

"Now you're just being ornery. You know I'm right." The growl got deeper. "If you're too stubborn—"

This time, it was Ted who clamped her hand over Alex's mouth. He didn't give an inch, snapping out and grabbing her ring finger between his teeth.

She wanted to scream because that shouldn't have been hot, but it definitely was.

Before he could argue with her, Ted said, "*Mortal danger.*"

He frowned and let go of her finger. "What?"

"Mortal danger, Alex. I'm the only doctor in town. If someone's having a heart attack, you're going to have to keep your pants on."

He narrowed his eyes, then gave her a shrug. "I'll give you mortal danger."

"Oh, that's so generous."

"But 'mortal danger' does not include one of your thousand and one cousins having a migraine."

"Fine."

"Or cramps."

"Fine."

"Or heartburn."

"Fine!" She shoved at his shoulders, wanting to get up. Still slightly pissed, even though the words he said—the conviction in them—hit her, and not in any shallow way. This man was in deep. As deep as she was. It was beautiful, and a little frightening.

"And if they interrupt us having sex, there better be massive blood loss."

She rolled her eyes. "Okay, I'm done with this conversation."

"Or there *will be* massive blood loss, if you catch my meaning."

"Wait, hold on..." Ted scrunched her face together and closed her eyes. "It's difficult. I think... because I speak rudimentary English..." She opened them and glared into his now-amused eyes. "I get it."

He smiled. "You're so damn cute when you're pissed. Want to make out on the couch before we go to Jena's?"

Since that was the question he led with as he walked through the door, she shouted, "Argh!"

Then she climbed off his lap and stomped to the door.

So Alex made out with her in the car.

"Let's lay things out," Caleb said.

Alex asked, "You sure you want to do this with everyone here?"

Ted glanced around the room. It wasn't just her, Caleb, and Alex. Jena was there, along with Sean, Allie, Willow, and Ollie, who was looming in a corner, obviously trying to ignore how close Sean and Allie were sitting.

Caleb looked around at the assembled crowd. "Is anything we say here going to leave this room?"

"No."

"Uh-uh."

"Hell, no."

Various grunts.

"Okay, then." Caleb turned back to the board where he'd pinned a bunch of pictures. Ted could spot a few crime scene photos, along with pictures of Marcus Quinn, Chris Avery, Frank Di Stefano, and a few people she didn't know. "Here are the players we have so far."

"You left someone out," Allie said quietly.

Caleb turned. "Allie—"

"I don't think he'd kill anyone," the small woman said quietly, "but he should be up there if he's a suspect. Or connected, Caleb. Don't try to spare my feelings on this."

Damn. Ted always forgot how tough Allie was. Even as a kid, she'd suck it up if she was hurt or sad. When things hurt the most, she just got really, really quiet. Her last baby, when Joe couldn't bother showing up at the hospital and Jena was holding her hand, had been delivered in almost complete silence. And there she was again. Allie's jaw was tight when Caleb pulled out a picture of Joe and stuck it on a blank corner of the board. Ted knew that's where it had been before Caleb pulled it down.

Damn.

Ted heard her pull a deep breath. Then she said, "Let's go."

Caleb turned to her. "Ted, why don't you start at the crime scene? Then we'll work backward."

"Fair enough." She rose and walked to the board. "First off, the crime scene wasn't where Marcus died. He was killed somewhere else. Then his body was dumped there. There wasn't enough blood at the scene. So somewhere out there is the real crime scene, but it's possible we'll never find it."

"So the coyotes?" Sean asked.

"Opportunistic. Just regular coyotes. His body was there, so they… did what they do. Luckily the pathologist in San Bernardino was able to get a clear cause of death. Shot in the back by a nine-millimeter. Prior to death, he'd been given a dose of Rohypnol. Roofies."

"He was drugged?" Jena asked.

"He would have been able to function, but he would have been much more vulnerable."

Ollie asked, "Does that mean we're looking for someone smaller than he was? Needed to even things out?"

Caleb said, "It's possible."

"Or is it someone who knew he wouldn't be able to shift if he took drugs?" Sean said.

Allie turned to him. "You can't shift if you take drugs?"

Sean grinned. "It's fucking adorable that you didn't know that. But yeah, it's almost impossible."

"Huh." Then she narrowed her eyes. "Wait, how do *you* know, Sean Quinn?"

"Don't worry, honey. I'm past my wild youth."

"I hope so."

"You're such a mom."

Ollie rumbled from the back, "Can we get back to Marcus getting killed?"

"Yes," Ted said. "The only other thing I'll add is that my initial estimate was right. The official report is that he died near one in the morning, but I'm still going to say it could have happened between midnight and two because reptile shifters have quirks in their body temperatures."

"Bigger window of opportunity," Willow said. "And you said he wasn't killed at the jobsite, so we have no idea where it actually happened. Was there anything at the scene…?"

Ted sat down and Caleb stood. "The thing of it is it's a construction site. There's all sorts of miscellaneous stuff that might be related but probably isn't. There was nothing on or near the body that would tie it to a location. I've asked for soil samples that were on his body to be tested, but that could take weeks."

Ted said, "More like months. Those things are slow."

"So," Alex finally spoke up, "the best chance of finding his murderer is not going to be forensics. We need to find out why someone would have wanted Marcus dead."

Sean shook his head. "He was a good guy. A genuinely good guy."

"He wasn't lily-white, Sean." Caleb crossed his arms.

"Did he have any outstanding warrants?"

"No."

"Then he's a choirboy in my family."

Ted tried to cover her smile, but she heard Alex chuckle.

Then he cleared his throat and said, "Marcus had ties with the Di Stefano family in Las Vegas. They're criminals, but it looks like their deal with Marcus was a straight—well, mostly straight—loan. He was paid in full, even had an ongoing legitimate business relationship with Cameron Di Stefano. As far as Ted and I could tell, any threat to Marcus was not coming from his background with Di Stefano. However, Frank did mention some concerns about the brother-in-law."

"Chris Avery." Caleb tapped on the picture. "Ollie?"

"He's quiet." Ollie shrugged a bit. "Doesn't come in much. When he does, he's with his sister or the kids."

"Wait." Ted held up a hand. "We almost came to blows about Alex and me looking into this case, and you'd already asked Ollie for help?"

"Ollie sees everything. So do the rest of the Campbells. Plus they keep their mouth shut unless you pry it out of them. Alex and I almost came to blows because you're my wife's best friend—a woman I care about—and he took you to a criminal's house for brunch."

Put like that, it didn't seem quite so irritating. It was almost sweet. Still...

Alex said, "Past is past. Ollie, what have you got on Avery? I know it's not just that."

"He doesn't like his sister moving here. At all. *Really* doesn't like the kids moving here. He's... weird around them."

Every body in the room tensed.

"Weird how?" Sean asked.

"Not like you're thinking. He's protective. Doesn't like them making friends here. Hear him talking about Las Vegas a lot. Almost like he's trying to get the kids on his side against their mom about moving back."

Willow asked, "Where's Josie on that?"

"Josie and the oldest girl are settled here or close to it. Boys are little. They're happy anywhere Mom is happy."

Allie said, "I think Kasey's already had a sleepover with my oldest niece."

"And I heard Bear mention her the other day," Jena added. "Says she's really nice. He's a grade behind her, but he noticed."

Ollie continued. "The girl knows the score, and she and her mom have obviously had the fur and feathers talk, since she's getting to that age. I'm not sure the younger boys even know about the shifting, to be honest."

"Does Avery?" Alex asked.

Ollie paused. "I can't say for sure."

Alex said, "Let's try to create a timeline. Who was the last person we know of to see Marcus Quinn?"

"You, as far as I can tell. And the other guys at work," Caleb said. "He left the site that day, and no one claims to have seen him until his body turned up."

"He was staying at his mom's?"

"Yeah, but his mom and his sister went to Indio that day to shop. Came home late. Marcus wasn't there. They're who they are, so it's not like they were concerned. His truck's in the drive. Wherever he went, he didn't drive himself."

"Anyone see him getting picked up?" Jena asked.

"Not that I've been able to find."

"I'll talk to Dad. See if anyone was flying that day and didn't think to mention it."

"So," Alex said, "sometime between six o'clock and midnight, Marcus Quinn left his mom's house with… someone. And that someone likely drugged him, shot him in the back somewhere, then left him at the jobsite where he worked. Didn't try to hide the body—"

"And there's plenty of places to do that out here," Sean said. "There's a million places to hide a body that no one would ever find."

Alex continued. "But he didn't. So whoever killed him wanted him found."

"A message?" Ollie asked.

"For who, though?" Ted tapped a finger on her chin. There was something she wasn't connecting that was bugging her. "He wasn't one of

Di Stefano's guys, even though there was a past relationship. This wouldn't hurt Frank, just piss him off. This must have had something to do with Marcus."

"He had life insurance," Willow said. "I talked to Josie. She mentioned it. Nothing big, but enough to pay off their house in Vegas. Give Josie a little money to start up again here."

Allie gasped. "No one thinks Josie—"

"No, honey." Sean grabbed her hand. "Josie adored Marcus. I think what Willow's implying is that if Marcus just disappeared, life insurance would take a while. Might be motive to dump his body if someone didn't want his family to wonder."

"Like a brother-in-law?" Ted asked, looking at Alex.

"That's what I'm thinking," Willow said. "He kills his brother-in-law and hides the body. It could be years before his sister can collect on that insurance. Or maybe he feels guilty and doesn't want her to wonder."

Ted saw Alex's mouth get tight.

"I don't like Avery," he said.

"Neither do the cops in Vegas." Caleb walked back to the board and pointed at Chris Avery's picture. "Avery doesn't know this—so this really, really can't leave the room—but they're investigating him for suspected payouts to code inspectors. It's been going on over a year, and according to my contact in Vegas, Marcus knew nothing about them."

"So why would he have been targeted?" Willow asked.

"He didn't know about the payouts when they were happening, but it's possible he knew about the investigation. Or suspected something was going on. The police hadn't contacted him, but he's not an idiot. And it's his brother-in-law. One of the detectives said it looked like Marcus might have been trying to take care of things before it became a problem with the police. Bring the projects up to—"

"He knew." Alex had shot up and was pacing, tugging a hand in his hair. "Shit! He knew about the payouts, Caleb."

"How do you know?" Caleb asked.

"We were delayed. Pissed me off, but Marcus said there were some environmental problems at another job he'd been working on. Something he had to go back and fix. Couldn't wait. Safety issue. Promised he'd be back on my job as soon as possible, but he was dead set on fixing this other thing, even though I was really, really mad about it."

Allie whispered, "He found out they weren't up to code."

"If it was a safety issue, he'd be the one to go fix it. Make sure things were okay, even if that meant pissing off a big customer like me."

Caleb asked, "When was this?"

"Couple months ago. Why didn't I think of it?"

Ted put her hand out and tugged on his arm until he was sitting again. "Because it could have been anything. It might not even be related."

"It's related."

"But there was no way of knowing anything like this was an issue, Alex. Give yourself a break."

Caleb said, "Is there any way you can find out what job that was?"

He nodded. "I'll ask his guys. They'd know."

"And so would Avery," Ollie said. "If Marcus was going back to fix the jobs that Avery had paid off, then Avery would know Marcus was on to him."

Sean nodded. "So why were they still working together?"

"Family?" Willow asked.

Jena shook her head. "I've gotten to know Josie a little. I don't think she'd back her brother against Marcus. She was *Marcus's wife*. If her husband wanted him out, I don't think Josie would have said a word."

"Agreed," Allie said. "So Marcus was keeping Avery in. Trying to avoid exposure?"

"It'd kill his reputation, something like that came out," Alex said. "And cost him a mint. Every permit he ever pulled would have been scrutinized. He might have lost his business."

"So he was trying to fix it without raising any alarms," Caleb said. "I still haven't figured out why he wouldn't have kicked Avery out. Or at least taken him off jobs. He was a fifty-fifty partner, but he could have just stuck him in the office."

There was silence in the room until Alex spoke.

"Avery had something on Marcus."

Sean asked, "But what? No skeletons that I've found except the ones his brother-in-law stacked up."

"Then we need to find out," Alex said.

Sean nodded. "I'm on it, cuz."

Allie's voice was soft, but Ted could hear her from across the room. "What about Joe?"

Alex's face got soft when he looked at her. "I don't think he's involved, Allie."

"But are you not looking at him because he's my husband?" Her mouth got tight. "Don't do that. You're not going to hurt my feelings, guys. I know he owed Marcus money. I knew he wasn't a nice person. If I'm really honest, he could be involved in something like this."

"Allie," Caleb said softly. "I really don't think Joe's involved directly, but I didn't ask you about drugs before. At the time, we didn't know Marcus had been drugged."

"So ask." Her chin came up.

"Did Joe take drugs?"

She was silent for a moment. "Define 'drugs.'"

Jena leaned toward her. "Allie—"

"I know he smoked pot. A lot of it sometimes. But there were other times... He didn't seem right. Especially toward the end."

"Could he have had roofies?" Caleb continued the soft questions. "They're blue now, but they used to be little white pills. Might not look like anything weird. You wouldn't think—"

"He had a baggie of... something. In the back of his sock drawer. I found it putting laundry away. He... he said they were antihistamines, but he didn't have allergies." She took a deep breath. "He never had allergies. I... I didn't know. Didn't ask."

Ted felt a chill settle over her. Felt Alex's arm go around her shoulders. What had Allie been living with for so many years? She glanced at Ollie in the corner and chanced a look in his eyes. She'd caught a glimpse of it before, but nothing like what he was holding in now.

Deep. Quiet. Rage.

Caleb knelt down in front of her. "You want to go in the other room for this? We don't need to do this with everyone—"

"No." Allie's hand was gripped in Sean's. "You have a question, ask it. I'm fine."

"You guys fought."

"Yeah."

"A lot?"

"Yeah."

"Because you thought he was cheating on you?"

"Maybe. I... I didn't... Toward the end, we didn't fight about that anymore."

She didn't have to say why. Ted knew Allie and Joe hadn't had sex in months. It was more than possible Joe was getting it somewhere else. Was he using a date rape drug to get it, though? Could Joe have drugged Marcus or been involved? Or was it all just a horrible coincidence?

"Was that bag with the pills still there after he left?"

"No," she whispered. "It was gone when I cleaned out his drawers."

Caleb took a deep breath. Sat back on his heels. "You knew him best. Do you think he could have drugged someone else? It's one thing to take something yourself, but it's another to use it on someone else."

"I don't know, Caleb."

"Did he... ever ask you to try some of that stuff with him?"

She looked close to tears, but she kept her chin up and kept talking. "I said no. The kids need... I never wanted to do that shit. Not even pot. He would make fun of me. Say I was stuck up. Thought I was too good for him. Shit like that. He could get mean."

Ted was disgusted. It was one thing to smoke a little pot, but to pressure your wife to do it when she obviously didn't want to, then try to make her feel like crap about *not* using drugs was more than messed up.

Then Caleb went somewhere Ted never would have expected.

"Sweetheart, you ever... Do you think Joe might have given you... anything? Ever?"

Allie paled and Willow sucked in an audible breath.

"Caleb?" Jena whispered.

He ignored Jena and kept looking at Allie. "Let's go in the other room with Jena, okay? We don't have to—"

"No." She sat up straighter and looked Caleb in the eye, but Ted could tell she was struggling for words. "There are some questions…" She took a deep breath. "There are some questions you don't let yourself ask when you're married to someone like Joe." She wasn't whispering, and Ted couldn't stop the surge of pride she felt for Allie's quiet strength. "Because asking them might make a lot of things a lie." Then she lost it, and her voice fell to a whisper. "Might make your whole life a lie."

Ted heard the slam in the corner. Her eyes flew there just in time to see Ollie disappearing out the back door, a massive hole in the wall where he must have driven a fist in. Alex flew out the door a few minutes later, following his friend into the night.

Chapter Eighteen

Alex tore off his clothes the minute he got out the door. The shift took him and he fell to all fours, nose lifted until he could track the bear's scent. Thick muscle rippled under the heavy fur of his wolf as he tore into the darkness. Dry scrub crushed under his paws. The night air called him as he lifted up his head and howled.

Ollie would know he was giving chase.

People underestimated bears because they tended to keep to themselves. But Ollie's bear could run as fast as Alex in wolf form. And he was a hell of a lot bigger and stronger. Shifters tended to be a little bigger than their full animal counterparts, and Alex guessed Ollie's bear weighed nearly six hundred pounds.

And he was enraged.

Part of him was tempted to let Ollie run it out of his system. But if his friend lost focus and hurt someone, he'd never forgive himself. Alex could hear him running past the springs and into the canyon. The large shadow looming on the canyon walls as the waning moon lit the night. He moved silently, listening for the deep huffs of grizzly breath.

He caught a glimpse of Ollie moving in the darkness.

The bear had slowed his pace, probably exhausting himself with the hard run from Jena's house. He could run fast, but not for long. Alex would always be able to catch him. He halted when he saw Ollie's hulking form pacing back and forth at the canyon wall. The grizzly huffed out his breath, and a low groan echoed through the canyon. The wolf pushed down the urge to howl and watched.

Then he bit back a growl when Ollie stopped pacing and ran straight into an outcropping of rock, crashing his shoulder into the sandstone, causing a minor landslide as chunks of rock showered down on his fur.

The bear was so angry he was hurting himself.

The wolf circled on silent pads until he was behind him. A low growl simmered in his throat a moment before he ran to the grizzly, leapt on its back, and sank his teeth into the thick hide.

The bear roared and reared up, throwing the wolf into the rocks. Alex scrambled to his feet and faced his friend, but there was no recognition in the animal's eyes.

Ollie turned and lumbered straight for him, his lip curling and a rumble growing in his chest.

Alex turned toward the dark canyon and ran.

He darted through the rocks with Ollie at his heels. Back and forth, leading him away from any areas where a human or shifter might wander when they ran at night. Hard at the chase, the grizzly followed, totally focused on the wolf who had attacked him. A frustrated roar echoed in the night, and Alex knew he was getting tired.

Not tired enough.

Alex came to a clearing surrounded by cottonwoods and hid in the trees, then watched as the bear entered the clearing, huffing out puffs of breath in the cold night. He circled, scenting the air a moment before Alex burst out, leaping straight at Ollie's flank and jumping on his back again. When he bit, he tasted blood. Ollie reared up and threw him off. Alex quickly dodged the paw that could break his back with one swipe. The grizzly's anguished roar was deafening.

They fought until the moon was high. Alex darting in to bite at Ollie's legs, the bear trying to grab the wolf in his deadly arms and landing excruciating blows to his legs. Ollie was stronger without question, but Alex was fast and focused. He could outlast Ollie, and he wasn't blinded by anger. But Ollie needed a fight, so Alex gave him one, until both animals were bleeding.

After a while, the bear sat, its giant chest heaving in the night. Then it blinked and Alex saw his friend reemerge from the ursine rage.

The bear shook his head, then shifted, and the giant man lay back in the dust, staring into the night.

"Fuck," he groaned. "Your teeth hurt like hell."

Alex shifted right after him. "I'm surprised you didn't break my leg."

He sat with his back against a rock, watching Ollie. Making sure the anger had burned down to something he could control.

"You okay?"

"No, I'm not fucking okay, Alex."

"You going to kill anything?"

"Other than Joe fucking Russell when I get my hands on him?"

"Your mom hear you use language like that, Campbell?"

Ollie said nothing, just raised a hand and flipped him off. Alex grinned through the pain.

"I forget how strong you are," he said on a grunt, stretching out his legs and rubbing his knee. "When was the last time we had to do this?"

Ollie's voice got quiet. "When Loralie was born."

When Joe hadn't even shown up at the hospital.

"He's gone now."

"He better be because if he comes back, I'll kill him."

It wasn't said as a boast or a threat. Just a statement of fact. If Joe Russell stepped foot in Cambio Springs again, Oliver Campbell, pillar of the community, would kill him.

And Alex had not a doubt in his mind that this would happen.

"He gave her that shit, Alex."

"We don't know that."

"I do. Think back to high school. You ever think of trying anything with Allie?"

"No. I was always thinking about Ted."

"Pretend you're sixteen for a minute."

He thought back and realized that, yeah, he'd looked. Allie had a fantastic ass and curves for days. But Ollie was right. He'd never, ever have gone there. Not with Allie. Neither would Sean. None of them had, though Ollie had probably been in love with her even back then.

"No," Alex said. "You're right. None of us would have tried anything."

"Allison Smith was one of the sweetest, cutest girls at school. And not a single one of us would have gone there with her because that wasn't Allie. She was shy about boys. Always. Not in a bad way, just her own way. And two months after Joe Russell hooks up with her, he's gone there, hooked her in, and didn't let her go. He wanted it. She gave it to him. Now, think about sixteen-year-old Allie and tell me that doesn't sound off to you."

"Man, we have no idea what went on back then."

"Maybe I need to hunt him down and find out."

"Ollie—"

"I can do it, Alex. And I wouldn't have a problem finishing the job."

Alex fell silent and thought about the best way to get Ollie back on track. Joe might have been trash, but he didn't need to be dead. He just needed to be out of Allie's life. For good. And not in a way that made Ollie a murderer.

"You think Allie needs you off hunting her ex or around her, helping her and the kids out?"

"I think I can't be around the woman and think straight, so maybe I need to be gone for a while."

Ollie didn't need to be gone. He just didn't know what to do with the emotion he was feeling. Because despite the fact that Alex was in love with Ted, Allie was family. And what Alex felt was rage, confusion, and guilt for not seeing things that were right in front of him for years. He couldn't even imagine what Ollie felt.

"You need to be here for her, Ollie. Get a grip on it. Be there for the kids. I know Kevin spends a lot of time with you. What would it do to him if you left town right now?"

"Fuck you, Alex."

"Fine. Whatever. But you know I'm right. Get it under control and do what you need to do. What you *don't* need to do is go hunting right now."

"Do you think he had a hand in Marcus's death?"

"I think…" All of a sudden, it clicked into place. "I think he spent a lot of time at casinos."

"So?"

"And so does Chris Avery."

"Almost every weekend." Ollie sat up. "You said Avery was on a job at the river when Marcus was killed?"

"Yeah."

Ollie fell silent for a moment. "Find Joe. Find out if he knows Avery. And do not tell me where he is if you want him to be breathing."

"Did he look as bad as you?"

Ted was kneeling by him as he sat on the couch, wrapping the knee that Ollie had wrenched. Shifting had pulled the bones back into place, but the muscles were still swollen. And his face was still cut up. He also had a few gashes on his side from Ollie's claws, but they weren't serious and were already healing.

"I think he looks worse, but he feels better." He flinched a little when she tightened the bandage. Then she grabbed the bag of ice and plopped it on his knee.

"Keep it on there. Even if it aches."

"Yes, doctor."

The corner of her mouth turned up. "Be a good patient, and we'll play a fun game of doctor when that knee's healed."

"You know, I'm really not all that injured."

She leaned down and let her lips brush his as she whispered, "You're going to need to be at one hundred percent for this game, wolf."

"Understood." He stole a quick kiss before she stood and held out her hand.

"Come on. Bed. We've both got work tomorrow, so we need some rest."

"Right." He managed to get up while still keeping the ice on his knee. By morning, the swelling would be mostly better, but it would be sore for a few days. No one knew why bones healed so quickly but muscles didn't.

Ted speculated that it had something to do with their skeletal systems being more fluid than their musculature, but he had no idea what the actual science was. No one did.

She lay down in bed and pulled down the covers. "How was Ollie when you left?"

"Pissed off but under control."

"Hurt," she said quietly.

"What?"

"He hurts for her." She curled into his side, and his arm came around her shoulders. "That man would take twice her pain if it would spare her any. And he can't. He hurts for her."

"Yeah," he whispered, gathering her close. "That's what you do for someone you love, Téa."

"I want Allie to understand that."

"Has to be in her own time."

She yawned and he felt her exhaustion in his bones.

"Sleep."

"Night, *querido*. Love you."

Alex smiled. He felt that in his bones too.

The next day, Alex took off at lunch to meet Devin Moon at the casino restaurant on the river. The hard sound of slot machines hit him as soon as he opened the door.

Yep. He hated that sound.

Still, the steak house was pretty good, and Dev was already there, gulping down a cup of coffee, his jacket hanging on the pole by the door.

"McCann."

"Moon."

They eyed each other for a moment. Then the waitress came over and Alex ordered a coffee too. It was starting to get cold, even when the sun was out.

"I hear you and Ted are back together," Dev said.

"Yep."

A smile twisted the corner of the man's face. If it were anyone but his woman, Alex would have no problem with Devin Moon. He knew the town's secrets, like many of the tribal elders on the Colorado River, but he kept them. He was a sheriff's deputy and good at his job. Trustworthy. He was a good man.

It hadn't stopped Alex from doing everything in his power to step on him when Dev had tried for a relationship with Ted.

"No one else ever stood a chance with her," Dev muttered.

"Nope."

"You're an asshole, McCann."

"Only to people trying to take what's mine. Other than that, I've got no problem with you."

"Ted let you get away with that possessive bullshit?"

"She may not like it, but she gets it."

"Yeah." Dev nodded. "If we're done braiding hair, why don't you tell me why you wanted lunch?"

He opened his menu and glanced at it as the waitress came by to get his drink order.

Coffee. He couldn't decide about the food.

"Chris Avery. You know him?"

Dev narrowed his eyes. "Know I checked him out when I started seeing his ass in this casino every other weekend."

"His company did the land leveling on the addition to the tribal offices. He oversaw the job."

Dev nodded.

"He was also Marcus Quinn's brother-in-law. Fifty percent partner in business with him."

"I hadn't put it together, but okay." Dev sipped his coffee. "This guy seems like a weasel to me, but you think he had something to do with Marcus's murder?"

"Don't know. Trying to figure out how much he knew about us."

"About...?"

"Yeah." Alex leaned forward. "His sister says she hasn't shared. Doesn't think he should know. But if there were guys at your site who knew—and knew he and Marcus were family—they might not have been as discreet as they normally are, you know?"

"Yeah." Dev sat back in the booth. "I'll ask around."

"It'd be appreciated."

Dev narrowed his eyes and watched as the waitress set the mug down in front of Alex. He took a sip, then set it down to cool.

"He still hangs out around here," Alex said.

"Yeah, I see him around."

"Anything... notable?"

"The people Avery hangs with now are not the most wholesome, but they're not criminal, either. If that's what you're wondering. They're also exclusively female, if you catch my meaning."

"Who does he hang with?"

Devin shrugged. "No professionals. But he has a type, and it's not far from it."

"The man dresses like a Mormon missionary."

"Trust me when I say he does not act that way."

Alex paused to try the coffee again. Still too hot. "You ever see Chris Avery hanging out with Joe Smith?"

"Allie's Joe?"

"Not Allie's Joe anymore. He's gone."

Dev let out a breath. "Thank fuck for that. She's a good woman. Doesn't deserve that shit."

"You ever see Joe and Avery together?"

Dev frowned. "Yeah. Didn't even think about it until you asked, but they did hang for a while. When Avery was working that job down here, Joe got friendly with some of his crew. You know how he could be. Joe could make friends with anyone if he wanted to. I saw them hanging out. Laughing it up a few times around here. Joe liked to gamble."

"Trust me. I know."

Tried the coffee again. Finally. Drinkable. He let the caffeine roll through him.

Dev leaned forward and said in a lower voice, "Are you telling me Joe had something to do with Marcus?"

Alex knew he would hate that for Allie's sake because he was a good guy. And Dev wouldn't think twice about handing Joe over to the council in the Springs. Despite his badge, he understood how things worked. Alex suspected for some things Devin worked just the same.

"I don't know. Can you ask around? See if anyone in that crowd has heard from him lately? He was in Orange County a while back, but he doesn't know anyone down there well enough to crash for long. And he doesn't have much money, unless he's getting it from alternative sources. I'm asking around. Caleb is too. We need to find him. Have a few questions about him and Avery."

"And Marcus?"

"It might have something to do with that. If you want more, call Caleb."

"Got it."

Looking at Devin, Alex expected Caleb would be getting a call soon.

"And Dev, if Ollie Campbell comes around looking for Joe, do not give him any information."

Dev raised an eyebrow. "You going to give me a reason that I should hold that back from someone I consider a friend?"

"Because I consider him a friend too. And if you're his friend, you want to avoid giving him any information about Joe Smith."

Dev locked eyes with him for a moment, read the situation like Alex knew he would, and said no more. He nodded and looked down at the menu.

"You actually going to sit here and eat with me, McCann?"

"No, I'm going to get a prime rib sandwich to go and head back to work."

"Counter's that way." Dev nodded toward it. "I'll call you or Caleb if I have anything."

And that was that. He and Devin Moon were never going to be best friends, but he figured they'd be okay.

By the time he got back out to his truck, sandwich packed into a to-go container, Alex was ready to go home. He'd had an early morning. The groundwork on the resort was a day or two from done, and he ached from the fight with Ollie. He wanted to go to Ted's place, eat lunch, and fall asleep. If he was lucky, she'd wake him with something sweet when she got home.

He felt his phone buzz in his pocket and closed his eyes. He knew—just knew—whoever was texting him was going to mess up his perfect plans for this afternoon. He pulled out the phone anyway.

Hopkin's Ravine. Pack meeting. Midnight.

The text from his father raised the hairs on the back of Alex's neck.

He texted back, *I'll be there.*

Chapter Nineteen

Ted finished the exam and smiled at Kasey Quinn. "You're all set."

"Thanks, Dr. Vasquez."

"You're welcome. Do I pass?"

"Yeah." The girl blushed slightly. "I like your games out in the waiting room."

Josie Quinn had brought the kids in for a routine physical at Ted's recommendation. They were due for one, and if she was going to be their new doctor, she wanted to meet the kids so they were comfortable with her before they got sick.

"Your brothers are probably messing everything up out there, huh?"

"Probably."

"You going to have to clean it up?"

"Nah." She shook her head. "I'll make them do it. If I don't, they'll just do it again."

Ted smiled. Josie's oldest could have walked into town with a total stranger and Ted would have known she was a Quinn. She had the same dark hair and light eyes as Sean, and she was going to be tall. She was still young, but signs of early development were there. She'd be sure to talk to Josie because Kasey could shift sooner than expected. And when that shift might be into a venomous snake, you had to be careful. Young snakes had more potent venom than older ones and tended to strike out if they were panicked.

"Do you have any questions?"

"I think I'm okay."

"You sure?"

Kasey blinked. "Is something wrong?"

"No." Ted sat on her stool so she was eye to eye with the girl. "It's just that I'm your doctor, I'm a girl, and I'm also a shifter. So you don't have to have any secrets with me. I have been through it all."

That got her a smile, so Ted continued.

"I know it's got to be tough losing your dad." Kasey's tears welled up immediately, and Ted reached for a tissue on the desk behind her. "I lost mine when I was grown up, and it still hurt. So much. And your mom seems pretty awesome to me—I can tell you guys are close—but she's not a shifter. And your dad is gone. So I just want you to know if you ever have any questions about what your first shift might be like, or other things that are happening with your body as you get older, you can always ask me. Okay?"

The girl nodded quickly. "Thanks."

"Promise me you'll ask me? If you get nervous about something? Or even just curious."

"I promise, Dr. Vasquez."

"Thanks, Kasey." She squeezed her hand and gave the girl another tissue. "So think about it. Is there anything you're curious about now? Or worried about?"

"Well…"

Ted was glad she'd asked because there was obviously something on the girl's mind.

"There are no silly questions, okay?"

"Is there any way to know what I'll shift into?"

"Nope." Ted frowned. "And every kid wonders. I did. But there's no way of knowing. It's most common to shift into something the same or similar to your parents. So it's very likely you'll shift into a snake, but there's no way of knowing what kind."

"What kind was my dad?"

"King snake." Ted grinned. "I saw him a couple times. Awesome. He was really cool-looking."

A hesitant smile tilted the corner of her mouth. "Yeah? When he told me, I kind of wished I was going to be a cat or a bird or something. Snakes just seem so... weird."

"No way. Reptile shifters are some of the most interesting shifters in the Springs. Some of the strongest predators and the smartest. I'm not one, but from talking with patients, I'd say reptiles have the strongest instincts in animal form. Combine that with your human intelligence. That's way cool."

"Will I still be me?"

"How do you mean?"

"Would I ever... bite someone without meaning to? My brothers or something?" The girl was getting upset. Ted could tell she'd been worried about this, and she was doubly glad Josie had brought in her daughter.

"That's a really good question, Kasey." Ted spoke in her most soothing kid-doctor voice. "I'm glad you asked me."

"I don't want to hurt anyone."

"It's very unlikely you will. And I'll make sure to talk with your mom. You *could* bite someone if you got scared. Especially when you first start shifting. But after a little while, you'll adapt and you'll start to recognize the signs. You'll be able to tell when you need to shift—like at the full moon—and when you just kind of *want* to. And you'll learn to control it. That way you can make sure you're in a place where you feel safe."

"Are you sure?"

"I'm sure. In fact, reptile shifters tend to catch on to those changes more quickly than other shifters. Maybe because your natural form is so different from your human one. You recognize the signs earlier."

"I... When I wake up sometimes, I feel these little pins and needles in my legs. Kind of like when your arm falls asleep. But all over. I've never had that before. Is... is that one of the signs?"

Oh yes. This girl was not far off from her first shift. Ted nodded calmly. "It is. So you'll probably shift in the next year or so. Are the tingles painful?"

The girl's face had paled, but she answered, "No. Just kind of itchy."

"Totally normal."

"Will you talk to my mom?"

"Mm-hmm."

"And there's no way of knowing what I'll change to?"

Ted smiled. "Sorry."

Kasey sighed. "Darn."

She leaned forward and tucked a curl of Kasey's dark hair behind her ear. "I bet it'll be something really cool."

"Snakes are scary. Not cool."

"They're totally cool."

Kasey finally smiled again. "You're kind of weird, Dr. Vasquez."

"I am. Thanks for hanging out with me anyway."

She giggled, then stood and got her backpack before she turned back one last time. "You'll talk to my mom? Make sure she knows everything so I can't hurt anyone?"

"I'll call her this afternoon, okay?"

Kasey nodded, and a little of the fear lifted from her eyes. "Thanks."

Ted walked Kasey out to the waiting room and caught Josie's eye. She gave her the "call me" sign and then waved at the two younger boys as they left the office. Kasey had been her last appointment of the day, so she trudged back to the office and started her charts, wishing she could curl up and take a nap. Or shift and hunt something small and tasty.

Her cat had been restless all day. It wanted Alex. They hadn't slept apart from each other since they'd come back from Las Vegas. In fact, it was starting to seem a little ridiculous that he even kept the trailer. Smiling, she decided to talk to him about moving in that night. There was no denying they were together now. Even her mother was only throwing up token objections. She knew it was useless to argue when Ted had her mind made up.

Speaking of her mother…

"Teodora?"

Lena Vasquez only ever knocked out of politeness when Ted was at work, no matter how many times she'd tried to explain HIPAA. Luckily, she didn't come to Ted's office often, and she had the manners to never intrude on exam rooms. Ted's office, on the other hand…

Lena walked in. "Hello, *mija*."

"Hey, Mom."

"Is your work done today?"

"Last appointment just left." She waved to her computer. "You're only interrupting paperwork. What's up?"

Lena sat down. "Has Alex called you?"

Ted blinked. "Uh… no."

Why was her mother asking about Alex? So far, her attitude toward her daughter's renewed relationship with Alex McCann was to pretend as if it didn't exist. Ted figured her mom would come around sometime after she and Alex started giving her grandchildren.

"What's going on?"

Lena actually looked nervous. Which made Ted nervous. Because Lena didn't really get nervous. She may have not been in the Elder's seat, but everyone in the clan knew her mother ran it. Technically, it was her Aunt Paula and her Grandfather Gabriel who ran the cat clan of Cambio Springs. They did have the final say, but the day-to-day headaches were sorted out by her mother. She was the most dominant female of her generation, and no one had challenged her authority once she'd reached adulthood.

So her mom being nervous made Ted doubly so.

"What's going on, Mom?"

"I heard some of the teachers talking at work today. McCanns. There's a pack meeting tonight."

"Alex didn't tell me, but then, I haven't seen him today. We've both been working."

"It sounded serious."

She tried not to react, but she was worried and a little pissed off. Her mother didn't lie and didn't exaggerate. So if she said it was serious, it was serious. Alex hadn't bothered to call or even leave a message all day, and he usually did. Which meant he was avoiding her.

"Why did you think it was serious?"

"Those girls were throwing off scent like a fight was coming. They were nervous about it. The wolves aren't like that about most pack meetings."

"I don't know anything about it."

Lena looked annoyed. "He doesn't tell you these things, and he calls you his mate?"

"I don't know what he's thinking because I haven't talked to him today, *mamá*."

"It's disrespectful. To you and to your clan."

"It's nothing but a rumor at this point, and I refuse to overreact until I've talked to Alex."

There was a gleam in Lena's eyes that Ted couldn't interpret.

"You've grown with him, Teodora."

"Sorry?"

"You're more patient. Calmer. Not so quick to react to things. I'm... impressed."

Compliments from her mother were so rare that Ted had to catch her breath. "I *have* to be patient. I'm mated to a wolf."

"Are you mated? Truly?" Lena's head was cocked to the side. She wasn't antagonizing; she was truly curious, so Ted decided to be honest.

"He makes my lion curl up and purr. He always has."

"He soothes you."

"Yes."

"I never had that with your father."

The lump formed in her throat, just like it did whenever her mom talked about her dad.

"You did, *mamá*."

"Not in the same way. He wasn't like us."

Salvador Jimenez had been one hundred percent human but had considered Cambio Springs his home and its shifters his people. Because of her mother. Her dad had adored her mother. Her father had been the kind of man who didn't just put up with having a strong-willed wife; he reveled in it. He never attempted to curb her mother's dominance. Sal was a man's man, but more, he was *Lena's* man. He'd taken her name when he married her. Given their daughter the gift of that history.

Her dad, somewhat surprisingly, had always liked Alex, even when they were friends in high school.

Her mother had not.

"So we wait?" Lena asked.

"Only thing we can do. I don't know what's going through Alex's head. He's been busy. It might not be a big deal, so he forgot to mention it. Or it might be a big deal and he's trying to figure out how to manage me."

"Manage you?"

Ted smiled. "He tries."

"*Dios mio.* You're the one who wanted him. That's all I'm going to say."

"Did you hear who called it?"

"Alex's father."

So it was a big deal.

Her mother read her annoyed expression and said, "You're mated to an alpha wolf, *mija.* You're going to have to figure that out on your own. I tried to warn you. This was your choice."

"He's not the alpha, *mamá.*"

"He will be."

Ted's eyes met her mother's intense stare.

"*He will be*, Teodora. And maybe sooner than you think."

Alex didn't come to the house after work. He didn't call her. And she didn't call him. She called Ollie.

"I'm kicking myself, Ted. I don't know if the old man planned it this way or if it's just a coincidence. But I'm kicking myself for losing it the other night. I met him for coffee this morning, and that knee's not one hundred percent."

The knot twisted in her stomach.

"He didn't come home?" Ollie asked.

"No."

"Shit. He's probably trying to get his head around things. He didn't expect this."

"Is it what I think it is?"

Ollie was silent for a moment. "Yeah."

Her heart started to pound. "Ollie, where is it?"

"Do not go out there."

"Is it Hopkin's Ravine?"

"You go out there, and you screw him. You screw yourself. You screw this town. Do not go out there."

"If he gets hurt—"

"He's a wolf, sweetheart."

"I know that."

"He's a *wolf*."

Sitting down had become too difficult, so she stood and paced.

"I can't do this. I can't just sit here and do nothing while he's out there."

"You'll sit there and wait for him because this is something he has to do. And he can't have your help doing it."

"Ollie—"

"It's who he is, Ted. It's always been who he is. He's been preparing for this since he was fourteen years old. Do you understand me?"

Ted was silent because she couldn't wrap her brain around that knowledge. Cats didn't establish dominance the way wolves did. It wasn't ingrained in them the same way. It was political. Personal. Dominance could shift over time and often did.

But Alex had lived with the knowledge he might have to kill his own father since he'd been fourteen years old.

She prayed he wouldn't have to. Prayed the stubborn old man would yield so his son wasn't forced to do something that would haunt him. If Robert McCann had been older, he could have yielded the fight without damaging his pride. But Robert was still in the prime of his life; he wouldn't allow himself to yield without a hard fight.

"Ollie, this is because of me."

"No, Ted, this is because Alex's old man is kind of a bastard."

"Alex loves him."

His voice softened. "He loves you more."

"Ollie…"

"Are you going to go out there?"

She whispered, "No."

"Good kitty."

She didn't want to laugh, but she did.

"You want me to come over, sweetheart?"

"Not right now. If it gets bad, I'll call you."

"Want me to call Jena or Allie?"

"Maybe Allie."

"I'll call her."

Allie knew more about the pack than Ted did, but being a fox, she wasn't a full member. Allie would be able to calm her down. Then she realized it was already late and the kids would all be in bed.

"Ollie, can you watch the kids?"

"I'll take care of it and send her over. You just stay there. Don't leave the house."

"Okay."

"You promise?"

"I promise."

A half an hour later, a silent Allie came to the house and wrapped her arms around Ted as soon as the door opened. The tears Ted had been holding back pooled in her eyes.

"Inside," Allie urged. "Come on, *chica*. Hold it just a few more minutes. Let's get you behind closed doors."

Because Ted couldn't show weakness while her mate was battling for his life. And on a night like tonight, every eye in the desert could be watching.

Chapter Twenty

He didn't call Ted. He stared at his phone for a while, but he didn't call her. She'd be pissed, but he could handle her being pissed. What he couldn't handle was her being scared.

And she would be. Because she wasn't stupid.

Alex got out of the car and slammed the door, ignoring the quiet murmurs of the other wolves nearby and the rumble of thunder in the distance. The ravine was too soft to drive into, so they had to walk. Most did in human form. A few trotted past in fur. Alex wished they were gathering for one of the good reasons. A marriage. A new baby. But they weren't. And Alex could tell by the way everyone was walking and casting furtive glances at him. They all knew why they were there.

He'd been expecting something since Vegas. Since his father knew that Alex had claimed Ted in a permanent way. But he hadn't expected this. Not yet.

His knee groaned in protest as he walked over the uneven ground. He'd be more comfortable on four legs, but he didn't shift. Not yet. There would be things to say first.

Alex heard Jeremy approach.

"How's the knee?" he asked quietly.

"It'll be fine once I shift."

"You sure?"

"Yep."

Jeremy glanced at the sky. "Is it going to rain on us?"

"Do I look like my sister?"

Jeremy wasn't officially his second because Alex wasn't officially the pack alpha. But the relationship was there. And if tonight went as he expected, that responsibility would shift from his uncle to the cousin standing next to him.

Willow was waiting for him on a rock near the edge of the ravine.

"I am so pissed at him I don't even know what to say."

He hooked an arm around his sister's neck and kissed her forehead. "I was surprised, but I shouldn't have been."

"This doesn't need to happen, Alex. Not now."

"I know. But it is."

"Why is he pushing this?"

Jeremy said, "You know why, Wil."

Alex's anger at his father only grew when he saw the tears in his sister's eyes. Willow rarely cried.

"He knows what this is doing to Mom, and he doesn't care."

He squeezed his hand on her shoulder, then let her go.

"Willow, we need to worry about the rain?"

"We've got a couple hours. And I don't smell any water in the ravine."

Willow and Jeremy fell behind him as he walked into the wide gorge in the middle of the desert. Hopkin's Ravine was a wide spot in a river that had shifted course sometime long before any people arrived. The walls were high, and heavy rock had tumbled into the sand below, pushed to the sides by sudden streams of water that still occasionally flashed during monsoon season. Winter rains could be just as dangerous.

Over time, the ravine had formed a natural amphitheater that the pack used for meetings. Most of the time, those meetings were to announce good news or settle the occasional dispute.

Not tonight.

The sand shifted under his feet as he walked into the ravine with Jeremy and Willow behind him. His pack watched him approach, but no one spoke. He took a seat, leaning against a boulder as he had so many times before. Small clutches watched him. Some human. Some wolf. Parents with teenagers. A few mated pairs, but only a few. McCann wolves were encouraged to look outside the pack for their mates, though a few were married to other shifters in different clans.

But none of them were the alpha.

His father stood next to his Uncle John at the top of the circle. His arms were crossed over his chest as he watched his children walk down. His uncle stood beside and a little behind his father, as always. Usually Fate balanced the two branches of the McCann family. The alpha came from one line. The water witch from another. But Fate hadn't been quite so balanced when it came to Robert McCann. He'd sired only two children. One was the future alpha. The other the most keen water witch in decades. Proving to most of the town that Fate liked Robert a hell of a lot more than anyone else did.

Some alphas faced challenges periodically. No one challenged his father.

"You ready?" Jeremy asked.

Would he ever be ready to challenge, fight, and possibly kill his father?

"Yeah, I'm ready."

Robert waited ten more minutes for everyone to settle, and still hardly a word was said. Then, with the half moon shining down on his steel-grey hair, he stepped forward and started talking, and the walls of the ravine carried his voice to every ear.

"Alex McCann, do you claim a woman as your mate?"

The old man wasn't wasting any time. Fine by him. Alex stepped forward and made a point not to yell.

"I do."

His father's eyes held his. "Who is your mate?"

"My mate is Teodora Vasquez."

A heavy silence fell over the ravine. He only heard the wind and his sister's desperate whisper, "Don't say it, Dad."

But Robert wasn't looking at his daughter.

"I do not allow this," he said to Alex.

In a blink, Alex's clothes ripped to shreds as he shifted and leapt at his father.

Thunder boomed closer as Robert met him in midair, his black wolf meeting Alex's silver-grey with a vicious snarl as the wolves around them howled.

He went for his father's throat, but Robert ducked his head and hit Alex with a ripping bite to his shoulder.

Alex faltered but didn't go down. He snapped his teeth in his father's muzzle, biting down until Robert was forced to let go of his hold.

They fell back, circling each other, tails held high and fangs bared.

Robert growled, blood dripping from his torn muzzle. Alex was silent. He didn't want this. He'd never choose this. But his father had.

And his father would lose.

The knee Alex had injured days ago still ached, but he ignored it, the surge of adrenaline pumping through his system as he felt the energy change around them. He didn't have to look to know that every pack member had shifted. Howls and yips sounded around him, and he heard the flap of wings overhead.

The birds had come to watch.

Robert lunged forward, his black pelt blending seamlessly into the shadows as he attacked his son. Alex dodged to the left, then circled around, trying to attack his opponent's neck from the side. Robert was too quick and twisted away, rolling—briefly exposing his vulnerable belly— before he was on his feet again.

But Alex was relentless.

He continued attacking, circling the older wolf, trying to wear him down.

The black wolf was smart and swift, but the raw power of the grey was starting to weaken him.

Alex drove forward, snarling as he met his father and they crashed together.

They pushed each other to standing, both wolves snapping at the other's neck, trying to topple the other to expose their belly.

Alex felt his father's teeth sink into the same wound on his shoulder. Then suddenly, the black wolf fell, throwing the grey off balance long enough for Robert to twist his jaws and sink his teeth into the knee his son was favoring.

The harsh yelp was involuntary, the first sound Alex had made. But as he twisted away from his father to stand on four paws, his mind focused.

The longer this went on, the more injuries both would sustain.

The longer this went on, the more dangerous it became.

He heard Willow's low howl behind him as he and his father paced in circles. He stopped. Crouched down. His father's bloody muzzle curled up, but his eyes were locked on his son's.

Finish it.

Alex snarled and lunged forward, rocking the black wolf from his feet, barking in his face and snapping his teeth around Robert's muzzle.

A lip tore beneath his jaws, and Alex tasted blood.

They rolled in the sand, black and grey spinning under the half moon as the McCann wolves howled around them.

His father bit again, going after the same wound he'd made in Alex's shoulder, but this time, the grey wolf clamped his jaws around his opponent's neck and threw him across the ravine.

Barking and snapping, he landed on the black wolf's flank before the older wolf could scramble to his feet. Alex leapt on his father, rolling him to his back as his jaws sank into his neck.

Robert twisted under him, his claws tearing at Alex's chest and belly, but he could not break free. Alex leaned forward, letting his jaws go slack only to grab more of his father's neck in his mouth, whipping his head back and forth. Until he felt the skin tear and the vulnerable windpipe beneath his teeth.

The black wolf stopped pawing. Alex could hear the raspy wet breaths as his father tried to suck in air. A dangerous bubbling cough.

Finally, the black wolf went limp beneath the grey.

Alex bit down harder, and his father's head fell to the ground.

It was finished.

Excited howls went up around him as wolves rushed to his side. He felt Jeremy's steady presence on his wounded left and his sister on his right.

Her teeth gave him an affectionate nip as he turned his back on the black wolf still bleeding in the sand.

His father was alive, but he'd need help to get out of the canyon. That was his uncle's job now, as the older wolves nosed around Robert's black body, some whimpering, some lying down beside him. But no one challenged Alex.

The raw energy poured through him as he trotted up the side of the ravine with the majority of the pack surrounding him. A wet wind whipped through his fur, bringing a dash of rain and the smell of creosote to his nose. Then the wind died down, and he ran.

There were excited yips and more playful nips at his back and tail. More than one younger wolf rolled over as he passed, baring their bellies as he ran.

Despite the pain in his shoulder, he needed to hunt.

They followed him, circling around in familiar patterns, playing with each other as Alex led them farther into the desert. He could hear the swift flutter of birds overhead. The occasional hoot or low growl as they passed other shifters in the night. The low slink of cats and the flutter of black wings. Creatures slithering away in the dark. A quiet rumble that told Alex the bears, as always, were watching quietly.

Cambio Springs had a new alpha, and by morning, everyone would know.

Alex rode the adrenaline as he scented a herd of mule deer in the distance, grazing on the lower slopes as the mountains grew colder. Jeremy went forward, scenting the herd a second behind Alex. A few quiet yips and barks, then the wolf pack bounded forward in formation, heading toward the rise of the hill and the prey beyond.

The storm clouds rolled over the moon, and everything went dark. Alex couldn't ignore the pained howls that still came from the ravine.

But his pack rushed around him, so he led them on the hunt.

Hours later, covered in his own blood, his father's, and the blood of the deer they'd feasted on, he went to her. Jeremy and Willow followed him to the edge of her territory, hanging back until they saw the mountain lion rise from the rock where she'd curled. She leapt toward the grey wolf, snarling at the others until his hackles rose and he curled up his lips.

She stopped and nosed at his neck. Then his shoulder. Checking him for injuries. As the cat bent her head to lap at the wound on his shoulder, he opened his mouth and bit down at the skin near her neck.

The lion froze.

A low rumble from her throat as he held her in a soft, firm hold. She didn't roll over, but she didn't twist away.

He heard the other wolves retreat.

As soon as they were at a distance, Alex shifted. Ted was only a second behind him, and his mouth was at her neck, kissing and licking the skin there, humbled by the gift of her submission in front of his wolves.

"Thank you."

"Are you okay?" She tried to push him away, tried to get to the wound on his shoulder, but he tugged her mouth to his.

"I'm fine," he growled against her lips.

"You're covered in blood."

"Need you. Now."

"Is this all yours?"

"No. Now, Téa."

They were both naked, and it didn't escape him that they were in her front yard. The night was alive with the sound of animals around them.

He didn't care.

Alex shoved her back, sweeping an arm under her back to make sure there was nothing that could hurt her. The pebbled walkway where they lay was far from luxurious, and his knee still ached, but he didn't care.

She held on to his neck, avoiding his shoulder, still trying to protest quietly.

"*Querido*, we need to get you inside."

"No."

He leaned down and bit into the side of her breast as she gasped his name. Her legs spread immediately, and he slid his hips between them. He brought his mouth down in a harsh kiss as he rocked against her.

"Are you ready?"

"Alex, we—"

He groaned and licked her neck. He was hard beyond anything he'd ever felt before. His skin burned as the scent of her arousal filled the air. He bit down on her neck, promising himself he'd go slower the second time. And the third.

"I need you," he growled in her ear. "Now."

He stroked his length between her thighs and felt it. Scented it. She was ready.

"Yes," she whispered a second before he drove in.

The lightning shock of their joining crashed through him. He rode her hard. Didn't feel the rain start to come down. Didn't feel the rocks at his arms or knees. Barely felt the bites she gave his neck or the licks at his shoulder. He felt her. The searing heat enveloped him. She wrapped her arms around his shoulders. Her legs around his hips. And she gripped the back of his hair as she gave herself over to it, shouting into the night when he thrust harder.

The wolf in him howled. Then he threw back his head and came in a rush a moment before the storm broke and the water poured down.

It was only in the shower hours later that Alex began to feel it. Pain. Anger. Exhaustion. And a weight of responsibility he'd tried to anticipate his whole life.

It was nothing to the reality.

His father was home by now, hopefully breathing easier. His mother would have called Dr. Anderson when he got home. Doc Anderson was ancient, but he was part of the tribes and he knew how to treat shifters.

He heard Ted on the phone when he stepped out of the shower.

"Uh-huh…"

The rain was still pouring down outside, and he'd heard the storm turn to hail once or twice, so he knew work at the jobsite would need to be canceled for the day.

Small blessings.

"Yeah. ... He's fine, Jeremy, but I heard the shower turn off, so I need to go. Thanks for calling."

Another pause. "I'll give him the message. ... Yeah. Tell Anderson to call me if there are any problems. I'm sure the old man won't want me there, but the doc will ignore him if he's in any danger."

Alex rubbed a towel over his head and checked his shoulder in the mirror. Damn, his dad had some strong teeth. His shoulder looked like hamburger. No wonder Ted had been alarmed. The edges of the wound were already beginning to heal, and the wound was clean. He didn't think there would be a scar, but you could never tell.

He scented something that smelled like chili cooking on the stove. Protein-rich food to help along the healing. He wasn't going to tell Ted he'd had a belly full of raw venison because her chili smelled way better.

His mouth turned up at the corner. Ted. Taking care of him. He was a lucky bastard.

He walked out and pulled on a pair of sweats, leaving his shirt off so his shoulder could have air. The lights were low in the living room. Ted had started a fire and left on a few lights in the kitchen. She was wearing an old flannel robe and standing at the stove. He came up and put his arms around her waist.

"Thank you, baby."

"I had it in the freezer. It should be hot soon."

"I love you."

She didn't say it back, but put her hand up to his jaw and pressed his cheek to hers. His stubble rasped along her smooth cheek, but she didn't pull away.

"Your dad will be okay."

"Good."

"Jeremy went over to check on him."

"Part of his job now."

"Your second?"

"Yeah."

She nodded. "Your female?"

"Willow."

"Good choice."

Because there were so few mated pairs in the pack, the female alpha was usually a close relative of the male. A sister or cousin was the most common. Willow was Alex's obvious choice, and he knew he could trust her to take care of the female half of the pack, even if she'd have to curb her more antisocial tendencies to do it.

Ted's voice was soft when she asked, "So it's done?"

"There were no challenges."

"You must have torn up your dad pretty bad."

He paused and laid his head on her shoulder; his arms got tighter around her.

"Yeah, I did."

She whispered, "I'm sorry you had to do that, *querido*."

"Me too."

She took a deep breath.

"I'm sorry I didn't call before, Téa."

"I know why you didn't."

"Still sorry."

She stirred the chili a little more. "And I'm sorry I couldn't be there."

"I'm glad you weren't."

Ted let out a soft, sniffly laugh. "Is it a wolf thing?"

"It's a wolf thing."

Then she put her hand to his cheek again and whispered, "I love my wolf."

"I love my lion."

His arms stayed around her, and they both fell silent as the rain pounded in the background.

There was nothing else to say.

Chapter Twenty-One

Ted tapped her fingernail against her cup of cold coffee. Silence blanketed the breakfast table, and not even the warm reassurance of Alex's thigh pressing into hers under the table could calm her nerves.

Breakfast could not have gone worse.

This was for a couple reasons.

One, Alex and his father were giving each other death glares.

Two, Alex's father and Ted's mother were giving each other death glares to end all other death glares.

Alex, thankfully, was immune to death glares.

Ted and her mother might have come to a tentative peace about her relationship with Alex, but Lena didn't like surprises. She'd consider this breakfast an ambush, but Ted had agreed with Alex that it was better to get the inevitable conversation out of the way.

"Well, this has been a ball of laughs," Alex said, "but since absolutely no one is eating, let's get down to the reason I asked you both over here."

"Without telling us," his father muttered.

"Has your health not recovered enough to sit down with a fellow clan leader, Robert?" Lena's voice was smoothly biting. "You're certainly welcome to get back to us when you're feeling up to it."

"*Mamá.*"

Lena turned hard eyes to her daughter as Ted felt the already chilly atmosphere in the room turn colder.

"Yes?"

"Lena," Alex said, "cut the crap and don't speak to my father like that again."

Ted's pulse spiked in instinctive anger as her mother's eyes flashed, but the hand he put on her thigh squeezed, just once, and she took a deep breath. They'd talked about this before. Planned how it would go. And now, after thirty minutes of silence, Alex was digging in.

Lena said, "You don't have the right to—"

"I do. And you know it." Alex held her eyes. "Has leadership in the cat clan shifted without my awareness?"

Ted was the one who replied, "No."

"Then I'm Alex McCann, the wolf alpha, speaking to a senior member of the cat clan," he said quietly. "You're not an Elder, and you've just insulted a member of my pack who is a guest in your daughter's home. So yes, Lena, I do have that right, unless you're looking for a challenge."

Ted saw the waves of fury pouring off her mother, but she knew Lena was stuck. She couldn't challenge Alex without a massive inter-clan incident, and no one wanted that. So she turned her attention to Ted.

"Teodora, you cannot be serious."

"Mom—"

"This? For you?" Lena curled her lip. "This disrespectful, *macho* wolf you could run circles around?"

Alex said nothing, letting Ted respond. "Yes, Mom. We've talked about this. You know my feelings. They have not changed in the last twenty-four hours."

"You could do so much better than him."

Ted heard Robert McCann growl, but she spoke over it. "Your idea of better is vastly different from mine. I've made my choice. Am I no longer welcome in my mother's house?"

"You should be the one stepping into leadership, not your cousin—"

"I don't want leadership. I have never wanted leadership. I'm a doctor. I need to be trustworthy to everyone in this town. And for that, I need to *not* be a leader in our clan. We've had this discussion over twenty times that I can count, and we've never agreed. So tell me now, am I no longer welcome in your home?"

Lena's eyes were ice cold, but she said, "Of course you're welcome."

"Wonderful. Don't insult guests in mine. Alex, could you pass me the cream?"

He released his hand from her thigh and reached across the table to hand her the pitcher.

"We're almost out," he said. "Want me to get more?"

"That would be great, thanks."

He rose and walked to the fridge to get the jug of milk while Ted tried to pretend her hands weren't shaking. At the last minute, he turned and winked at her behind their parents' backs.

"United front, baby. No matter what they throw at us."

She started drinking her cold coffee, looking for all the world like breakfast between a pissed-off cat and a pissed-off, injured wolf was something that happened regularly at her table.

Thinking about it, she figured it probably *would* be happening regularly, so she might as well get used to it.

Alex came back to the table and reached for the carafe, warming up her coffee before he handed her the small pitcher of milk.

"Lena? Dad? A warm up?"

Robert's voice was wary, but Ted could see the admiration in his eyes as he looked at his son.

"Yes," he said. "Thanks, Alex."

"None for me." Lena's voice was acid, but she'd backed off. Ted could feel it.

"Now," Alex started again, "we're here because…" He looked at her and smiled. "Well, we're here."

Ted couldn't help but smile back. He was just too damn charming when he put his mind to it.

He let her eyes go and continued. "Ted and I are making plans to have a life together. This shouldn't be a surprise to anyone. We asked you both here for two reasons. One, we don't want awkward Christmases." Lena curled her lip, but Alex ignored her. "And two, while you two both think this is going to cause problems, Ted and I think this might be a way to solve some."

Lena arched an eyebrow. "Do tell."

Ted said, "Despite the recent change in the wolf clan, you two both represent your packs. Robert, you're on the Elders' Council. Mom, you will be. The wolves and the cats have always been the two most powerful clans in Cambio Springs. This should be an alliance, not a source of contention."

"Like we would bow to the wolves on anything," Lena said.

"Woman, have we ever asked you to bow?" Robert snarled. "We have no interest in your grudges and political bullshit. That's not how our kind work. So you do your thing, and we do ours. You think I'm any more pleased about them being together than you are?"

"On that, we are in total agreement."

Ted heard the low growl from Alex, but the old man kept speaking.

"If you think that, you'd be wrong. I may not be pleased my son chose your daughter, Lena, but I'm damn pleased he knows his own mind to stand up for her when he was pushed. And I'm pleased as hell your daughter doesn't put up with your crap, either. I may not like her for my boy, but I can respect that."

"Enough, Dad."

"I don't like it," Robert said. "Or her. But you fought for her. Bled for the right to have her. And you earned that respect."

Ted found herself warming to Alex's dad. She was fine with him not liking her. She could even respect it because he clearly had his reasons, even though she didn't agree. After a while, he'd warm up. Or he could just stay being an ornery bastard. If Alex could put up with it, she could too.

Her mother, on the other hand, was being pissy because she didn't like being bested. She'd return to ignoring Alex and Ted when she got over it.

"This—" She waved between them. "—is a perfect example of what we should avoid. Petty fighting should be beneath both of our clans. If we have an issue, we discuss it. Come to a consensus privately so we provide clear leadership for the town in public."

That shut up both of them because Ted saw they were both considering it.

The wolves didn't like arguing. Thought it made them look weak to have to bicker about matters on a council they thought they ran. But it was necessary at times. All council decisions had to be unanimous. And most of the bickering was between the cats and the wolves.

The cats, on the other hand, had always been the second strongest, and they knew it. It was partly by design and partly their nature. Most cat shifters had little interest in any matters but those that affected their immediate family. Their loyalty was deep but only extended to blood relatives. And frankly, Ted knew most had no interest in the real responsibilities of town leadership.

In forming an alliance, the cats got equal footing in decisions and the wolves avoided public bickering. It could be a win for both clans if Alex and Ted worked things right.

Alex said, "Think about it. Talk it over with your Elders, Lena. I can speak for the wolves that we're open to a private alliance. With Ted and me together, the other clans will suspect it, but they won't say anything."

"And the first topic for discussion is the mayor's position," Robert said.

Lena agreed immediately. "Yes. And Ted, I know you don't—"

"Not going to happen," Ted said with a groan. "Mom, seriously? I told you I don't want to be in leadership."

Lena waved a hand. "The mayor's position is in name only. You would just implement what the Elders' Council wants."

"No," Alex said quietly. "That needs to change."

Robert asked, "Why?"

"Because the cats and the wolves already have enough power, Dad. The mayor needs to come from one of the other clans. And he or she needs to not be a rubber stamp. Look what happened with Mayor Matt."

"Cat." Robert sneered.

"Matt Marquez was a decent guy." Alex continued. "He got frustrated with the lack of respect the council gave him, and that was part of the reason—"

"His wife went nuts and killed people?" Robert broke in. "I don't think anyone can take that blame but Missy Marquez."

Alex leaned forward. "We don't have to run everything. The town won't fall apart if we share the load."

Robert didn't have any response to that.

"I'm going to have a resort to run along with managing the business in LA. I don't have time to micromanage. That's not the kind of leader I'm going to be. You know this. You've always known this."

After a few more moments of silence, Robert sighed and said, "Not a Quinn."

Lena sipped her coffee and said, "A bear would be ideal. The Campbells are steady and involved in the community. The birds are even more insular than the cats and they have a tendency to wander. A bear would provide enough of a counterweight to our representatives on the council to make the other clans feel as if they have a say. Everyone trusts them."

Ted said, "Or we could—I don't know—give democracy a try and let people vote on it."

"Fine," Alex said. "But I'll be instructing my clan that none of them are going to run." He looked at Lena.

She said, "I'll speak to my father and my aunt."

"And I'll speak to Old Quinn," Robert said. "Need to talk to him about something else anyway."

"Will Quinn be a problem?" Ted asked.

"I don't think so. He's got enough on his plate right now." Robert glanced between Ted and Alex. "Any news on Marcus's murder?"

"Caleb is working with both of us now," Ted said, feeling her mother's eyes on her. "And I know he has Ollie checking out some leads too. Jeremy is smoothing things over with the sheriff's office and doing what he can. He's still got a lot of friends there. But we need to find Joe Smith. Put the word out that if anyone sees him, they contact Alex or me. We have some questions."

Lena said, "That woman and her children deserve to know what happened. Marcus was a good father."

Robert asked Lena, "How are the kids doing?"

"They're adjusting well enough," she said. "But the attention and uncertainty are wearing on them. The other children are mostly kind. I'm keeping an eye on things."

Robert grunted and Ted tried to suppress a smile. Alex's dad may have disliked her mom, but no one could deny, for the children of Cambio Springs—no matter their clan—Lena Vasquez was their champion. Every child in that town was hers, and she made no bones about it. More than one neglectful parent had felt the edge of her claws if they didn't straighten up.

Alex leaned over and whispered, "We need to work on giving them some grandkids. They won't be able to fight about other shit when they're fighting over our kids."

"Slow. Down."

She felt his grin against her neck when he kissed her.

"Not a chance."

The swoop of steel guitar hit her as Alex swung her around to the Bonnie Raitt tune on the jukebox. Ted decided that "Something to Talk About" was their tune because every eye was on them as they danced around the Cave, and more than a few of them were talking.

Partly it was the fact that they were together—very, very together—but most of it was about the fact that Alex was the new McCann alpha.

She couldn't say he looked different, except for the red bites and claw marks that were almost healed. She couldn't say his voice was different or that he walked differently.

Except he did.

It was that indefinable quality that had marked him when he was fourteen. The one that had always caused friction with his father. And now it was the settled confidence of knowing he *was* the biggest and baddest. And no one—at least no one who didn't want their ass kicked—was going to challenge him.

Being alpha looked good on Alex. So it was probably a good thing he'd mated with her. A lesser woman, Ted decided, would let the man walk all over her because that walk was damn sexy.

They'd spent the day poking around the construction at the resort. The site had dried out from the rain, but more storms were in the forecast so they were hustling. Ted had the day free from the clinic so she'd asked Alex to show her around. It was the first time she'd truly allowed herself to feel excitement.

The Cambio Springs Resort and Spa was clearly Alex's labor of love. He treasured it and was involved in planning every inch. From the mineral water pools to the guest cottages, he explained it all. The treatment rooms. The restaurant and private dining nooks. The landscaping. Watching him talk about it made her fall in love with him all over again because she was finally starting to understand his passion. And that understanding gave her peace.

They'd lost years, but that sacrifice meant something when it could lead to something so beautiful.

The resort would be stunning. But more than that, it would be a lifeline for the place they both called home. And the complete privacy Alex was cultivating as the hallmark of the resort would also be the thing that kept the town safe. It would be an oasis, but a private one. And in a little over a year, it would be complete. According to Alex. They were already taking reservations.

She was startled out of her thoughts when his mouth swooped down and kissed her hard.

"Don't think so loud, Vasquez."

She smiled and curled her hands around his shoulders. "You're so lucky I'll have you, McCann."

"Yes," he answered. No hesitation. No bickering. Just a cocky smile. "And you'll have me again when we get home."

"You're insatiable."

"You're irresistible."

And how was she supposed to resist when he said stuff like that? Ted had to raise her voice a little to hear over the crowd. "When are you moving in your stuff?"

"When do you want it?"

Ted couldn't pass that one up. "I want it whenever you want to give it to me, McCann."

He burst out laughing and stopped dancing to lift her in his arms and swing her around. He met her lips for a lingering kiss on the slide down.

Happy. Ted didn't think she'd ever seen Alex so happy.

She didn't think she'd ever been that happy, either.

Ted saw Sean and Allie dancing in the corner of the room. Sean bent down to whisper something in her ear just before Allie threw her head back and laughed.

"Playing with fire," Alex muttered.

She glanced behind the bar. Ollie's jaw was set, and he was pointedly ignoring anything but the drink he was pouring.

"What's Sean up to, Alex?"

"Other than being an idiot?"

"Hey." She tugged on his hair. "He's not being an idiot."

"He's playing with her. She doesn't need that."

"He's not playing her. Sean adores her the same way you do."

"Do you see me flirting with her in front of the bear? Right after her husband took off?"

"No, but you're not Sean," Ted said. "He's a flirt. Always has been. And I'd say right now having a good friend give her some harmless flirtation probably makes her feel pretty damn good since her asshole husband has been ignoring her for years."

Alex looked surprised. "Years?"

"Years."

His shoulders tensed. "You're right." He bent down and inhaled the scent at her neck. "She probably needs that."

They danced for a few more minutes, winding down as the song switched to a slower one.

"I'd never ignore you, Ted."

"I know." Her head lay on his shoulder as the room spun around. "I'd kick your ass if you ignored me like that."

She felt his soft laughter as he held her. Spinning around, feeling the mellow of two beers and a full dinner sink into her. Peace. Quiet. When things settled down, this would be her life. Working at her clinic. Visiting Alex at the resort. Maybe taking off to Vegas or LA for the weekend. Sunday dinners with friends and slow dances at the Cave… Her eyes drifted closed as she relaxed on Alex's shoulder.

And when she opened them, the panicked face of Joe Smith was looking at her through a window.

Chapter Twenty-Two

"What are we doing?" Alex frowned as Ted pulled him toward the door of the Cave. "Ted, what's—"

"Outside. Now. Quiet, *querido*."

He shut up and walked.

"And make sure no one is following us."

Holding the door open as she walked out, Alex glanced behind them but saw no one taking note. They probably thought the two new lovers were ducking out to go home early. He glanced at Ted and hoped no one noticed her purse sitting at the end of the bar where Ollie had stashed it for her.

She led them out to the parking lot, not halting until she heard a low whistle from the bushes. Then Ted frowned and stalked toward it.

They were only a few feet into the dark brush when she stopped. Her hand flew into the darkness, and he heard the solid thud as it collided with someone.

"Fuck, Ted!"

Alex stepped forward and held her back, blocking her with his body as he searched the night.

Sprawled on the ground was Joe Smith, looking dirty, ragged, and beat as he rubbed a hand over the jaw Ted had punched.

She let loose a stream of furious Spanish, all the while reaching down to hit him again. Alex had to hold her arms, and he felt the animal energy ripple along her skin. He squeezed her arms. "Focus, Ted."

"You bastard!" she hissed. "What are you doing here? And it had better not be trying to get back with Allie, unless you want to die. You take off on her. Abandon those kids. Then come skulking in the parking lot? What are you up to, you sneak?"

"I needed to talk to you two!"

That brought both of them up short. Alex was only a few seconds away from letting Ted loose on the man, even though he knew they needed to talk to him.

He asked, "Why do you need to talk to us?"

"Don't tell Ollie, okay?" He was dusting off his pants, and Alex took the opportunity to assess him.

Joe had always been lean, but his clothes were now hanging off him. He looked like he hadn't shaved in weeks, and by the scent of things, he wasn't getting regular showers.

"What's going on, Joe?" Ted demanded.

"I'm trying to do right. I know I fucked up, Ted. But she's better off without me anyway. You all knew that. So did she. She's just too damn loyal to—"

"We are not your marriage counselors," Alex interrupted. "What's this about? Is it about Marcus?"

Even in the moonlight, Alex could see Joe's face pale.

"I didn't know," he whispered.

"You need to explain that, Joe."

"He… I owed him some cash. He said it was a way to pay him back. Hell, I hadn't used that shit in years. Didn't even think it was good. But he —"

"Who are you talking about?" Ted hissed again, glancing over her shoulder to check the parking lot when the door swung open.

"I didn't know. I know me and Marcus fought about stupid shit. Cards and stuff, but I didn't know. Wouldn't have even given him that shit, but he knows! Man, he knows. And he said he'd tell everyone."

"Tell everyone what?" Ted asked.

Joe kept rambling. "I'm an asshole, yeah? But my kids, man. My kids. I can't let my kids—"

"Joe, shut up." Alex stepped closer and stared into the desperate man's eyes. He let his anger rise, knowing Joe would scent it. Knowing even outside the pack, the coyote would react to the stronger predator in front of him.

He did. Alex smelled the urine as Joe let out a whimper.

"Tell me who you're talking about."

"Avery," Joe whispered. "I owed him money, and he asked me to—"

Joe's voice cut off with a gasp a second after the door to the Cave slammed open and his eyes flew over Alex's shoulder.

A ferocious roar filled the air as Joe yelled, "Fuck!" and shifted in a blink.

Seconds later, the coyote had disappeared into the darkness and Alex tackled Ted to the ground to escape the path of the thundering grizzly.

She scrambled to her feet and yelled, "Ollie, stop!"

It was too late. Both animals had disappeared into the night.

"Shift!" she yelled, shoving him. "You need to catch him. Catch them. Joe knows—"

"Joe knows a million burrows in this desert. More than you or me. And definitely more than Ollie. He's fast and smart." He kicked his boot in the dust. "Shit! He's history, Ted."

"You don't know that."

She stepped toward the bushes, acting like she was going after them.

"Ted, do not chase that bear."

"It's Ollie. It's not like he's going to hurt—"

"A few things you need to know about Ollie, Ted, and one of them is when that man loses it, he goes into a bear rage that does not listen to reason or understand much past his animal."

She blinked but stopped walking. "What? He's Ollie!"

"It takes a lot to get him there, but when he does, you do not fight him. You do not provoke him. You get the hell out of his way and hope he doesn't run into anything but full animals."

"But he's Ollie," Ted whispered.

"Yeah." He put his hand on her jaw. "It doesn't happen often. But even the quiet ones need to roar every now and then."

"Is he going to be okay?" Ted's voice was shaky.

"If he doesn't come back within an hour or so, I'll track him down."

There was more movement in the parking lot. Sean and Allie had joined them.

"He had your purse," Allie said. "He went to the window. I think he was going to bring it to you, but he…"

Sean took a deep breath. Then his eyes cut to Alex. "Who was it?"

"Joe," Alex said.

Allie's eyes got huge. "Joe?"

Ted walked over and grabbed her hand. "He was talking to us. Something about Marcus. Then Ollie came out and—"

"He can't hurt him." Allie interrupted her, looking at Alex. "You have to stop him. He can't hurt the kids' dad. He'd never be able to live with himself."

Sean and Alex exchanged a look. "Don't think he's going to see it that way, Allie."

"He will eventually." She stepped closer. Desperate. "Find him. Stop him."

"Joe's fast, honey," Sean said. "He'll be all—"

"This isn't about Joe!" she yelled. "You have to keep Ollie from doing this, Alex!"

Alex met her desperate eyes. Saw what was swimming behind them. Then he turned and ran into the dark.

Hours later, exhausted and bleeding, he walked into the house.

"Alex?"

She was still awake, calling from the bedroom.

"I'm coming back," he called. "Don't get up."

"Is he all right? Is everyone okay?"

He shrugged out of the jacket he'd retrieved from the bushes behind the Cave and started unbuttoning his shirt as he walked to the bedroom.

Ted was already standing, so he went to her, gave her a brush on the jaw and a quick kiss. "I'm beat. Everyone's fine. Go back to bed and let me shower. Then I'll fill you in."

She grabbed his arm before he could turn, holding him in place.

"Ted—"

"Are *you* okay?" she whispered. "Should have asked that first."

He smiled, reached for the back of her neck, and pulled her into a harder kiss. It was slow, deliberate, and thorough. He tasted every part of her mouth before he let her go, biting her lower lip as she let out a soft sigh.

"Let me shower," he said. "I'll meet you in bed."

"Okay."

He cleaned off quickly, always amazed at just how dusty his ears got when he shifted. Shaking off after he turned the water off, he stepped into the foggy bathroom and stopped at his cloudy reflection.

He didn't look different, but he felt it.

Older. Stronger. Harder.

He'd taken Ollie down quickly that night, and he knew part of it was because the bear had been exhausted and distracted. But part of it wasn't.

"Alex?"

Older. Stronger. Harder.

And happier.

Having that voice to come home to, that woman at his back? He'd never been happier in his life.

Reasonably dry, he walked to bed and collapsed onto it. Ted rolled to him immediately, checking a new gash on his shoulder.

"I can see you're going to be a full-time project, McCann."

"Yep."

"Can you tell me what happened?"

"Bear claws."

"So you found Ollie."

Alex took a deep breath and focused on the soft feel of Ted's fingers, not the pain of his body's healing. They healed plenty fast, but it still hurt.

Sometimes it seemed like the healing hurt more than the wound, but that was probably only because it took longer.

"I found him. He was already exhausted and distracted when I did, so it only took a few hard bites to snap him out of it. He hadn't found Joe. We looked after he'd calmed down. I tracked his scent to a burrow near Gerry Wash, but after that, he was gone. Once he goes underground…"

"Yeah."

She knew from tracking desert animals herself. The ground was the best fortress a small animal could have. And as long as you could avoid snakes…

"Should have taken Sean with us."

Ted snickered. "I have a feeling he'd spend most of his time avoiding those big bear paws."

"Yeah… Ollie doesn't like him much right now."

"He'll get over it." She paused. Took a deep breath. "What does he know?"

"Ollie?"

"Joe. He kept saying 'he knows, he knows.' Can we assume he's talking about Avery?"

Alex thought. "Probably. Piece it together for me, baby. I'm wiped."

"Joe and Avery knew each other. Gambled together. Maybe picked up women together too."

"Mm-hmm." He blinked hard, trying to keep awake. "Did Joe use drugs to pick up women? Did Avery do it, too? Is that the connection?"

"I don't think so. Remember what he said. 'I hadn't used them in years.'"

Which meant at some point, Joe Russell *had* used the drugs for something, and the most likely scenario was on the women he met and possibly even with his own wife. He felt the skin on his neck prickle, despite his exhaustion.

Ted sensed it and put a hand on his chest.

"He's gone," she said. "Never getting to Allie again."

Alex cleared his throat. "He hadn't used them in years, but he kept them. The drugs. Maybe he said something to Avery when they were drinking. He remembers it, then goes to Joe when it becomes useful."

"Joe gives him the drugs because…?"

"He owed him money? It seemed pretty clear Joe didn't know he was going to use them on Marcus."

Ted asked, "Are we sure Avery killed Marcus, though? The man is clearly an asshole, but there's no evidence he was directly involved."

"No. Nothing but what Joe said, and he's underground."

"So there's no connection directly, but—"

"'He knows. He knows.'" Alex repeated Joe's panicked words. "What does Avery know, Ted?"

"About the payoffs? The investigation?"

"I don't think Joe Russell would be worried about a criminal investigation in Las Vegas that didn't involve him."

They both fell silent.

"He knows about the town," Ted whispered. "He knows about us."

"Avery, a minute?"

The man looked up from the bed of his truck where plans were spread out on the tailgate. He lifted his chin at Alex before he said a few more words to his foreman and started walking toward the office trailer.

Alex took a seat, mindful that he needed information, but he'd have to tread carefully. He needed to know if Avery knew about the town. If he did…

He didn't know how he'd handle it. In his grandfather's day, someone like Avery would have just disappeared. But Alex was trying to bring the town into the modern age. Secrecy was important, but there had to be a better way to conceal who they were without violence.

Not that killing Chris Avery would cause Alex any sleepless nights if the man had drugged and killed Marcus Quinn.

The job was almost done, and according to Caleb, they didn't have anything that tied Avery to Marcus's death. Nothing that could warrant an arrest. The police in Vegas were drawing their own conclusions regarding the murder and its relationship to the bribery investigation, but they didn't have enough either. There were still no eyewitnesses that put the two men together and still no plausible reason Avery would kill his brother-in-law when the man was keeping him in the business and covering for him.

"Alex," Avery said as he sat in the chair across the desk. "How the hell you doing? Looking good, man. End of the week and we're out of your hair."

"Great." He nodded. "That's excellent news. Of course, you'll be around as we're building."

"I'm already seeing your concrete guys come in. They have any issues, let me know. Crescent Construction will have crews in the area, and we'll be parking some equipment on the project until you're finished."

"Appreciated."

"Helps me out too. People coming in see our name, like our work, we get more."

"True." Why the hell was the man being so friendly?

"This job," Avery continued, "it meant a lot to Marcus. Means a lot to me, too, now that Josie and the kids will be here. We'll take care of you, Alex."

Did he suspect they were looking at him? Or was he just that confident his tracks would never be found?"

It didn't matter. Alex could bullshit with the best of them. "Well, we appreciate that, Chris. More than you can know. Josie's a hell of a woman, and her kids are already making friends here. I hope they're feeling right at home."

A slight twitch at the corner of his eye before Avery secured his friendly expression again. "They are. Kasey talks about her new friends all the time."

"They may not have been born here, but their dad was. So they're some of our own now," Alex said, noticing the twitch again. Chris Avery sure didn't like his niece and nephews being considered part of the town.

Alex decided to push a little more.

"We take care of our own, you know? Marcus was like that too. Kept a lot of guys from the Springs in work when things were slow."

"It's unfortunate that a lot of his crew has moved on."

Alex cocked his head. "Is that so?"

Avery shrugged. "Guess he was just that kind of guy to work with. With him gone, a lot of his guys left too."

He forced himself to nod instead of growl. "Did that put you short-handed?"

There was the eye twitch again. Alex was betting the man didn't know his own tell, which might be another reason he was such a bad gambler.

"We're fine," Avery said. "We had a lot of guys out for the season, so we just called them in. They were happy to be working."

And Alex was betting those men were ones Avery had hired, not Marcus.

Alex bared his teeth in a smile. "Well, I hope they're the right sort."

"I know they are." His eyes were dead. How easy would it be to make the rest of him dead, too?

"I appreciate you keeping me up to speed," Alex said, shuffling papers on his desk. "Your crew works hard. I look forward to seeing them around when we have more building projects in town."

"Appreciated, Alex. Take care." Avery stood and walked toward the door before he turned back to Alex. "McCann?"

"Yeah?" Alex was still making a show of shuffling papers on his desk so he didn't leap toward Chris Avery and tear his throat out.

"Good to know you take care of your own around here."

He stopped and looked up, his eyes going cold at the gleam he saw in Avery's.

Alex heard Frank Di Stefano's voice in the back of his mind. *Secret eyes...*

Avery continued. "I'll look forward to getting that call for the next project that comes around."

"Is that so?"

"Marcus always said the Springs people take care of their own."

That gleam. That cocky gleam. Chris Avery actually thought he had something over Alex McCann. That he was a shoo-in for future contracts because he knew their secret.

The stupid bastard had just signed his own death warrant.

Alex leaned forward and let his hands come together.

"Marcus was right, Chris. This is Cambio Springs. We *always* take care of our own."

Chapter Twenty-Three

"He knows."

"Are you sure?"

"Yep."

Alex was pacing at the station house with Ted, Caleb, and Jeremy.

"Are you sure, boss?" Jeremy asked.

"I'm sure."

Caleb sighed. "Do you have any proof that we can use to actually—"

"He knows, Caleb!" Alex leaned over the police chief's desk. "He found out about the Springs. I don't know how. But he used that to force Marcus to clean up after him. Not go to the police about the bribery thing."

Ted said, "That was probably also self-preservation."

"Self-preservation would be cleaning that shit up, keeping quiet, and making your criminal brother-in-law ride a desk until you could figure out a way to get him out of your business. Marcus wasn't doing that. Marcus was covering for Avery and keeping him in the business."

Jeremy asked, "Because you think Avery knows about the Springs?"

"I know he does."

Caleb looked between Ted and Alex. "Ted, you think—"

"If Alex says he knows about us, then he knows." Ted answered Caleb's unasked question. The chief of police *had* to start trusting the McCann alpha. "He's not going to read something like that wrong."

"Thanks, baby." The quiet words warmed her, despite the chill wind that had swept into the desert that afternoon bringing rain and even a few flurries of quickly melting snow.

"So Avery knows." Caleb leaned on his desk. "What the hell do we do about it, McCann?"

Jeremy and Alex exchanged glances, and Ted knew exactly what they were thinking. Once upon a time, human law wouldn't have had much to do with how Chris Avery was handled.

It wasn't that every human who found out the secret of the Springs disappeared. For most, they were trusted friends or family of the shifters who lived there, vested in keeping their secrets. And for strangers, wild stories were easy to brush off. Most humans didn't want to see anything out of the ordinary. They had an excuse for the most bizarre signs. And if the town had gained a somewhat mysterious reputation over the years, that was just fine. It worked to their advantage, most of the time.

But this was different.

This wasn't a shifter killing another shifter in a rage. This was a human who had killed a shifter, quite possibly because of what he was. It was cold-blooded murder, but Chris Avery wasn't a man who could just disappear without questions asked.

Caleb and Alex had their eyes locked. Ted wondered if Caleb understood just how much authority Alex was granting him to keep his eyes like that without tearing out the chief's throat.

"We have to find something," Alex said. "Something that will prove he murdered Marcus so he can be arrested and tried. He's a human; this is a human problem."

Caleb sat back. "It's not that easy."

"There's got to be something," Jeremy said.

The weariness slipped into Caleb's eyes. "Do you know how many murders happen in the state of California that are never solved?"

"No," Alex said.

"Four in ten."

Ted was shocked. She had no idea it was that high.

"*More* than four in ten, as a matter of fact. Over forty percent of murders are never solved. Never closed. And that's not because the evidence is inadmissible in court. Sometimes there is no evidence. Sometimes people do cover their tracks. Sometimes the bad guys are the ones with luck on their side."

"We've got to find something, Caleb."

"There might not be anything to find. That's what I'm trying to tell you, Alex. The autopsy didn't reveal any trace evidence we can use because the remains were compromised by the coyotes. The body had been moved. The gun was a common caliber. There is no clear motive without the bribery investigation, and officially I don't know about that."

"What?" Alex said. "So this is the perfect murder?"

"You don't have to commit the perfect murder to not get caught. You just have to have luck on your side."

Jeremy piped up from the corner. "We need to focus on finding Joe Smith."

"Russell," Ted said. "His name is Joe Russell. He doesn't get to keep anything of Allie's."

"Whatever. We need to find him. He's the only link between Avery and Marcus. We might even be able to get a warrant to search for the drugs if we bring Joe in."

"You're not going to bring him in," Alex said. "He's scared shitless."

"Yeah," Jeremy said. "Of Ollie."

"Of everything." Ted corrected him. "He's panicking, but he doesn't have money. Not by the look of him the other night. He couldn't get far. So we should look close."

Caleb picked up the phone. "I'll call Dev. See if anyone has spotted him near the river."

Jeremy pushed off from the wall. "And I'll start canvassing the cheap motels around the interstate. Those are probably going to be our best bet."

Ted watched Alex. Saw him struggling to control his instincts. The instincts that told him Chris Avery was a threat, and threats to his people and his home should be eliminated.

"Come on," she said, rising to her feet. "I have lunch stuff at home."

"Ted—"

"Food, Alex. You need to step back for a little while. Let these guys do their work."

Caleb mouthed, *Thank you,* as she pulled Alex to the door. She felt for the chief. It couldn't be easy trying to operate legitimately with a near-feral shifter breathing down your neck. Caleb was doing the best he could, but he was right. In the real world, sometimes luck was on the side of the bad guys.

Alex followed her back to the house, but he was still brooding. She started to make sandwiches as he stared out the window.

"How's the clinic?" he finally said.

"Fine. Slow. No new strep epidemics to keep me on my toes. It was so slow I moved the one appointment I had to take the afternoon off."

"Want to roll around in bed for a while?"

Her pulse spiked a second before her mouth turned up at the corner. "Need a distraction, do you?"

"You're the best kind."

"Are we really just going to roll around in bed, or are more illicit activities going to be indulged in?"

"Illicit." He pulled her into the bedroom, and Ted forgot about the food. "Very illicit."

Alex spent the next hour exploring the boundaries of what Ted considered "illicit" and pushing them very close to "depraved." But she loved every second of it. And she laughed as much as she moaned. It had always been that way with Alex.

"It'll all work out," she whispered, fingers running through his thick hair as he laid his head on her breast.

He lifted his head. "When did you get so relaxed?"

"Me?" She arched a haughty eyebrow. "I'm always relaxed."

"Right."

"You just irritate me more than most people."

"Mmmm." He pushed up and slid a hand behind her back. "That's because I get under your skin."

Her breath hitched and she arched her back, bringing her body closer to his mouth. Never one to pass up an opportunity, he took it.

"You know what?" he whispered, his mouth trailing down to her belly button.

"What?"

"I like being under your skin," he said. "Makes it a little more fair you're so far under mine."

The phone rang in the middle of the night. Before she could lift her head, Alex was answering it.

"Hello?"

Silence. Then his voice growled, "Tell me where you are."

The motel in Barstow was on the edge of town, a rundown relic just off the interstate that still offered rooms for twenty dollars a night and had posted hourly rates. There were a few big rigs parked across the street and a few more cars in the parking lot. The lights flickered as they walked across the cracked asphalt toward room 10, a ground floor room at the very end of the building. Ted didn't see any eyes in the night. No curtains flickered.

Some places, you chose not to pay attention.

There was a low light under the curtain when they stepped up to the door. A slight movement, as if a fan might be running inside. Alex tapped on the door with two fingers, the low sound still echoing loudly down the covered walkway.

It cracked open, and Joe was behind it.

"Is it just you?"

Alex didn't answer, just walked in, and Ted followed. She looked around the room, took in everything. The room had a queen bed with a sad comforter she wasn't going to sit on. There were no lamps, just an overhead light Joe had switched off. The only light came from the yellow glow of the bathroom fixture. It was enough to see, but not enough to see well, which was probably a good thing. The smell alone told her Joe had been smoking, but she could also see an overflowing coffee mug near the only chair in the room.

"Talk to me," Alex said as Ted walked around.

He had no luggage. Not even a backpack. But there was a plastic grocery bag on the small dresser, a bottle of Black Velvet peeking from the top. Ted walked over and opened the top drawer.

"Ted, you can't—"

"You called us, Joe," she said.

Just as she suspected, the top drawer held a bag of weed and a few pills she couldn't see well enough to identify. She slid it shut with a bang.

"What the hell have you done to yourself?"

"Ted—"

"You had a home. A family. Kids who love you. A pretty wife who cooked you dinner every night. And you threw that all away?"

Alex stepped over and took her hand, squeezing it before he looked back at Joe, who'd gone deathly pale.

"Ted," he said softly.

"Done." She threw up her hands, disgusted. Angry that they had to talk to the scumbag because he might know something about Marcus's death.

Alex stepped forward and said, "Joe, you need anything? Have you eaten lately?"

He jerked his head in a nod. "I'm cool. I just… I heard you were looking for me. And I figured, as long as you didn't bring the bear, I could talk to you."

"What did you want to tell us?"

"I need to warn you. About Avery."

"He killed Marcus."

Joe winced, as if he were in physical pain. "Now… I don't *know* that. I mean, he might have. But I didn't see it or anything. I know Marcus was pissed at him. So maybe…"

"He did it, Joe. Why are you covering for him?"

"Hey." Joe stepped back and raised his hands. "No. Uh-uh. I ain't covering for that bastard. Just saying I don't know he's the one that killed Marcus, you know? Marcus didn't get on with his family, either."

"The Quinns did not kill Marcus," Ted said.

"How do you know?" he asked. "They do all kinds of shit to each other. They're mean."

"Old Quinn was grooming Marcus to take over the clan, Joe."

Joe looked at Alex, then said, "Oh. I guess they probably wouldn't, then."

"Tell us more about Chris Avery."

Joe started shaking his head, looking down at the floor. "He seems cool, but… he is not. Avery knows. About us. About us shifters, Alex. He knows about the kids. All our animals. Doesn't like it."

"What does he know?"

"I don't know, man!" Joe threw up his hands. "He was asking about the water and shit, but I didn't tell him anything more. Not after I figured out…" The scruffy man stepped back, guilt written all over his face.

"*You told him.*" Ted stepped forward, lip curled up. She wanted to shift and leap on him. Sink her teeth into the spineless waste of a human who trembled before her. She could smell the blood under his skin.

"Joe, what the hell?"

"He already suspected something!" Joe was up against the wall again, hands raised. "He asked these questions. Made me think Marcus had already clued him in, you know?"

"So you told him more?"

"I was drinking! Needed money from him. Thought we were friends and all. Hell, he was family. Why *wouldn't* Marcus have told him the truth?"

Ted shouted, "I don't know. Because he's an asshole?"

"I know that *now*! I didn't know it when… you know."

Alex said, "When you were drunk, probably high, and needed money from him."

Ted asked, "When did you give him the pills?"

"I don't know."

"Joe!"

"I don't!" He was blinking rapidly. "It was a while ago. A week. Maybe two, before Marcus was killed."

Ted asked, "Why did he kill Marcus?"

"I don't know. I really don't. I thought they were tight. Maybe... I know he didn't want Marcus's wife and kids moving to the Springs. He mentioned that. When he was asking about the water and springs and stuff."

Alex narrowed his eyes. "He ask a lot of questions about that?"

"Yeah. I guess." He looked at Ted. "Teddy, my kids okay?"

"You don't get to call me that. You don't get to ask me that anymore."

"I just want to know they're doing okay." His voice broke a little.

"Maybe you shouldn't have left them, Joe. Maybe even when you decided you didn't want to be a husband, you should have stepped up and *been a fucking man,* a father to your kids."

"I'm a piece of shit!" he yelled, his voice breaking as a fist from an irritated neighbor pounded on the other side of the wall. Tears were sliding down his face and his nose was running. "I know that. They're better without me. They'll forget me. I just want to know how they are."

Ted couldn't answer, so disgusted with what Allie's husband had allowed himself to become.

"You were never good enough for her," Ted whispered, leaning toward him. "You stole something that shouldn't ever have been yours."

"I know."

"Your children will be fine because they have a good mother. And they have people around them who love them. And hopefully, they'll forget you ever existed."

Ted saw his eyes empty out, the life draining away in a blink. She'd seen it happen before, just not to anyone who wasn't dying.

"Joe." Alex stepped forward and pulled her behind him. "I need you to pull yourself together. We need to go to the police. You need to give a statement about giving Chris Avery those pills."

Joe shook his head.

"We'll go to Caleb. He'll know how to write the report so we can get a warrant. Get Avery in jail for what he did."

"Can't, Alex."

"You have to."

Joe looked up, eyes bouncing between Alex and Ted. Then to the door. Then back to the bottle sitting on the dresser. "Can I take my whiskey?"

Ted let out a disgusted breath.

"Yeah," Alex said. "You sit in back. You can take your whiskey."

"Okay, then."

He walked over, grabbed the neck, and headed toward the door. But as soon as he opened it, he swung back, clocking Alex on the temple with the glass bottle. He fell back into Ted, who was walking behind him, and they both tumbled to the floor. Joe darted out the door, but by the time they were up and running, all they saw was the last of his shredded clothes in a small pile on the edge of the parking lot.

The phone rang just as the sun was peeking through the window. This time, Alex was sprawled out, dead to the world, and it was Ted who tagged the phone.

"Yeah?" she whispered.

"Ted?" It was Sean. "Is Alex there?"

"Sleeping. We had to drive to Barstow last night. Can he call you back?"

"I need you both to get out to Josie Quinn's place."

She sat up, goose bumps prickling over her skin. "Why?"

"Her kids are gone, Ted."

She gave a strangled cry that had Alex bolting up in bed.

"Someone took her kids."

Chapter Twenty-Four

This did not happen.

The thought kept circling his mind as he strode up the walkway to Josie Quinn's house. The wolves were already circling. Some shifted. Some walking. Jeremy and Alex's father stood at the center of a clutch of muttering, dark-eyed men.

This did not happen.

He felt Ted at his back. Felt her fingers reach out to grab his as the door opened and Josie Quinn rushed out. Her hair was pulled up in a knot at the top of her head. Her face was streaked with tears. She threw herself at Alex.

"This town! This *fucking* town!" Her fists pounded down on Alex's chest.

Alex ignored the pain on his still-healing shoulder and wrapped her tightly in his arms.

"Josie."

"You find my babies, Alex McCann!"

"I'll find your babies, Josie."

The sobs wracked her body. Terror. That's what he held in his arms. Pure, undiluted terror.

"You hear me?" he asked, one hand cradling her head. "I will find them."

"I can't lose them." She shook. "I can't lose them too. Not my babies. Not my babies, Alex."

He felt hands pulling her away. Then Sean Quinn took her, pulling her into his strong arms and back to the porch where Old Quinn stood. He looked at Alex, his mouth in a hard line.

"This does not happen," the old man said.

"You have people underground already?"

Alex and Old Quinn were standing a little ways from the porch where Sean sat with Josie, who was still barely holding on.

"A few. Most didn't know the kids. No scent. Came here to get it," he said. "Then they're gone."

"They'll have first scent."

"No one takes Quinn children from their home, McCann." All his natural humor had fled, and looking in the old man's eyes, Alex knew the Quinns were after blood.

"We can't kill him, Quinn."

"People get snake bites all the time, wolf." His grey mustache twitched. "Weird shit happens in the desert."

Jena came out the door, holding sheets as pale as her face. Little trucks on one. Spaceships on the other. Willow came behind her, holding a set with butterflies, and he felt Ted squeeze his hand again.

"Dad's already in the air," Jena said. "We have anything we're looking for yet?"

"Chris Avery drives a white GMC pickup."

Willow's eyes got sharp. "We sure it's him?"

Ted was the one who answered. "We caught up with Joe last night in Barstow. Sounds like Avery killed Marcus, though Joe didn't know for sure. Said he knew about the Springs. Didn't like it. Didn't like Josie and the kids moving here."

Chris Avery didn't like shifters. Didn't like his sister being married to one.

Now the man had three shifter children in his possession. What was he capable of?

"Alex?" Jeremy was waving him over.

"What's up? You catch a scent?"

"It's definitely Avery. His scent's all over the house."

"He's Josie's brother. Spent a lot of time here."

"It's recent in the kids' bedrooms. No reason he'd be in there, according to Josie. She says he hasn't been to the house in days."

Old Quinn overhead them. "Avery's a dead man."

Alex turned. "Joe—"

The old man threw up a hand. "It's done, boy. He's a dead man walking."

Jena's face was still pale, and she was clutching the children's sheets in her hands.

"Alex, do you think he'd hurt the kids? He's their uncle."

"I don't know. We need to find them before he has the chance." He nodded toward the sheets. "Get those spread out so the trackers can get their scent. We don't want to delay any longer."

The sun was barely over the horizon when Jena and Willow spread out Kasey, Mark, and Trevor Quinn's sheets on the cool grass in front of Josie Quinn's house. As soon as he did, Jeremy stepped forward, his shirt already off. Alex held out a hand.

"Quinns first."

No one saw them shift, but as soon as the sheets were out, dozens of snakes started circling them, split tongues out, tasting the air. They circled and twisted around each other. Then in a blink, they were gone, and only Sean and Old Quinn remained.

The old man walked to Josie and put his arms around her.

"We'll find your babies, girl. Our people travel places others can't."

Then he looked over his shoulder to Alex.

"Let your pack go."

Alex nodded to Jeremy. Then one by one, the pack shifted and circled the sheets as the snakes had. There were barks and pants. A few lifted their heads and let out a mournful howl. Then they started breaking into groups, heading out in twos or threes.

Jeremy said, "We'll focus our efforts along the highway and the back roads. He'll be in a vehicle."

"He's got hours on us."

"He may be already gone, but we have to check. Caleb's on the phone with Vegas PD. It's likely Avery will head up there since that's what he knows."

"Go. You're in charge of the search around here. Call in when you can. Keep me updated."

"Who are you calling?" Alex asked Ted after the pack had dispersed.

Sean had taken Josie inside to sit with Old Quinn and Allie. Now he was pacing the porch. Caleb was still on the phone with the sheriff's department, and Devin was in his car, driving to the Springs. Jena had her eyes to the sky, waiting for more of her people to gather.

"I'm calling Frank Di Stefano."

"Ted—"

"I don't care if he's a criminal. You think he's going to have any problems looking for someone who kidnaps children?"

She'd read Frank well. Cam's dad would go ballistic.

Alex shook his head. "Jena?"

The hawk-eyed woman turned to him.

"Yeah?"

"Can you get your dad a message about Avery's truck?"

"Shirleen!" Jena called, and a sleek black crow landed in front of her. "Get a message to Dad and the others. Chris Avery has a white GMC pickup. He's probably heading up to Vegas. Anyone sees him, they get to a phone as fast as they can and call the house here. You have the number?"

The bird cawed once, then flew into the air.

Sean said. "If we're done here, I'm going to go look."

Jena clenched her jaw and rubbed a hand over her swollen belly. "I want to shift. So bad."

DESERT BOUND

"Relax and focus." Alex put a hand on Jena's arm. "But get some more of your people over here. I want a few ready if we hear anything. Sean's here. And the birds are the fastest."

Jena glanced at Sean. "Are you thinking—"

"Who's the fastest? Other than you?"

"My cousin Harper. Her natural form is a golden eagle."

"She in the Springs?"

"Coachella."

"Call her."

Jena nodded and turned back to Josie's house. Sean glared at Alex.

"No."

"The birds can get anywhere quicker than the cops. And an eagle can carry you."

"And drop me."

Alex gritted his teeth. "This isn't up for debate."

"You're not my alpha."

"Marcus's kids are missing, Sean!"

"Shit," Sean muttered. "Fine."

"She won't drop you," Jena said as she walked out of the house. "As long as you don't bite."

"Snakes were not meant to fly," Sean said.

Ted closed her phone and walked back to them. "Frank Di Stefano was not pleased. He says he'll get men out looking right now."

An old Ford Bronco pulled up to the curb. Ollie and Rafael Flores, one of Ted's cousins, hopped out. Rafael's animal was a big black cat that no one had ever managed to identify. Probably because no one ever got close enough. He was an anomaly in the cat clan. An unapologetically dominant male who showed no interest toward any of the female cats in his clan. Rafael kept to himself.

"Alex," Ollie called, "what are we doing?"

"Ollie. Rafa. Appreciate it. You have the town covered?"

Ollie said, "No unknowns that we've spotted. One of my guys is watching the main road. Caleb says we'll be getting sheriff's officers in?"

"Probably within the hour. Escort them to Caleb's office, and he'll take it from there. Rafa, anything back in the hills?"

"Lena sent them out as soon as she got the call. We've had people looking in the canyon and the hills, but so far nothing. One of the women did catch a trail that smells like the children, but we don't know how old it is."

"It's not likely he'd go on foot, but we have to check."

"We'll keep some people back there. Keep looking."

"Good." He took a breath, wishing he had something more to do. Something to break up the unrelenting worry eating his gut.

Three children. Out there with the man who killed their father. The boys might not have any idea they were in danger, but Kasey would know by now. The little girl would be terrified.

"Alex."

He heard Ted calling his name, but his eyes were locked on Josie, sitting on the porch again with Old Quinn, staring out into the desert with hollow eyes. The old man was talking, but she was miles away.

"Alex."

"Yeah?"

Ted held up her phone with a grim smile. "Organized crime is efficient this morning. Frank says Avery was spotted at a motel in Henderson. No sign of the kids. Wants to know if he should call Vegas PD."

"No."

"But—"

"Avery knows about us. God knows what he'd tell the cops if they found him, and we don't need the extra attention. A murder and a kidnapping is bad enough. We'll take care of this, but it needs to be quiet."

Ted let out a deep breath and stepped closer so only Alex could hear. "Are you sure?"

"No," he said, equally quiet. "But we need to get the kids first. Then we'll figure out what to do with Avery. Whatever we do needs to be quiet."

"Okay."

"Are *you* sure?" He didn't want another weight on her conscience.

"Yeah.

Alex turned to his friends. Jena and Sean were standing silently with an enormous golden eagle who hadn't shifted. "Jena, send Harper with Sean." He looked at the eagle, who stared back, head cocked to the side with a golden-brown eye trained on him. "Avery is at a hotel in Henderson. Look for the children first. He may have them at the hotel, and whoever spotted Avery missed them. Kids are the priority."

Ted crouched down and held out a small map on her phone. The eagle chirped and hopped away. A few seconds later, a stunning woman with chestnut-brown hair stood naked before them.

"Sorry," she said. "I can't see computer screens like that in my natural form." Ted showed her the image again. Harper nodded. "I know the road." She glanced at Sean. "You ready?"

"Yeah."

Ted said, "Frank says he sent a couple guys over to keep an eye on the hotel. Avery's truck has mysteriously slashed tires, so he's not going anywhere."

"Good."

Alex heard clothes rustling. Then something thumped against his legs. He looked down at the diamondback who was head-butting him in the calf.

"Stop bitching, Sean. She's not going to drop you."

"Unless you bite me," Harper said. "Then all bets are off." A moment after that, the eagle shimmered to life, hopping over the grass until she hovered above the snake. She jumped up, wings spread, and grabbed the twisting snake in her talons. Alex heard Sean's rattle a second before Harper's wings beat against the air, and the two lifted into the sky.

Alex opened his phone and hit Frank's number as he and Ted got in the truck.

"Alex," Frank answered. "How's Josie?"

"Terrified," he said over the engine roaring to life. "What the hell was Avery thinking?"

"I do not know, my friend. But he's not going anywhere now. There's still no sign of the children, but my men are there, keeping an eye on the room."

"I have people headed toward you, and Ted and I will get in the car now."

He waved at Old Quinn, who nodded back, arm still around Josie's shoulders.

"But no one's seen the kids?"

"No. But that doesn't mean anything. They saw the car and called it in. Identified Avery when he walked out to get groceries from the car. The children might be in the room and away from the windows."

"Groceries are a good sign."

"We'll keep watching. Are you sure you don't want us to go in to look for the kids?"

Josie said her brother had doted on the children. She'd never imagined he would hurt them. Alex didn't know where Avery's mind was, but he was guessing—in his own twisted way—Chris Avery thought he was rescuing his sister's kids.

"Not... yet."

"If that changes, you let me know."

"I appreciate this, Frank," Alex said, "but I need another favor. I have people headed your direction, and they're going to need some sweats or something."

"Sweats?"

"Sweats. Coveralls, even. A man and a woman. He's around six feet. She's tall too. Just get them something to cover up with when they get there, a phone they can use to call me, and please no questions."

There was silence on the other line. Ted turned left on Spring Street just as sheriff's cruisers turned.

Finally, Frank said, "Is this part of those secrets you and Ted keep?"

"Don't ask questions you know I can't answer, Frank."

"It's hard when you're making me curious, son."

Ted pulled up to the stoplight at Spring and Main. The truck's back door was wrenched open just as the light turned. Caleb Gilbert jumped inside.

The chief of police barked, "Go!" and Ted took off.

"Is this Alex?"

"Harper? What's happening?"

Two hours later, Ted, Caleb, and Alex were still driving, but Harper flew as the eagle flies, which meant he'd been expecting her call, so he put it on speakerphone.

"We're here," she said. "Sean's still alive and wearing really ugly coveralls. Some guys are here. They say they're Frank's men? You want them to stick around?"

Alex turned to Caleb, who was frowning. Slowly, he shook his head at Alex, and he got the message.

"Send them home," Alex said. "Avery's human. The sheriff's department is already involved. We need to call Vegas PD."

Chapter Twenty-Five

By the time they arrived at the Rest E-Z Inn outside Henderson, the parking lot was swarming with cops.

Caleb leaned forward over the front seat. "What the hell?"

He flipped open his phone and in a few seconds was shouting at it.

"Devin, what the hell is going on? I call in a possible sighting and pull into a mobile command unit with SWAT presence!"

Ted was just trying to figure out where to park. She pulled into a spot outside the lighted area and sat back, listening to Caleb rail.

"How did it turn into a hostage situation, Dev? This didn't need to be a hostage situation. I told them I was coming up here to talk to the guy. I told them the kids were his—"

The sudden silence made Ted's stomach clench.

"What do you mean there's only one kid in there?" Caleb switched to speakerphone.

"—couldn't stop them from calling backup. He was yelling and screaming. The next-door neighbor called the cops too. Management. They said they've heard one kid crying. An officer went to the door, and Avery shot through it. They followed procedure. Called it in. They're trying to make contact, but no one's answering the phone."

Alex was fuming. "What the hell's going on in there?"

Caleb said, "Dev, I'll keep you updated."

"Talk to a Lieutenant Eric Boxer. He knows you're coming. He doesn't know Ted and Alex are with you."

Caleb hung up the phone and moved to get out of the car. Alex put a hand on his arm.

"What can we do?"

"Nothing until I find out more. They might be willing to let you talk to him since you know him. I'll play it up like you're a friend of the family."

Ted said, "I'll try to find Sean and Harper."

She got out of the truck and hiked toward the lonely pay phone at the corner. She stopped and turned, scanning the parking lot for any familiar faces.

"Sean?" she hissed. "Harper?"

Voices came from behind her. "Here, Ted."

She turned to see Harper in a black sedan, wearing blue mechanic's coveralls.

"Where's Sean? And whose car is this?"

"It's either Vito or Guido. Not too sure."

"Vito?"

Harper got out, holding out the keys to Ted as she shrugged. "Frank's guys. Someone came and picked them up. Left the car here for me and Sean."

"Where's Sean?"

She nodded toward the lit-up parking lot. "He shifted to get closer. Went around the back."

Ted took a deep breath. "Let's hope no one on the SWAT team is phobic about snakes."

Sean felt the cool crawl of dust on his belly. The unmistakable taste of panic in the air. Two of the children were in the room, but not the third. And Chris Avery was not in good shape.

It was an old building with a raised foundation, so he slipped underneath, into the shadows past the brightly lit parking lot. Bullhorn shouts beat against his ears. The subfloor of the motel was rotten with garbage and dead rodents. He could hear scrambling on the floor.

Two children.

No, one child.

No, two.

His rattle trembled when the puzzle pieces locked into place.

He had to get into that room.

Sean was lucky. Not only because his snake could shift to four-legged forms, but also because rodents had gotten there first, burrowing into the walls, following the pipes that led up to where the food and water would be. He slid along one, seeking an entrance. He spied a pinprick of light, and in a blink, he'd shifted.

The tiny lizard crawled up the back of the wall, poking his head through to see the dark shape of Chris Avery thrashing on the floor.

"L-little... freak," the man spat out. "Fucking... little... bitch."

Before he lost his temper and shifted through the wall, he darted into the room.

He could smell her venom in the air. The lethal neurotoxin had already started working on Avery. The young snake had struck twice. Once on his hand and another on his face. Avery was muttering partly because his jaw had already swelled to the point that Sean was surprised he was able to talk at all. The hand must have been the first bite. It was bleeding and raw. Instead of going to the door and getting help, the man had huddled against a wall, clutching his hand and spitting curses at the bed.

He could hear a boy crying in the bathroom. He shifted, the shivers wracking his body as he stretched and twisted. Pinpricks of pain rushed along his newly human skin, and he broke out in a cold sweat.

Blinking, he lay staring up at the ceiling as Avery began choking on his own spit.

"What the f-fuck?" he moaned. "What the—"

"Shut up." Sean snarled. "Where is she?"

Avery's eyes widened. "I don't know."

"Are the boys okay?"

"Fuck you. I would never hurt them. I was trying to get them away from you freaks. Kasey—"

He started choking again. Sean knew Avery had less than an hour to live unless he could get medical treatment. Young snake venom was especially toxic. And shifter venom was even more toxic than most. Since he'd smelled the neurotoxic venom in the air, he knew what form Kasey had taken. He had to be very, very careful.

"Kasey?" He shuffled along the floor. The lights were still shining through the closed drapes, and he didn't want to give the cops a shadow to shoot at. "Kasey, it's Uncle Sean."

"Uncle Sean?" a small voice from the bathroom called.

He ducked and scrambled to the door. Little Mark was huddled in the bathtub, clutching a stuffed otter. There were tears in his eyes.

"Hey, buddy."

"Uncle Sean, Kasey—"

"I know, bud. Can you stay here while I look for her? Keep quiet so we don't scare her?"

He nodded.

Sean's eyes swept the bathroom, but his senses hadn't been mistaken. "Where's Trevor?"

"He ran away. Uncle Chris was taking us to the car to see Grandma and Grandpa, but Trevor ran. Is he with Mommy?"

Trevor hadn't been at the house, so Sean was guessing the boy had sensed the danger and run off. Hopefully, the trackers had already picked him up.

"Stay here, Mark. Stay in the bathtub. I'm going to close the door, okay?"

The boy nodded, and Sean eased the door closed, then crawled back to Avery.

Chris Avery had lost consciousness, and his body was starting to seize. Sean had to decide. Let Avery choke on his own vomit or find Kasey before the police came crashing in?

Not really a question.

The room phone started to ring. He ignored it.

"Kasey, honey?"

He heard a soft rattle from under the bed, but he didn't approach.

"Kasey, he isn't going to hurt you anymore. It's safe."

Another rattle, but no sounds of movement. He took a deep breath and tried to calm the panicked girl.

Ten was young for a shift, but it could happen. Sometimes traumatic injury or fear could flip the switch early, throwing a child into a shift as a survival mechanism. But shifting back for younger kids was harder. The old people said at the beginning of things some young shifters went wild and couldn't find their way back.

"Kasey," he whispered. "I need you to come back, honey. Mark is scared right now. We need to get him back to your mom."

There was a shifting under the bed, and a small Mohave green rattlesnake slid out from the darkness. Its body was curled and wary, braced for danger as its tail shook back and forth. Kasey's tongue was out, tasting the air. Sean took deep calming breaths when he saw the spot of blood on the crown of her head.

The phone rang, but Sean kept his eyes on Kasey.

"I'm going to stay right here. I won't come any closer."

The rattling stayed steady, but the snake's body relaxed on the ground.

"Good girl. Now, you need to picture—"

A sharp bark from one of the police bullhorns sent Kasey back under the bed.

"Shit!" They were growing impatient. He had to get the girl safe. Sean didn't think he could get her to follow him in snake form out of the room. And if the police burst in and saw Avery dead from a snakebite, they'd kill whatever bit him as soon as they found it.

"Ignore them, honey. We need to get you back with your mom. Just picture yourself in the mirror. Try to imagine lying in your bed first thing in the morning, okay?"

The rattling stopped.

"You ever do that? I do. I love to lie around in bed. Used to make my mom really mad. But the way my window was when I was your age, the light would come in just right and hit my bed if I let the curtains open…"

He kept talking, trying to distract her from the sharp shouts of the men outside. The flashing lights that still broke through the curtains.

"Just picture it in your mind, honey. Feel yourself stretching out like you're getting aaaaall the kinks out of your back. You feel your legs? Point your toes, Kasey."

There was a shifting on the other side of the bed.

"Stretch your arms out. Feel the muscles there?" He battled back the instinct to shift and hide when he heard footsteps. "You're such a strong girl, Kas. I bet you were the one who told Mark to get in the bathtub, huh? That was smart, honey. You're a good big sister."

Sean kept his voice steady, even as he heard the footsteps coming closer. The police were going to break through the door. It had been quiet too long.

"Kasey—"

A rustling on the opposite side of the bed. A small cry of pain.

"I'm here."

He closed his eyes in relief.

"I can't find my nightgown though. I'm all naked."

He spied it in the corner of the room and threw it to her.

"Put it on. Quick. The men coming through the door are police, so I need to—"

The door crashed open and light poured into the room. Sean's eyes flashed to the first figure in the room.

"What the fu—"

It was a second before the man disappeared and the lizard skittered under the bed.

Within seconds, he was in the wall.

"Kasey?" he heard one of the officers call.

"What the hell was that?"

"What are you talking about?"

"There was a guy. Then there wasn't."

"Clear! Suspect on the ground. Unconscious. No weapon."

"Kasey, we're the police. We're gonna take you home."

"My brother's in the bathroom. Mark!"

More feet and the sound of doors opening cautiously. "Mark? Trevor? I'm a police officer. Don't be scared."

"We're going to take you back to your mom now, okay?"

The officers were being gentle with her. Calm. He heard one of them calling for a medic for Avery. Heard him calling out medical information over the radio, but Sean focused on the kids. He heard Mark start to cry in the bathroom again, but Kasey was there.

"It's okay, Marky. The policeman's going to take us back to Mom."

"What happened?"

"—boy and a girl. No sign of the other boy. No injuries apparent. We're bringing them out now."

"Kasey, are you hurt?"

The sound of gagging.

"She's vomiting. Pete, get a trashcan or something. And get another medic—"

"Pulse is irregular. Get a board. We need to get him out of here as soon as possible. No antivenom in the truck."

"—might be shock. She's sweating like crazy."

"Where's the other boy?"

"—on the phone with San Bernardino."

"Kasey, honey? Kasey, what happened to your uncle?"

"—wait until she's at the hospital, Brannon."

"I need to know what this is! I've never seen this kind of reaction before. Did it bite the kids?"

"Kasey?"

Sean waited for her to speak. Skittered closer to the hole in the wall to look through.

The girl was huddled in the corner, clutching a trashcan. Her brother hung on her shoulder, but the girl sat up straight, her eyes plastered to the seizing man they were strapping down to the board in front of her. Sean blinked. Looked again. But the girl's eyes didn't waver. The police crouched around her, waiting for her to speak.

Finally, she whispered, "There was a snake."

"Let me through!" Ted shouted as soon as she saw the kids. "I'm their doctor. Let me through!"

She ran toward Caleb, who was shouting at someone in a black uniform.

"Caleb?"

"Yes, she *is* their doctor," he yelled. "And a friend of their mom. Get her over there and let's focus on finding Trevor!"

Ted walked toward Kasey and Mark. No one stopped her.

"Kasey!" she called out.

"Dr. Ted?" The girl walked toward her, shoulders slumped.

Just then, a stretcher raced past her. As soon as Ted saw Chris Avery, she knew exactly what had happened. Her eyes met Kasey's, and the girl started to cry.

Ted ran to her, pulled her away from the officer in black BDUs and into a fierce hug. She was shivering, but Ted guessed they were the normal shakes that happened after a first shift.

She whispered, "Good girl, Kasey."

"I didn't mean to—"

"You were scared, and you protected your brothers. Good girl."

"Trevor's not here."

"What?" She looked around. Mark was sitting in the back of an ambulance, sucking on a juice box as a ponytailed paramedic checked him out, but there was no Trevor.

"Trevor ran. I don't know where he is."

"Okay, sweetie. Don't worry. We'll find him."

"I'm sorry, Dr. Ted. I didn't mean—"

"Shhhh." She pressed the girl's face to hers and whispered, "Not here."

Kasey clammed up immediately and nodded.

"Let's get you checked out, okay? How are you feeling?"

"I threw up a lot, and I'm really cold."

She squeezed the girl's hand and brought out her phone at the same time. Then she flipped to Alex's number and hit 'call.'

"Ted, what's going on? They won't let me close."

"Avery was bit by a snake." She let the silence hang until she knew Alex must have caught on. "Not sure what kind, but he's in bad shape. Kasey and Mark are okay. No injuries. Get on the phone to Old Quinn. We don't know where Trevor is."

"He ran away," Kasey whispered. "Before we got in the car. He ran behind the house, but I don't know where he went. I thought he was going back inside for Mom. That's why I didn't yell."

"You get that?" Ted asked.

"Yeah," Alex said. "I'll call the old man. Who has my keys?"

"I sent Harper to wait in your pickup. She has them. You might send her ahead and see if she can find anything."

"Got it."

"I'm staying with the kids here. Catch a ride with Caleb or something. Go find Trevor."

"Yes, ma'am." She could hear the smile in his voice. "If he's around the Springs, we'll find him."

"I know you will."

"With any luck, they've already picked him up. Love you, baby. Take care of those kids."

"Later."

"Later."

A half an hour later, Ted got the call that a giant black cat walked out of the desert with Trevor Quinn clutching its back. He'd been found at the old cave behind Alma Crowe's house. He had no injuries, but was pretty hungry and worried about his brother and sister.

Chris Avery lapsed into a coma while doctors pumped over fifty vials of antivenom into him. He was breathing, but the prognosis wasn't good. Officers tore the room apart, but no one could find the snake.

Within a few hours, Kasey and Mark Quinn were released into the custody of Caleb Gilbert and Dr. Teodora Vasquez after paramedics determined the children had no injuries or health problems other than an inexplicable fever in Kasey that the paramedics put down to stress.

Official statements could wait. The children needed to go home. Ted gave them her phone to call their mother from the car.

Five minutes after the call, Josie Quinn started making pancakes, and the nightmare was over.

Chapter Twenty-Six

"How are they doing?" he asked, sitting on the top step of Jena's porch.

Ted looked across the yard to Josie and Kasey, sitting side by side at the curb, watching the little boys play on their bikes, racing up and down the quiet street on Sunday afternoon. The sun was almost down, and Alex could smell dinner wafting from the house.

"Physically, Kasey's fine. It was early for her to shift, but we all know trauma can bring it on. Other than that, I just told Josie we'd watch her. But everything seems fine. Emotionally, we'll have to wait and see. Josie's keeping a close eye on her. Sean too."

"Thank God he was able to get to her right after. And that he was able to talk her out of the shift."

Ted smiled. "I think 'Uncle Sean' has a shadow now. If anything can convince him to stay, that sweet little girl's hero worship might do it."

"Avery is still in a coma."

"Good."

They sat in silence, listening to the kids' shouts. Kevin and Low, perched on their bikes, Jena's son Bear, Allie's Justin and Austin, and Josie's two boys were running around them. Allie's daughter, Loralie, hung on the back of Ollie's big mastiff, Murtry, following behind the older boys. Ollie and the surprising addition of Rafael Flores were leaning against Ollie's Bronco, keeping watch.

"What's that about?" Alex asked, nodding toward Rafael.

"Josie says Trevor keeps asking for him," Ted answered. "I guess Rafa slept on their couch in the front room the first night back. Only way Trevor would calm down enough to go to bed."

"Hmm."

"Rafa won't mind. He's quiet, but kids like him." Ted sighed. "The boy lost his dad and his uncle tried to kidnap him. It's understandable that he's scared."

"He's also got a great mom, lots of new friends, and a town full of bodyguards, one that seems to be keeping a particular eye on the situation. So, eventually, he'll be okay."

"Yeah."

She leaned her head on his shoulder, and he said, "Still sucks it all happened, though."

"Yeah."

"But it's done."

Her arm slipped around her waist, and Alex put his around her shoulders, tugging her closer.

It was done.

Once the police in Las Vegas were able to search Chris Avery's house, they found the evidence they needed to link him to Marcus's murder. They may never know exactly what happened, but Avery was stupid—or arrogant—enough to keep the gun that shot his brother-in-law. There was no evidence of the drugs, but the gun would be enough. Along with Chris Avery's cover-up and his actions afterward, even if he came out of the coma, he'd be in jail for a long, long time.

The bribery investigation had destroyed Crescent Construction though. Josie was talking to two of Marcus's foremen, Quinn cousins, who were looking to buy the existing equipment and start something new. Josie seemed more than happy to sell, and Alex was happy that out of all the heartbreak something could be salvaged. It wouldn't be much for Josie and the kids to live on, but since Alex already had her in his sights to manage the resort spa, he had a feeling it was all going to work out.

As for his friends, it all seemed to be settling.

Sean Quinn was back. For how long, nobody really knew. But Old Quinn was working hard to get his nephew to corral the crazy group of snake shifters he grudgingly called family. There was no love lost, but at the same time, no one really had the guts to challenge Sean. The old man was in charge for now. How the future would shape up, no one knew.

Caleb and Alex had come to a truce. Caleb didn't want Alex to poke his nose into any more murder investigations. Alex was hopeful no one else would get murdered. Since neither one wanted to anger a very pregnant and very cranky Jena, they'd just decided to be friends.

Or at least act like it in her presence.

Allie seemed to be fine, though Joe had yet to reappear. Her dad and one of her sisters helped her hire a lawyer in Indio to start divorce proceedings. Kevin had stepped up, as Alex knew he would, and was helping out his mom.

Alex watched him with the younger kids. He was careful never to let one fall too far behind. Lifted his little sister in his arms when she fell and bumped her knee. Watching. Already a young man at only fifteen.

"If we have a boy," Ted said, "I want him to be just like Kevin."

"I was just thinking the same thing."

Allie had also asked Ollie if she could pick up evening shifts at the Cave to make some extra money now that she was on her own. Ollie, being one of her oldest friends, said yes.

Everyone was curious how that would go.

Alex and Ted were back. In some ways, it seemed to Alex like the years they'd been apart had never really happened. They still bickered with each other. Their families both gave them headaches, though Lena Vasquez and Julia McCann were now seen at the Blackbird Diner at least once a week, sharing coffee and laughing about something or other. Alex didn't ask. His mother didn't share.

All he wanted was Ted.

Ted in his bed at night. Ted under him every morning. Ted at the table while he cooked dinner for her. Ted in the bathroom, nagging him about using too much hot water or dropping his towels on the floor. Ted in his arms, dancing at the Cave. Ted laughing at anything.

He'd lost her once. He'd never take her for granted again.

He was at the fridge, grabbing a beer while Ted took her shower after work. She needed it. In fact, the array of scents she regularly came home with, combined with his preternatural sense of smell, was making Alex seriously consider an outdoor shower added on to their bedroom.

Two months after the moon night they'd first shared together, the most recent one seemed to have triggered a rash of adolescents changing. Four new wolves in his pack, two bears that he knew of. A bird. Five cats. And nine snakes.

The Springs was growing, and most of the time, Alex couldn't be happier.

Ted could do with a little less nausea during office checkups, though. Young shifters puked a lot.

"*Mi querido?*"

"*Si, mamá?*"

She snickered every time he called her that. Then she teased him about being her *lobo macho,* and he usually ended up kissing her. So he kept calling her *mamá.* If he had his way, she would be one soon enough.

"Who's cooking?"

"I'm exhausted."

"Yeah, so am I."

"Pizza?"

"Yesssss," she groaned in relief as she collapsed on the couch. He opened another beer and brought it to her just as someone knocked on the door.

She cocked her head. He shrugged and sniffed the air. Human, not shifter.

"I'm not expecting anyone. You?"

"Nope."

Alex opened the door and tried not to show his surprise at Cameron Di Stefano standing on the other side.

"Cam!"

"Hey, Alex."

"How do you know where I live?"

Cam's mouth curled up in the corner. "This town really *is* friendly. It's almost scary how quick they'll tell a stranger where you live."

That's because they know a full-grown wolf and large mountain lion live here and we're not afraid of one guy in a suit.

Alex didn't share that. "Well, you know small towns."

"Not really."

Alex chuckled. "Not to seem unwelcoming, but—"

"Why the hell am I out in the middle of the desert?"

"Yeah, kind of wondering that."

"Chris Avery came out of his coma last night."

He felt Ted at his back before he even opened the door.

"Come on in," Alex said. "Beer?"

"That'll work. Heya, Ted."

"Hey, Cam. What's up with Avery? He's awake?"

"Kind of."

Alex tried to control his hackles while he opened a beer for Cam and Ted led him to the living room. He knew Avery knew about the shifters—had seen his own niece turn into a Mohave green rattlesnake—but no one knew how much he remembered. According to Ted, a patient in a coma this long rarely woke up, and more rarely were they the same person.

So no one knew how this would go.

"Here you go." Alex handed Cam a bottle of beer.

"Thanks." Cam settled back in an armchair while Alex sat next to Ted.

"Has anyone told Josie?" Ted asked.

"I don't know." Cam took a long pull on the longneck. "My dad had a… friend watching him. Keeping an eye on things. She called this morning, said he woke up last night. He's been going in and out of consciousness all day."

Alex squeezed Ted's shoulders. "He's Josie's brother. Even though he did what he did, they probably contacted her first."

She nodded. "I'll call Caleb later. Make sure he and Jena know too."

"Good idea." Alex turned his attention back to Cam, who Alex was fairly certain wasn't here just because a suspected murderer and kidnapper had regained consciousness somewhere in Las Vegas. "So what's up?"

Cam shook his head. "You hear crazy shit out in the desert, man."

He forced himself not to react. "Yeah? Like what?"

"Oh… little girls turning into rattlesnakes. Men disappearing into thin air. Wolves and coyotes and all sorts of stuff."

Alex let his eyes fly open. "What? That's… crazy."

Ted said, "Is this something Chris Avery is saying?"

"He's saying all sorts of shit." Cam's gaze was keen on her. "Every time he wakes up, it's a new story. Though, according to the cops, he did confess to killing Marcus so the man didn't 'infect the children,' whatever that means. Police aren't sure they can use that in court, though."

Alex took another drink of beer. "Brain damage from the coma, you think?"

Cam shrugged. "The doctors are baffled. The cops are pleased. The DA is not."

"He can't use a confession from a suspect who is clearly hallucinating," Ted added, her voice clinical. "I was told he was bitten by a Mohave green rattlesnake, which is an unusual variety. Its venom is a neurotoxin. Did you know that?"

"I didn't."

"Neurotoxins attack the nervous system, including the brain. It's fascinating because most rattlesnake venom is *hemotoxic*."

"You don't say…"

She was piling on so much bullshit they'd have trouble wading to the kitchen. Mohave green bites caused swelling and vision impairment. Muscle spasms and seizures if the bite wasn't treated. They weren't going to cause a man to start hallucinating, but Cam didn't need to know that.

Alex wondered if he would buy it. He had a pretty strong bullshit sensor.

Ted rambled about the clinical properties of antivenom and the research possibilities of snake venom in neurology until Alex saw Cam's eyes start to glaze over.

"That's, uh, really interesting, Ted."

"Isn't it?"

Alex was trying not to laugh. He finished his beer about the same time Cam finished his.

"Cam, you staying for dinner?"

"What are you having?"

Ted said, "Pizza."

Cam shuddered and stood. "Think I'll head back."

"Snob."

"Whatever, Ted. Enjoy the heartburn. Alex, walk me to my car?"

Alex looked over to Ted, but she only rolled her eyes. "Whatever, *macho lobo*. I'm ordering pizza."

"No olives."

"With *so* many olives."

"On your half."

"Why do you have to make our order so difficult?"

"Ted, it's pizza. It's not difficult. Just tell them to leave the olives off my half."

"You're so high maintenance."

"I am not!"

Cam smiled and said, "Do you guys fight about everything?"

Ted said, "Yes."

Alex said, "No."

Cam burst out laughing.

Alex tugged her hair until she pointed her face at him.

"What?"

"Kiss me."

"Not in front of company. I'll blush."

He laughed against her mouth before he kissed her in a way that made it clear he didn't care what kind of company they had.

"*Lobo macho*," she whispered.

"Let me get rid of him. Then I'll show you macho."

She grinned back. "Cam," she said, standing up. "Nice to see you. Thanks for letting us know about Avery."

"No problem."

The two men walked to the door. Alex spied the driver and the black car idling at the road.

"It must be an oven out here in the summer," Cam said. "It's December, and it's still warm."

"You live in Vegas and you're calling the Springs hot?"

"Yeah, but we have acres of air-conditioning too."

"Why are you here, Cam?" Alex leaned against his truck. "You could have called about Avery."

"Yeah, I could have." Cam looked around. "I was curious."

"About?"

"What brought you back here?"

"It's home." He nodded toward the house. "It's Ted."

Cam let his eyes drop to the ground and kicked at the pebbles in the driveway, chuckling quietly. "It's Ted."

"Yeah."

He looked up and into the cottonwood trees that rustled beside the house. "It's an interesting town."

Alex shrugged. "Old. Lots of history. Lots of places like that, I guess."

Cam smiled. "Yeah."

They held each other's eyes for another minute before Cam nodded and turned around.

"Drive safe," Alex called.

"I will. You and Ted don't be strangers."

"We won't."

Alex watched Cam's driver ease away, careful not to kick up too much dust as they rolled back toward Main Street and the highway.

Ted came out to stand at his side.

"He knows?"

"He suspects something."

She took a deep breath and let it out slowly. "So we'll be careful."

"We always are, Ted." He threw an arm around her shoulders and walked back to the house. "Always."

Chapter Twenty-Seven

She woke without the heat of him at her back. The alarm hadn't gone off. In the back of her drowsy mind, she knew that meant it was Saturday. Their day to sleep in. Their day to laze in bed if they wanted. Ted could shift and lie on the rocks behind the house. They could go hunting that night. No meetings. No appointments. No family drama.

She felt his fingers playing with the ends of her hair.

"You awake?" he whispered.

"Mm-hmm?"

He didn't pounce like he usually did in the mornings. Alex was a fan of morning nookie. Some things changed, but that did not. He liked it anytime, but he especially liked it when she was sleepy and sweet. Probably because she didn't argue with him as much.

And yes, they argued. About sex. During sex.

Arguing was what they did.

"Alex?"

He still didn't say anything. Just kept stroking her hair.

"What's up?"

"I don't know how to do this."

She rolled over, blinking at him. The morning sun streamed across their sheets, and Alex sat up against the headboard. His eyebrows were furrowed and his jaw was covered in morning stubble. His eyes were pointed down to something he was flipping in his hand.

"What are you talking about?"

It flashed in the light, and Alex held it up.

A diamond ring hung on the end of his forefinger.

"I don't know how to do this."

"We've only been back together two months," she protested quietly. "It's fast. We don't need to—"

"I've loved you for as long as I can remember."

"Alex—"

"I don't remember being with a woman—even a friend—and not comparing her to you. Even when I was a kid."

She said nothing. Alex scooted down next to her.

"We've been together for years, baby."

"We broke up."

"It was only ever you for me," he whispered. "Tell me you know that."

She smiled. "I know that."

"It's only ever been me for you."

"Cocky."

He held up the ring. "This isn't fast."

Her smile grew. "I guess not."

"Marry me, Téa."

"Yes," she whispered. "Even though that wasn't actually a question."

Alex grinned and pulled up her hand, sliding the ring on her finger.

"That's the wrong hand, Alex."

"Told you I didn't know how to do this."

"Téa," he panted into her neck. "Hurry."

He twisted his hips, rocking them, tilting her up until she…

Yes.

"Alex!"

"Mmmm." He caught her cries with his mouth. Lips pressed to hers as he moved faster and she felt him groan against her mouth.

Needless to say, Alex did know how to *celebrate* an engagement, even if he was unsure about the asking part.

He was still kissing her. Long, drugging kisses that didn't stop, even when their bodies ceased to tremble. One hand at her jaw, the other curled in her hair, he lingered at her mouth. Lips swollen with pleasure, she took it. Took him. She curled her arms around him, the light warming them as frost melted from the glass.

"Love you so much."

"Love you too."

"Thank you," he whispered.

"You give as good as you get, *querido*." Her hand trailed down over the tight muscles of his back. "Always have."

"Thank you for marrying me."

Was he going to keep being sweet like this? Ted didn't think she could handle that. She felt the tears at the corners of her eyes.

"You're welcome."

"I want to have babies with you."

"I know," she said, smiling. "I do too."

"*Lots* of babies."

Her smile fell a little.

"How many is lots?"

"Five? Six?"

She blinked and pulled her head back. "Do you think we're going to have a litter?"

"I'm just saying," he continued, "we should get started soon. Because we're going to have a bunch."

"Oh really?"

"Yep." He rolled back and pulled her to his side. "They can come one at a time, but I want lots."

"Alex."

"I'll add on to the house. I know an architect that would be perfect for the job."

"Alex!"

"What?"

"Is there some previously unknown technology that will now allow you to carry and birth children?"

"You'd really know the answer to that better than me."

"No. There's not. Which means *I* have to carry this football team you're planning—"

"Football is excessive," he said. "Basketball team. We can have a basketball team."

"Which, clue in, is *not* going to happen."

"Now you're just being unreasonable."

"Alex!"

"What?"

"You don't get to just *decide* how many kids we're having."

"I didn't decide. We're discussing it."

"We're fighting about it! When we should be celebrating."

He rolled over her. "Of course we're fighting," he said with a grin. "It's what we do."

"I'm rethinking the marriage thing."

"No, you're not."

No. She wasn't.

"Ted?"

"What?" she snapped.

Alex nibbled up her jaw. Then his mouth was at her ear, teasing it.

He whispered, "We're going to have so much fun."

THE END

Epilogue

Allie took a deep breath and locked the front door, glad that the last of the patrons hadn't put up too much fuss about leaving. Sometimes they could get rowdy, but that was rare as long as the tall man behind the bar was on the premises.

Ollie Campbell was six and a half feet of pure muscle and, lately, silence. She didn't know where her friend had gone. She just knew for the last few months he'd been quiet. And not his usual quiet, which had always prompted her to draw a smile from him, no matter how silly she had to get.

No, it was a heavier silence.

She didn't try to draw him out. Didn't try to draw a smile. Allie no longer had anything to give.

"Allie girl, what do you need?"

A better job. A full night's rest. A hug.

Everything.

Allie couldn't remember the last time she'd felt full. Fifteen years with Joe Russell had wrung her dry. Some mornings she woke up and felt like a husk. She liked to remind herself that the cactuses that surrounded her home got through life on practically no water. They just stored up when the rain came down and used that for the lean days. Bursting into bloom for brief, dramatic periods, they filled the desert with joy.

But other than her children's love, no rain had fallen in Allie's life for a good long while.

Ollie wiped down the bar in silence, ignoring her as he did most every night. He was busy, she knew. So was she. Though not *that* busy. During the week, the tips were abysmal because the bar wasn't full unless a band was playing. Great for training new waitresses. Not great for her bank account. Still, Tracey said she'd start putting her on more Fridays and Saturdays when she had more experience. And anything—even minimum wage—was better than sitting at home at night, worrying about the bills after the kids were quiet in bed.

"Ollie, I'm about done."

"All right." He put down the rag and waited for her to grab her purse from his office. He'd walk her to her car, just like he did with all the girls. Allie walked down the hall and stretched over the desk to open the file drawer where she and Tracey put their stuff while they were working. No one messed with Ollie's office. Ever. So his waitresses always knew their stuff was safe. It was a little thing, but working at the Cave made her feel safe too. Everyone in town—and out of town, for that matter—knew Ollie Campbell took care of his people.

When she turned at the door, he was there waiting for her. Leaning against the doorjamb, watching her. She blushed as her eyes rose to meet his, realizing she'd probably given him a show while she stretched over his desk to grab her purse.

Not that Ollie thought like that about her. No one did. She was a single mother of four whose husband had left her. Most days, she felt like the single most *un*sexy woman on the planet. And she'd seen the kind of women Ollie had dated over the years. Tall, voluptuous knockouts. Nothing even bordering on the "cute" she could barely rock on her best nights.

He cleared his throat. "I haven't asked for a while."

"Asked what?"

"You all right?"

Such a good guy.

"Yeah. Thanks for the extra hours this week. Christmas kind of wiped me out. And it's getting warmer again, so the kids are going to need new clothes. Though the boys are mostly taken care of with hand-me-downs, and I think my sister has some stuff for Loralie. So that's good. And—"

"I didn't ask about the kids." He stepped into the office, grimacing.

"I don't—"

"How are *you* doing, Allie?"

She took a deep breath. "I'm fine."

"You say that every time someone asks, and every night you walk in here, the circles under your eyes are a little darker."

She stiffened. "I'm doing my work, Ollie. Tracey says I—"

"That's not what I'm talking about," he clipped, stepping even closer.

"What are you trying to say, then?"

He gritted his teeth. "Seriously?"

She felt crowded. And Ollie never made her feel crowded. She knew other people probably felt that way, but she never had. From the time he'd been a boy, Ollie Campbell had been the kindest, most considerate boy in the world to her. And having three of her own boys now made her realize kind and considerate were not the natural states of male children.

But he wasn't acting very kind or considerate lately. Mostly, he seemed annoyed.

All. The. Time.

"Why are you mad at me?" she whispered, trying not to cry. She cried when she was angry or nervous or just overwhelmed. She hated it. And she felt the tears gathering at the corners now.

He scowled. "I'm not mad at you."

"Yes, you are. All the time now. It's like… I've done something to piss you off. And I don't know what. Ever since Joe—"

"I don't want to talk about your husband, Allie."

"Ex."

"You signed divorce papers I don't know about?"

She blinked and looked up. Ollie towered over her. Well over a foot taller than she was. The tears dried up and her temper rose with her chin when she glared at him.

"No. I have not signed divorce papers because my lawyer can't find my *ex*-husband to give them to him. He's run away, leaving me with four confused children, a lot of debt, and bills I can barely pay. So when I say my *ex*-husband, it's because nothing in this world—*nothing* he could say or do—can make up for having to explain to my four kids why their dad, my *ex*-husband, is no longer there to say good-night. Why he can't even be bothered to call them. So in my mind, Joe is my *ex*-husband. And he was the minute he stepped foot out of the door while I was serving meatloaf!"

"Allie—"

"I worked my ass off to try to make that marriage good, and my *ex*-husband gave me nothing. It's over."

"Allie girl—"

"It was over before he walked out the door. *That's* how over it is."

Ollie stepped another foot toward her, and suddenly his hand was on the back of her neck. The heavy weight of it shut her up. The dark look on his face made her suck in a quick breath as something foreign, warm, and a little scary curled in her stomach.

"I get that you don't want me to call Joe your husband," he said in a low voice.

His hand stayed on her neck, and she couldn't look away.

"Good."

"He's your ex. Even though the papers aren't signed."

"Exactly." Why was she out of breath?

"Good to know."

His head dipped down. Not a lot. Just a fraction. But for a second, her mind was consumed with one thought.

Kiss me. Please.

She blinked and pulled back. His hand left her neck, and he took a full step away from her. Which, with Ollie's giant legs, was something like halfway to the door.

He cleared his throat again. "You got your stuff?"

"Yeah."

"Come on, then." He nodded down the hall. "I'll walk you to your car."

"Thanks."

She couldn't read the expression on his face, but at least he didn't look annoyed anymore. His face was shut down, but his shoulders were relaxed. Something in her heart eased. Maybe he was just worried she'd make the mistake of taking Joe back if he came begging. It was probably that. Her dad had been worried about the same thing for a while. It must have been that.

But when she walked past him, the hair on the back of her neck stood on end, and that curl in her belly didn't ease.

It just got a little warmer.

About the Author

ELIZABETH HUNTER is a contemporary fantasy, paranormal romance, and contemporary romance writer. She is a graduate of the University of Houston Honors College and a former English teacher. She once substitute taught a kindergarten class, but decided that middle school was far less frightening. Thankfully, people now pay her to write books and eighth-graders everywhere rejoice.

She currently lives in Central California with her son, two dogs, many plants, and a sadly dwindling fish tank. She is the author of the *Elemental Mysteries* and *Elemental World* series, the *Cambio Springs Mysteries*, the *Irin Chronicles*, and other works of fiction.

Website: ElizabethHunterWrites.com

E-mail: elizabethhunterwrites@gmail.com.

Twitter: @E__Hunter

Find me on Facebook!

Acknowledgements

There's a point in the process of writing every book—whether it's my first or my tenth—where I sit back, stare at the computer, and am convinced that I am the absolute worst writer in the history of the entire world and should probably toss the whole manuscript away and find a "real job."

If you're not in agreement with this sentiment and like my books, then you owe a debt of gratitude to these brave people:

Kelli and Gen, who read this craziness while I'm in the process of writing, ply me with wine and questionable advice, and nag me when I'm not writing fast enough.

Sarah and Iriet, who give me wonderful and amazing notes, often catching things that seem obvious, but are not.

My mom, who usually will not touch one of my books until it is in final form, but made an exception in this case because I was nervous about a certain plot point and wanted her opinion.

And dear author friends, Colleen Vanderlinden and Killian McRae for their invaluable input. Having writing peers like you makes this job a heck of a lot more fun.

My editor, Cassie McCown, and my proofreader, Linda at Victory Editing, for always having my back and making my work professional.

I have never been a writer able to work within a vacuum. Though the thoughts and ideas are always my own, I owe so much to the readers who pre-read for me, giving me valuable feedback about what works, what doesn't, and—*holy cow, Elizabeth, you left a gigantic flaming plot hole in Chapter Twenty-four, how could you miss that?* (Sarah gets a special acknowledgement this go round for catching that one.)

Many thanks also go to my readers, who make this job, not only possible with their financial support, but so much fun with their interaction on social media and email.

Thanks to my agents, Jane Dystel and Lauren Abramo, for their unwavering support. Also thanks to my publicist Morgan Doremus, who came on in the middle of this project ready to roll.

Thanks to the staff and management of Two Bunch Palms Resort in Desert Hot Springs, California, where I started this book and found so much quiet inspiration.

Thanks to my family. To my parents, brothers, and sisters who make life a little crazy and a lot of fun.

As iron sharpens iron, so one person sharpens another.
Proverbs 27:17

Everyone needs an Alex or Ted in their life—whether it's a romantic partner, a friend, or a family member—who challenges them and makes them think. Keeps them sharp and keeps them real. I hope you have yours. I know I have mine. Thank you to everyone who keeps me sharp.

The Elemental Mysteries

Get the best-selling series by Elizabeth Hunter that readers, writers, and reviewers have raved about.

"Elemental Mysteries turned into one of the best paranormal series I've read this year. It's sharp, elegant, clever, evenly paced without dragging its feet, and at the same time emotionally intense." Nocturnal Book Reviews

Welcome to the Elemental Mysteries, where history and the paranormal collide, and where no secret stays hidden forever. Join five hundred year old rare book dealer, Giovanni Vecchio, and librarian, Beatrice De Novo, as they travel the world in search of the mystery that brought them together, the same mystery that could tear everything they love apart.

Praise for the first book, *A Hidden Fire*, semifinalist in the Kindle Book Reviews Best Indie Books of 2012:

"A tantalizing paranormal romance, full of mystery and intrigue. One of the best books I've read in a long time. Sign me up for book 2!" Nichole Chase, best-selling author of *Mortal Obligation*, Book One of The Dark Betrayal Trilogy

"Lush with detail and sweeping in scope, the emotional depth that you get is almost unheard of in recent years." Stephany Simmons, author of *Voodoo Dues*

"A Hidden Fire is saturated with mystery, intrigue, and romance...this book will make my paranormal romance top ten list of 2011." Better Read Than Dead Book Reviews

Get the complete series in e-book or paperback at all major online retailers.
ElementalMysteries.com

THE IRIN CHRONICLES

Hidden at the crossroads of the world, an ancient race battles to protect humanity, even as it dies from within.

THE SCRIBE:
Irin Chronicles Book One

"A perfect marriage of urban fantasy with tinges of romance... [Hunter] leads us on a riveting journey through the streets of Old Istanbul and old magic. An awesome ride!"—Killian McRae, author of 12.21.12

THE SINGER:
Irin Chronicles Book Two

"Passionate, spellbinding, and heartbreaking -- "The Singer" is all this and so much more. Hunter is at the top of her game, drawing you into a story of love, loss, bravery, and redemption. If you loved "The Scribe," you will absolutely adore this sequel."—Colleen Vanderlinden, author of the Hidden series

THE SECRET:
Irin Chronicles Book Three

COMING WINTER 2015

For more information, please visit
ElizabethHunterWrites.com

Made in the USA
Las Vegas, NV
09 March 2022

45275965R00173